The Secret Play

A Silver Fox Hockey Romance

Mia Mara

Sign up to the Mia Mara exclusive mailing list here:
https://sendfox.com/miamararomance

A wild night at a masquerade ball should have stayed anonymous.
Except it didn't.

Five years later, I'm a single mom, starting fresh in Atlanta, writing a piece on the NHL's most respected coach—Casey McConnell.

He's a silver fox with piercing blue eyes that ignite a spark in my soul.
A man who commands the ice and his team with sexy authority.
And completely off-limits, given I'm one of his player's younger sister.

Despite our age gap, I didn't think we'd get this close this fast...
Until I notice the birthmark on his shoulder—the same one I saw on my masked lover five years ago.

OMG. He's the one who left me with a little surprise that night.
He has no idea he's her father.
And I plan to keep it that way.

But when he starts piecing the clues together, I realize the truth could spark a career-ending scandal that threatens to shatter the team.

And for my daughter—and my heart—I can't afford to puck this up.

Chapter 1

Casey - 5 Years Earlier

I adjusted my mask again, trying not to feel ridiculous. The elastic strap bit into my scalp. A quick glance around the ballroom told me I wasn't the only one fussing with theirs, but somehow everyone else looked like they belonged.

It was always that way for me at formal events. Tonight, the women were in shimmering gowns, and the men were in perfectly tailored tuxedos, their masks ornate or elegant, making it all look effortless.

Meanwhile, I was a forty-three-year-old man in a penguin suit, fidgeting like a kid at a school dance.

Get a grip, McConnell.

The ballroom was elaborate—polished marble floors, towering floral arrangements, and chandeliers that dripped with crystal like they'd been plucked from some Gatsby fever dream. The Atlanta Fire's newly promoted PR manager, Whitney, had outdone herself, and for her, that was saying something.

I'd never complained about these events to her face, but

she always seemed to know they were not my style. Whenever we talked about them, she did that subtle head tilt thing women do when they know you're putting up with something. Sympathy and patient humor.

From the auction tables piled high with team memorabilia to the cocktail waiters gliding through the crowd with trays of champagne, every detail was perfect.

Every detail but me.

The whole scene made me feel like I was wearing someone else's skin.

I felt most at home in my skates and the Atlanta Fire team jacket with 'COACH' stamped across the back.

"This is for the kids," I muttered to myself. That phrase had been my mantra for weeks now. It was why I'd agreed to this masquerade ball in the first place, even though black tie formals were not my thing.

Hell, tuxedos weren't my thing. But this wasn't about me. It was about raising money for Atlanta Children's Hospital, helping fund a new wing for kids who deserved a fighting chance. If dressing up like a waiter at a Michelin-starred restaurant got that done, then so be it.

Still, I felt out of place. Maybe it was because most of the people here were half my age, all young professionals and twenty-something influencers who probably didn't know a puck from a football.

Or maybe it was because every time I was in a room like this, I couldn't help but think about how much simpler life had been twenty years ago, back when all I needed was my skates and a stick.

"Looking sharp, Coach."

I turned to see Sebastian Blue grinning at me, his own

mask tilted slightly askew. Seb was one of our oldest centers, an oddity in the league. He was the son of a tech mogul, and everyone had thought he'd burn out in his first year. A spoiled brat with a complex. But he'd shocked everybody with his hard work ethic and determination.

I'd watched him grow into a solid, dependable player. Tonight, though, he looked more like he was trying to survive a family wedding than attend a charity gala.

"Seb," I said, nodding. "You clean up well."

"Don't get used to it," he said, tugging at his bow tie. "This thing's choking me."

"Try wearing a mask," I muttered.

He laughed. "You look good, Coach. You should dress up more often."

"Don't push your luck."

Seb's grin widened. "The guys are betting on how long you last before you ditch the tux."

"Tell them to focus on staying out of trouble," I said, though I couldn't help smiling.

"Will do," he said, giving me a mock salute before disappearing into the crowd.

I watched him go, shaking my head. The thing about coaching players like Sebastian—and most of the team, really—was that they reminded me of just how long I'd been at this.

The younger guys called me "Pops" behind my back, and though I pretended not to care, some days it stung. I wasn't just older than my players. I was as old as some of their dads.

"Casey!"

I turned to see Matthew Edwards, the Fire's owner,

shuffling toward me with his cane. At seventy-four, Matthew was one of the few people here older than I was, though he carried his age with the kind of confidence money could buy.

His tuxedo fit perfectly, his silvery hair was tucked beneath his top hat, and his mask—simple black with gold trim—looked like it belonged on the cover of a magazine.

"Matthew," I said, shaking his hand. Minus the mask, he was dressed like the Monopoly Man, but I'd never tell him to his face. "You're looking sharp."

"So are you," he said, his voice warm. "Though I don't think I've ever seen you in a tuxedo."

He had. I'd worn a tux to four other charity events for the team. But Matthew wouldn't remember any of that. His memory was starting to go. I wasn't sure who else knew it, and I certainly wasn't going to bring it up. The old man was a kooky oil tycoon and a good team owner. He loved the Atlanta Fire, doting on everyone at every possible chance. So, bringing up his diminished capacity would have been cruel.

I merely smiled. "First time for everything."

"I wanted to thank you for everything you've done for tonight. Whitney says you've been a big help."

"It's her show," I said. "I'm just here to nod and follow orders."

"Don't sell yourself short," Matthew said, his gaze steady. "The players look up to you. They trust you."

The words caught me off guard, but before I could respond, he gave my shoulder a pat and shuffled off toward the silent auction table.

I sighed, turning my attention back to the crowd. The

team was spread out across the ballroom, mingling with sponsors and donors like we'd trained them to do. Beau Fournier was at the bar, his hulking frame making him impossible to miss, while Victor Sokolov held court near the dessert table, his Russian charm on full display. The rest of the guys had scattered, blending into the crowd as best they could.

And then I saw her.

She was standing near the edge of the dance floor, her long red hair catching the light like embers in a fire.

Her gown, a deep teal blue, shimmered with every subtle movement, and her mask—a dazzling peacock design—was a perfect match. The long feathers on the sides framed her face, drawing attention to her sharp cheekbones and the faint curve of her lips.

I couldn't explain why she held my attention, but my breath stopped as I watched her.

The room was full of beautiful women, all of them dressed to the nines, but there was something about this woman that made it impossible to look away.

Whatever it was, I was captivated.

She wasn't trying to draw attention to herself. She wasn't laughing loudly or surrounded by admirers. She just stood there, poised but unassuming, her gaze drifting across the room as she observed the goings-on.

She was like me. In the room, but not a part of it.

For a moment, I wondered who she was. A player's date? That didn't seem likely. She was too refined for their tastes. I loved my team, but they were notorious for hooking up with puck bunnies, and this woman was no puck bunny. Maybe she was someone connected to the hospital? There were plenty of them here—administrators, managers, and so on.

Before I could stop myself, I took a step toward her. Then another. But just as I reached the edge of the crowd, Whitney appeared at my side, her clipboard in hand.

"Casey," she said, her tone brisk. "I need you."

It was hard not to bristle at hearing my first name. She was one of the few team-related people who used it. "Not now, Whit."

Whitney followed my gaze and smirked. "A woman is enough to distract you from work? Since when?"

I turned to her, narrowing my eyes. "What do you need?"

"The hospital's CEO wants to meet you. He's over by the photo wall."

"Right now?"

"Right now," she said firmly. "And after that, you're doing a lap around the room to thank the donors. Remember, this is your event as much as it's mine."

If I thought I could have changed Whitney Dobson's mind about anything, I might have argued about it. But there was no point. I'd once tried to argue my way into a better parking spot that she wanted, and by the time I'd left her office, somehow she had gotten me to agree to personally handwashing her car for a month.

The woman was a word ninja, and I was smart enough to know when I was beaten.

"Lead the way." I reluctantly followed her across the ballroom. But as we threaded through the crowd, I couldn't help glancing back.

The peacock was still there, standing by the dance floor, her head tilted slightly as she scanned the room.

For a brief moment, her gaze landed on me, and my breath caught in my chest and my cock twitched. It was just a second, maybe less, but it was enough to leave me wondering who she was—and how I was going to meet her.

Chapter 2

Gemma

I wasn't supposed to be here.

I should've been home, packing boxes for my move to Los Angeles in two days.

Instead, I was standing on the edge of a dance floor, swirling a glass of champagne, trying and failing not to look completely out of place.

It was impossible.

"Relax, Gemma," Nico said, leaning down to mutter in my ear. "You look like you're waiting for someone to throw you in a penalty box."

I rolled my eyes, glancing up at my older brother, a center for Atlanta Fire. "That's because I am. This whole thing is ridiculous. Why are we even wearing masks? We're adults and this isn't Halloween."

"Because it's classy," he said, smirking as he adjusted his own mask—a sleek navy one with gold detailing that somehow made him look even more like the charming, over-confident flirt he was.

The mask matched the navy tuxes he and the rest of the

team wore. The Atlanta Fire's colors were navy and gold, so the players wore navy tuxedos with navy and gold masks, each one a little different from the other.

He continued, "And because I promised you'd have a good time tonight. It's like a costume party. That's fun, right?"

"This isn't really my scene. You know that."

"It's no one's scene," he said with a shrug. "It's for charity. Have a drink, relax. You might even meet someone interesting."

"Among debutants and guys hunting for a trophy wife?" I snorted. "I doubt it."

Nico put an arm around my shoulders, pulling me close. At six years older than me, he'd always taken his role as big brother very seriously, even when I didn't want him to.

"Breathe."

"I *am* breathing."

He gave me the look, the one that told me I was being petulant. He had perfected that look back when we were kids, and I hated being on the receiving end of it.

"You deserve to have some fun, Gemma. You've worked hard. Let yourself enjoy a night out of your comfort zone. You might even figure out that you like high society."

I sighed, because as much as I hated to admit it, he was right. Not about high society. They could kick rocks for all I cared. I'd seen how they treated him back when he sang at a charity event at the opera. He was a beefy, kind, charismatic man, smarter than anyone gave him credit for. And all the wealthy women of Atlanta saw was a good time and a story to tell over brunch. None of them took him seriously.

"Fine," I said, nudging him with my elbow. "But if this night sucks, you owe me."

"Deal," he said, grinning as he kissed the top of my head, careful of my mask.

Then his gaze shifted across the room, and his grin turned into something more mischievous. "Now, if you'll excuse me, I need to say hi to someone."

I followed his gaze to a petite woman with a dazzling smile who was chatting with a group near the bar. Her eyes said it all—Nico had this in the bag. "Let me guess. Staff massage therapist?"

"You know me too well," he said with a wink. "Be good."

"Seriously, Nico? Haven't you had enough of pointless one night stands?"

He smiled. "Right now, all I'm looking for is fun. And you're even younger, so you should be too."

"I'll try," I said, watching as he sauntered away, his charm already dialed up to eleven. As much as I loved my brother, I worried he was losing himself in the pro lifestyle. But it was his life, not mine.

With Nico gone, I was on my own. I'd never been the kind of person who thrived at parties, especially not ones where everyone else seemed to know someone except me.

I wandered toward the edge of the dancefloor, my champagne glass still clutched in my hand, and tried to look like I belonged.

That was when I spotted him.

Again.

He was leaning casually against the bar, his red satin mask gleaming in the dim light. It was simple but striking and accented with black filigree. It matched the sharp lines of his tuxedo.

He wasn't like the other men in the room—instead of easily laughing with the people around him, he looked like he was counting the seconds until he could politely excuse himself.

And he was hot. Old-time movie star handsome. He had one of those strong jaws. His casually styled grayish hair made him look older than his posture said he was.

A sexy silver fox in a tux.

Before I could think twice, he turned his head and caught me staring.

I froze, my cheeks heating under my peacock feather mask.

But instead of looking away, he smiled—a slow, easy smile that made my heart skip a beat.

He raised his glass in a silent toast, and I felt my lips curve into a smile of their own.

And just like that, he was walking toward me. It was more like a confident swagger, his muscly build gliding across the room.

"Breathe," I muttered to myself, remembering Nico's advice from earlier in the day. *Try to have fun. This isn't an execution—it's a party.* He had hyped me up so much for the party that I had almost believed I wouldn't be this nervous.

I was wrong.

"Good evening," he said, his voice low and smooth in a way that curled up my spine and made me fight a shiver. "I couldn't help noticing you over here, looking like you were trying to disappear."

I laughed softly, feeling a little more at ease. "Is it that obvious?"

"Only to someone who knows what it feels like." His crystal blue eyes sparkled.

That made me smile. "Were you dragged out to be here, too?"

"Not entirely. These functions are part of the job," he said with a shrug. "Someone had to drag you out to be here?"

"Drag might be too strong a word for it. Coerce is more accurate." I hesitated to say more, because I was sure I'd screw this up. But I wanted to hear him speak. His voice made my knees weak. What was the harm in a little conversation? We were in masks, so I decided to play up the anonymity of it. "It's nice to meet you, Red."

He smiled, and all thought drained out of me. He took my hand in his, warm and firm. "Nice to meet you, Blue. Care to dance?"

"Yes," gasped out of me before I could stop myself. I looked past him, toward the dance floor where couples were swaying to the soft strains of the band. It wasn't something I'd normally do, but tonight felt different.

Tonight, this masked stranger made me feel like someone else—someone who could say yes.

He led me onto the dance floor, his hand resting lightly on my lower back as we found a rhythm. I wasn't a great dancer, but he didn't seem to mind. He moved with an easy confidence, guiding me through the steps as if we'd done this a hundred times before.

"You're good at this," I said, trying not to trip over my own feet.

"So are you," he replied.

There was something about the way he looked at me—something that made me feel seen, even behind the mask.

It was intoxicating, the way his presence seemed to fill the space around us, blocking out the rest of the room as though we were the only dancers in the ballroom.

Being so close to Red, smelling his woodsy scent, the tension I'd held onto for the past two years had faded to nothing.

We danced for what felt like hours, though it was probably only a few songs. By the time we stepped off the floor, my heart was racing for reasons that had nothing to do with the dancing. And I could feel a warmth between my legs that told me what a turn on my body thought he was.

"Come on, let's get some air," Red said.

I hesitated, my pulse pounding in my ears, feeling this kind of pull toward someone I didn't even know.

But tonight wasn't about being cautious. Tonight was about stepping out of my comfort zone, about letting myself live. Having fun.

With a mask on.

I licked my lips and watched as his eyes flickered to my mouth. My heart kicked up as I anticipated the words coming out. I hoped they came out seductively and not as a desperate blurt. "My room has a balcony. We can get plenty of air there."

His lips parted in surprise, then spread in a playful smile. "Lead the way."

He took my hand and led me to the elevators. When the doors closed, he grabbed my chin and lifted my face up for a kiss.

He didn't disappoint.

Once he knew it was game on, he pressed me against the elevator wall, caging me with his arms as he kissed down my throat.

When the doors opened again, we found our way to my hotel room, the champagne still buzzing in my veins and his hand warm against mine.

I swiped my key card and we fumbled into the room, hands scrambling for clothing, mouths colliding and bruising.

I was naked before I knew it, save for my mask. He reached for that, too, but I drew back, shaking my head. "Leave the masks on."

His mouth shaped into a wicked smirk. "As you wish."

Once he was naked, I took a moment to memorize his body in the faint city light that poured in from the balcony, grazing every inch of him with my fingertips.

I had no idea who he was or where he came from, but his body told a story I suddenly wanted to hear in full detail.

He looked like sin wrapped in muscle—broad shoulders built for holding a woman in place, a firm chest that begged to be touched, licked, tasted.

The birthmark on his shoulder that looked like Italy.

Scars marked his skin, whispers of past battles, and I had the sudden, wicked urge to trace them with my tongue.

His body wasn't sculpted for show; it was built for power, for endurance.

Every inch of him radiated strength, from the carved

ridges of his abs to the deep-cut lines that led my gaze lower, making my breath hitch.

His waist was trim, tapering into powerful hips that promised control.

But it was his legs that really caught me—thick, solid muscle, the kind that spoke of brutal strength, of speed, of unrelenting force.

My fingers brushed over his hard glutes, aching to feel, to explore.

And then he moved. Just a shift of his stance, a flex of his fingers at his sides, but it felt deliberate—like he knew exactly what he was doing to me.

His gaze caught mine, dark and knowing, a slow smirk playing on his lips. Heat pooled low in my stomach.

I still didn't know his name. Didn't know why his body looked like it was made for both destruction and pleasure.

But I knew, without a doubt, that I wanted to find out.

My gaze dragged lower, and my breath stalled.

He was already hard. Thick, heavy, the kind of size that made my pulse stutter and my thighs clench.

He stood proud, the flushed tip glistening, the veins along his length pronounced, like he was barely restraining himself.

My mouth went dry, my body reacting on instinct, heat licking up my spine at the sheer intensity of him.

He gave me a slow, knowing smirk, wrapping a hand around his base like he had all the time in the world, like he enjoyed watching me squirm.

"See something you like?" His voice was a rough rasp, thick with desire.

I swallowed hard, my body screaming in response. Like? No. I was about to be wrecked.

He stroked himself slowly, deliberately, his grip firm as his dark gaze pinned me in place. "You have no idea what this does to me, do you?" His voice was playful, sexy. "Watching you like this, wearing that mask—fuck, it makes me harder than I've ever been. It's like you're mine, a forbidden temptation just waiting to be claimed."

He gave himself another slow stroke, eyes locked on me, reveling in the power he had, the way my breath hitched, the way my thighs pressed together.

"You want to know what turns me on?" He stepped closer, towering over me, his body radiating heat. "Knowing that under that mask, you're already wet for me. That you want this as badly as I do." He tipped my chin up, his thumb brushing over my lips, his cock thick and heavy between us. "And when I finally bury myself inside you? You'll be begging me to ruin you."

In a blink, he had me against the wall, kissing his way down my body. He licked my nipples and lightly sucked, sending heat all the way down to my clit. "Do you taste this sweet everywhere?"

I panted. "Only one way to find out."

"Get on the bed."

My knees went weak from the command in his voice. I crawled onto the bed, but he captured my ankle. I turned to ask what he wanted, but he spoke first. "Just like this. On your knees for me, Blue. Face down."

Oh.

I stayed like that for him, and his weight shifted the bed between my feet. His strong hands kneaded my ass for a minute. "Damn," I heard him growl. "Your ass is incredible."

Then he spread me wide open for him and dove against me, his tongue swiping up over my pussy. I gripped the bedding and groaned. Red grabbed my hips to hold me against his face as he devoured me from behind.

He drove me to the brink over and over, his tongue or fingers on my clit, I couldn't tell, exploring me, too. It was like he knew my body and exactly how to drive me crazy.

That deep throb built inside, and I wanted to beg for more, but I couldn't speak.

Finally, he pulled back, and I had the chance to breathe again.

But then Red laid onto me, his hard cock digging against my glute.

"If this is all you want tonight, say it now. Otherwise, I'm going to fuck you so hard that you're not going to walk straight tomorrow," he murmured in my ear, his voice rough, wrecked with need.

I shuddered beneath him. "Yes, Red. Fuck me."

"Condom?"

I fished one out from my purse and passed it to him.

"You were prepared for this, eh?"

"You know, just in case."

He leaned back to put it on and rolled me onto my back. "You're sure?"

"If you don't, so help me I will find someone who will."

He smirked before brushing the head of himself over me. "Don't even think about it."

"Stop teasing—"

He slid in halfway, and I was so on edge, I thought I might come right then.

He watched where our bodies joined and an animal growl came out of his chest. Fuck, there was something so primal about him, and I couldn't get enough of it.

As he began a rhythm, I thrust up to meet him, and soon, we were as close as two people could be.

Inside, he was filling me up. And he rolled against my clit with every thrust.

But I still couldn't come.

It had always been that way for me. Orgasms on my own were great. Orgasms with a man were elusive. Not impossible, but difficult all the same, so I usually ended up finishing myself off. If I finished at all. I still enjoyed sex, but it was never a climax guarantee.

But being close with Red like this felt different.

He leaned on his forearms next to my head and stared deep into my eyes. "You're so damn beautiful. Especially when I—" He cut himself off to dive deep inside and make me arch beneath him. Then he bent to my ear, his hot breaths caressing the shell. "You're right there, aren't you? So close you can taste it?"

"Yes," I whispered.

"What's stopping you?"

"I don't...I don't know." No point in getting into it now. I wanted to enjoy him and the moment. If I didn't come, it wouldn't be a surprise. But I didn't believe in faking it, either, so I hoped he wouldn't make a big deal about it.

Red reached down, taking my hands in his and pinning them to the bed while he practically danced inside of me.

I felt so full.

His cock brushed against that magic spot inside, and I gasped hard. I hadn't seen that coming. But he worked himself right there, over and over, until the throb became something more.

"I've got you. Just relax."

And for once, I did. There was no logical reason for it, no sane reason for me to trust him. But the last of my usual tension fell away. No more worrying about if I was going to come or not. I was just enjoying the moment.

And it felt so good.

He felt so good.

The next thing I knew, I was coming so hard I thought I'd black out. Heat flashed through me, and something ecstatic burst inside, unleashing a howl from my throat.

"Oh, fuck yes," he snarled as he pounded into me.

One became two which became more, and I wondered what the hell was happening. I never came like this, not even with toys. But Red worked my body over again and again until I was weak from it. From him. I patted his shoulder with a shaking hand, and he slowed to a stop, kissing me deeply.

"Need to stop coming?"

"Yeah," I barely gasped.

He pulled out and let me breathe for a moment before flipping me onto my stomach. "There we go." He spread my legs and hoisted my hips up. "My turn." He entered me from behind, filling me up before he laid on my back again. "And you're not done coming, are you?"

"I'm not?"

"You're young. You can take it." He reached beneath my hip and felt around until he found my clit. "Can't you?"

"Yes?"

"Good girl." He played with me as he fucked me, and I couldn't have stopped coming if I'd wanted to. I lost count as I bit the pillow.

His groans became growls and he sped up right as I felt him swell inside of me. "I can feel you coming on me, Blue. Fuck."

Between weak breaths, I panted, "Are you—"

"Right now!" He slammed deep and his hips jerked forward as he came, too.

Chapter 3

Casey

I stared at the ceiling, feeling both completely drained and utterly disoriented. Within the room and within myself. The room was quiet except for the faint hum of the air conditioning, and my pulse still thrummed from activity.

It wasn't like me to lose track of time, or to give in to something—or someone—without thinking it through, and I'd done both tonight.

But Blue. God, *Blue*.

How the hell was I supposed to refuse an opportunity like this? Maybe that was a self-serving thought, but I hardly cared.

I'd always thought I had too much principle for this kind of thing. She was young enough to be my daughter, for fuck's sake.

Turns out, nope. I was as susceptible to chemistry as any man.

I turned my head to where she stood by the window, her back to me, the city lights catching the deep red tones of her hair as she adjusted the strap of her dress. I wanted to take a picture of her like that and capture the curve of her bare backside. She was truly breathtaking.

Her mask still hung on her face, as if she wasn't quite ready to take it off.

I couldn't blame her. I'd left mine on, too, except when I was devouring her from behind.

The mask changed everything.

It was a line in the sand, a boundary erased, a reason to take what I shouldn't want. Without it, I might have resisted. Might have reminded myself she was too young, too off-limits, too much of a temptation I had no business touching.

But with it?

Fuck, it made me harder than I'd ever been. It gave me permission to stop fighting, to indulge, to take her the way I craved. The anonymity, the secrecy—it blurred the edges of right and wrong, made it easier to let go, to let myself have her.

Blue turned around then, her gaze catching mine, and I felt the stirring of something I couldn't quite name. She looked the same as she had when we met, but now, there was a lightness to her, like she'd shed whatever weight she might've been carrying.

"Good morning," I said, my voice rougher than I intended. My throat had dried out from breathing too hard, too fast, for so long. But it had been totally worth it. I could take a scratchy throat for a few days if it meant I got to share the night with her.

"It's after midnight, so yeah. *Very* good morning," she replied, a faint smile playing on her lips. She slipped her earrings back on and gestured toward my shoulder. "That birthmark of yours—it looks like Italy."

I blinked, caught off guard. "What?"

She gestured again, stepping closer. "On your shoulder. It's shaped like Italy. You've never noticed?"

I frowned, glancing down at the spot she was talking about. The mark had been there my whole life, but I'd always thought it looked more like Florida without much of a panhandle. "Huh. You're right."

"Have you ever been there?" she asked, her tone casual as she reached for her shoes.

"No. But I've always wanted to go. Haven't had the chance."

She slipped on her heels and stood, adjusting the hem of her dress. "You should. It's worth the flight time."

There was a moment of silence as she tucked her clutch in a drawer and gave herself a quick glance in the mirror.

I watched her, still not decided on my next play.

She was a lot younger than I was and surely there was no future for us. *Should I ask for her number? Suggest we meet again? Where would that lead? Or should I just walk away*. Every option felt wrong.

"You don't need to overthink this, you know," she said, breaking the silence. Her tone was light, but there was a firmness to it, like she'd read my mind. "You don't need to take my number or promise to call or anything like that."

I frowned, sitting up straighter. "I wasn't—" I stopped, realizing I had no idea how to finish that sentence.

She smiled faintly, her mask still hiding most of her expression but not the warmth in her voice. "It's okay, Red. We had a good time. Or, at least, I did. So—"

"I did, too." The best time ever, but I didn't want to commit to anything by saying that.

"Then, let's leave it at that."

"Are you sure?"

"I'm sure," she said. "There's no point in complicating things. It doesn't need to be more than that, right? Making hollow promises to call each other won't do either of us any favors. Besides, I'm moving out of state in two days. Well, one and a half now."

My chest tightened, though I wasn't sure why. "Where are you going?"

She hesitated, then shook her head. "Does it matter?"

I didn't answer. It felt like it should matter, but she was right. It was better this way.

She walked toward the door and gathered my clothes where she'd torn them off of me. "Here you go."

I dressed, regretting not having taken control of the situation. I finished the buttons on my shirt. "I'm used to being the one taking charge, maneuvering through things, planning everything. It's part of my job. I'm the—"

She pressed a finger to my lips. "No details. We are two people who shared a night of mutual attraction. Let's not pretend it's anything other than that by getting to know each other. I'd rather keep expectations to a minimum. Wouldn't you?"

"I agree." It was the right thing to do but part of me didn't want to let her go. I wanted more of her, again and again. This had been the best sex I'd ever had. I'd been in love, for God's sake. How had I never had sex this good before? But I hadn't, and I wanted...well, I didn't know what I wanted.

But it was clear she was done with me. *Must be a Gen Z thing.*

"Let me walk you to the door." She hooked her arm in mine and escorted me to the entry.

I wasn't about to let it end here.

Not like this.

I moved in closer and pinned her against the wall. She caught her breath and I felt my cock fill with blood.

"This is so you don't forget me," I said, kissing her like I've never goddamn kissed anyone. I could have tasted her forever but I ripped my mouth away from hers and glanced intensely into her eyes, burning my soul onto hers.

"Take care of yourself, Red," she said with a flirtatious tone, opening the door. Then, as I stepped through the doorway, she added, "And go to Italy one day. I promise, you won't regret it."

And just like that, the door closed and she was gone.

I stood there for a few moments, my thoughts a jumble of emotions I didn't know how to untangle.

Part of me felt like I should've stopped her, should've asked for her name, her number—something. But the other part of me—the part that had been too drawn to her to think straight all night—understood why she hadn't let me.

She was leaving, or so she said. Whatever the case, she didn't want strings. And maybe, just this once, I didn't either.

And she was probably half my age.

Still, I couldn't stop myself from wondering more about Blue. Who the hell was she? And would I ever see her again?

Chapter 4

Gemma - 5 Years Later

The humid Atlanta air clung to my skin as I watched the moving truck pull away from my new house.

They had left behind a driveway full of boxes and furniture that still needed arranging. Well, at least the weather was starting to cool down.

My new neighborhood wasn't too far from where I grew up.

The street was lined with trees just beginning to turn to their autumn colors, and the house—a modest two-bedroom bungalow with peeling shutters that I'd already planned to repaint—felt worlds away from our cramped apartment we'd left behind in L.A.

I hoisted a small table to my hip, ready to get a move on. But then Nico's voice rang out, "Don't lift that—your back is garbage!"

I turned to see my older brother jogging up the driveway, his tall frame balancing two chairs stacked awkwardly in his arms. He had the same easy confidence he'd always carried, even if his gait was a little slower these days.

At thirty-five, Nico Grimaldi was nearing the end of his contract with the Atlanta Fire, but he still had the same charm—and the same protective streak—that he'd wielded like a weapon since we were kids.

"You're not exactly a spring chicken yourself," I shot back, crossing my arms as I leaned against the doorframe. "Be careful with that. Wouldn't want you to strain something and not be able to sing."

"Don't worry, Gem, I'm a professional," he said, grinning as he set the chairs down inside the house. "You're the one I gotta worry about."

I rolled my eyes, but I couldn't help smiling. Nico had convinced me to come back to Atlanta, after years of me insisting I'd be fine on my own in Los Angeles.

And I had been, but fine wasn't enough anymore.

Not with my daughter Winnie starting school soon and rent skyrocketing out of reach.

Atlanta wasn't just more affordable. It was family. It was Nico.

And for the first time in years, it felt like home.

"Where's Winnie?" Nico asked, his voice softening.

"Inside," I said. "She's helping Megan unpack her toys."

"Megan's a saint," he muttered, shaking his head. "No way I'm stepping into the whirlwind that is your four-year-old."

"You mean your *delightful* four-year-old niece," I said, arching an eyebrow.

He grinned. "Sure. Delightful."

Before I could respond, Megan appeared at the door,

her face flushed but smiling as her glossy chocolate bob swung side to side in front of her eyes. She'd packed on muscle in my absence, and I was glad she was hitting the gym to burn off her nervous energy. Her job was sedentary —a work-from-home medical scheduler—and she had never been one for sitting still. Sitting still only worsened her anxiety.

Megan O'Reilly had been my best friend since elementary school, and though she'd stayed in Atlanta when I moved across the country, we'd never lost touch. She was the kind of friend who showed up when you needed her, no matter what.

"Gemma, your kid just made me an imaginary smoothie in her toy kitchen and tried to charge me five bucks," she said, laughing.

"What flavor?"

"I am a pineapple and mustard person, according to her," Megan said, wrinkling her nose.

Nico snorted, and I couldn't help laughing as Megan joined us outside, brushing her hands off on her jeans. Nico stared with too much interest as she straightened herself out, so I smacked his arm. I knew that look of his, and the thought of my brother and my best friend together was too much.

He cleared his throat and smiled. "Better than the shrimp and gravy one she offered me."

Megan grimaced. "Guess I lucked out."

"Where's your cavalry?" I asked Nico, nodding toward the driveway.

"They'll be here, don't worry. So, Megan, been a long time since I've seen you."

"That's your own fault, Grimaldi," she said, hands on her hips. Her minty green eyes flicked up and down over him. "I've been here the whole time, but you're too much of a big shot these days to keep in contact with the little people."

He smirked. "You're not the little people, O'Reilly. You're something special."

I didn't like that one bit.

"So, anyway," I said, sharply cutting their sexual tension that made me want to barf. "When did you say the guys are coming here—"

"Guys?" Megan brightened at the thought.

"Eh, now," he said, gesturing to three massive SUVs pulling up in front of my house.

As a dozen of the Atlanta Fire's best hopped out of the vehicles, Nico quickly introduced us and by the end of it, I'd forgotten most of their names.

I knew a couple of them from before I'd left—Beau, Victor, and Sergei—but the rest were a blur.

It was less than a minute before they were hauling boxes and furniture like it was a pre-season training drill. As soon as Winnie came out of her room to make me an asparagus and lime smoothie, she saw the players and jumped up and down, clapping. "Uncle Nicos!"

Nico laughed and scooped her up in his arms. "That's right. It's a whole fleet of Uncle Nicos to help get you all moved in."

"Yay!" Winnie had always been that way. As much as I tried to drill stranger danger into my kiddo, she had never met a stranger in her life. When the guys passed by her, she greeted them with the poise of a Disney princess high on too much candy. A couple of the guys ruffled her red pigtails as they worked, and she basked in the attention.

It worried me.

Any of the players who were on the team five years ago could have been her father.

Being back home had made me paranoid.

I had never asked Nico if any of the players hadn't worn a navy tux that night. I didn't want to know, and I didn't want him to suspect anything—it would have been a weird question to ask.

As far as he knew, her father was a one night stand that left me with a present. I didn't tell him when it happened, because telling him would have opened up a can of worms.

The truth was, her father was probably one of the hospital employees. My kid was whip smart, so he was a doctor or a lawyer in my imagination. Had to be.

Not that a hockey player couldn't be smart, but it seemed more likely to be one of the other men at the event. For that matter, he could have been some society douchebag who didn't like going to events.

Or I was just kidding myself and her father was standing in my house right now.

I put the thought out of my mind to focus on the present. We were rebuilding our lives in Atlanta, and I'd never see her father again, so the whole thing was moot. Life had moved on while I was gone.

Megan had a new career that she liked and which let her stay home so she didn't have the stress of leaving her house. Nico had made himself a family in my absence, even if that family was technically his coworkers.

They seemed to be a good group. The guys apologized

when they cursed in front of Winnie, and one of them shooed me away from moving an end table and took it himself. It was sweet, but it also made me feel like I should be paying them.

"You didn't have to drag them into this," I told Nico.

"They volunteered," he said, waving me off. "They owe me for all the times I covered for their asses on the ice."

"Well, I appreciate it," I said. "I was going to hire movers, but this is...better."

"You mean cheaper," Megan teased, nudging me.

"There's that," I admitted.

"And it's a good show."

"That, too." We watched as the guys got hot and sweaty, moving everything into the house. It was fun to boss them around, but a little awkward. But being a single mom meant I had to take all the free help I could get.

By the time the last box was unloaded, dishes were stored, and the furniture was mostly where it needed to be, the sun was dipping low on the horizon, casting a steamy glow over the neighborhood.

I'd baked cookies as a thank you, so I brought the tray out to the front porch where they hung out, and Megan delivered lemonade and milk.

"Cookies?" Beau asked, his eyes lighting up as I handed him the tray.

"Yeah, cookies!" Winnie sang out as she reached for one from Nico's lap.

"Freshly baked chocolate chip," I said as I passed the tray around. "It's the least I can do."

"Coach wouldn't like it if we cheat on our diets," Nico said, grabbing one anyway.

"Your coach sounds like a pain in the ass," I said, grinning.

"He is," Nico admitted around a mouthful of cookie. "But he improved our game, so his methods work."

"Better how?" I asked, curious despite myself. The other guys helped themselves to cookies, and Megan flirted with every one of them as she passed out drinks.

Nico was distracted by that, his eyes on her as he told me, "He's tough, but fair. He's got this way of holding us accountable without making us feel like we're getting lectured. And he knows the game, inside and out. Guy's a walking hockey encyclopedia. Can't imagine the Fire without him."

Nico was always talking about his coach when I asked him about work, and every time, it made me wonder about him and how much he missed Dad. I shoved the thought away.

"You sound like you admire your coach."

"I do. He's earned everyone's respect. I'd call him the hardest worker on the team, but our trainer probably takes that title," Nico explained.

"Esai is slave driver," Sergei said, his Russian accent hitting hard. "Good man."

Megan lit up at the thought. "So, you like being worked hard?"

"Megan," I hissed as a warning, jerking my head toward Winnie.

"What?" she said as faux-innocently as possible. "It was just a question."

"Right."

Nico looked perturbed, but as soon as Winnie passed

him another cookie, the frown subsided. "You should meet him."

"Who?"

"Coach."

"Why?"

"For your new job. Interviewing the head coach of the Atlanta Fire? That'd be a hell of a way to kick things off."

I blinked, caught off guard. "You think he'd agree to it?"

"I can make it happen," Nico said. "Coach likes me."

"Debatable," Megan muttered under her breath, earning a laugh from Sergei.

I looked at Nico and thought it over. My new job as a sports writer for a major outlet in Atlanta was a fresh start, a chance to rebuild my career closer to family. And an interview with the Fire's head coach—someone who'd taken a team with a mixed reputation and turned them into serious contenders—would be a huge get. They'd even won the Stanley Cup since he joined the team. I couldn't say no to that.

"Okay," I said, nodding. "Let's do it."

Nico grinned, and for the first time in what felt like forever, I felt like I was exactly where I was supposed to be.

Chapter 5

Casey

The aroma of freshly brewed coffee hit me as I stepped into the breakroom for a welcome reprieve from the whirlwind of meetings and practice schedules that had been my life since dawn.

I reached for a mug from the cabinet, vaguely aware of the sound of typing and frustrated muttering behind me. Turning around, I wasn't surprised to see Whitney parked at the small table, her laptop open, her fingers flying across the keyboard.

"They call it a breakroom for a reason, Whit," I said, pouring myself a cup. "You're supposed to be taking a break."

She glanced up, her angry expression softening slightly when she saw me. "Morning, Casey."

Whitney Dobson was the backbone of the Atlanta Fire's PR machine, a wizard at crafting stories and putting out fires—both literal and figurative—when the team's reputation was at stake.

She'd been with the organization since before I came on

board, and in all that time, I'd never seen her crack under pressure. But lately, there'd been a tightness in her shoulders and a strain in her voice that even her carefully polished professionalism couldn't hide.

"Working through lunch again?" I asked, taking a seat across from her.

She sighed, pushing a strand of dark hair behind her ear. "It's not like I have much of a choice. The team's image took a beating last year, and I'm still trying to clean it up. Besides, breaks are for losers."

"To my understanding, breaks are for humans. Come on, let me get you a cup of coffee so you might look up from that screen for longer than a blink."

"Are you insinuating I am a human?"

I chuckled, shaking my head as I poured her a cup of coffee. "Wouldn't dream of it."

As I passed her the cup, she snatched it and sipped before uttering, "Thank you."

I nodded. The past year had been rough. Between a string of bad press and a few serious high-profile scandals—most of them revolving around Luke Smith, our former playboy winger—Whitney had been running damage control nonstop. Things had started to settle down since Luke's sudden wedding a few months ago, but Whitney clearly wasn't ready to relax just yet.

"What's the latest?" I asked, genuinely curious. "Is Keke doing okay since having the baby?" I wasn't sure how she had survived the birth—Luke had a big head, so I doubted her labor would have been easy.

"Keke's great, and Oscar is the best baby who ever babied, they are not my problem."

"I thought having her around would mean your job got easier."

She sighed and sat back, running a finger around the rim of her mug. "She tries. And she's great at what she does. But that doesn't change the fact that this team is *my* show, and with so many players doing their level best to make my life interesting, there's only so much Keke can do. She's a miracle worker, and I need something bigger than a miracle."

"Well, how come? I thought things simmered down after their wedding and the baby."

"It's not Luke this time." She leaned back in her chair, crossing her arms. "The buzz around the Fire isn't what it used to be. Ticket sales are steady, but they're not growing the way we need them to. We need to get butts in seats. People aren't excited about the team like they used to be. Which means putting your faces out there—positive press, feel-good stories, things that remind people why they love hockey."

I took a sip of my coffee, mulling it over. "Any ideas?"

"That's the problem," she said, groaning softly. "I've brainstormed everything from community events to social media campaigns, but nothing feels big enough. We need something with real impact. Not just events. Something big on the ice, and that's out of my hands. All I can do is make what you do look good, and that means the guys have to be perfect."

I frowned, thinking about the balance Whitney had to strike every day. As much as she was the best in the business, she depended on having a good team to sell.

The Atlanta Fire was still a big name in the city, but we

were a city with multiple professional teams, and tickets weren't cheap. We had to convince people to part with their hard-earned money, and to do that, we had to provide them with a good show.

Or at the very least, good gossip, according to Whit, and to do that, we needed the press on our side.

A sticky proposition.

The press could be a double-edged sword, as we'd seen all too clearly with Luke. Granted, he was no Boy Scout, but he didn't deserve the reaming the press had given him. One misstep, and the media could turn a puff piece into a feeding frenzy. Or in his case, several missteps. It was a reality I didn't like but had learned to live with over time.

Before I could respond, the breakroom door swung open, and Nico Grimaldi strolled in, carrying an empty water bottle. His easy grin widened when he saw us, and he gave a mock salute to each of us. Even if all they ever wanted to do was play the game, everyone understood how integral Whitney was to the business side of things.

"Coach. Whit. What's the crisis today?" he asked, heading for the water cooler.

"Just trying to figure out how to make you all look good," Whitney said dryly, though there was warmth in her tone. "Any suggestions?"

"Come on, that's gotta be the easiest part of your job," Nico teased, filling his bottle. "You've got nothing to worry about. We're the best looking, best playing, best all-around team in the league. You're smart enough to know how to use us, right?"

She merely rolled her eyes and went back to her tablet.

I chuckled, shaking my head. Nico was in the final year

of his contract, and while his skills on the ice were still sharp, his goofy humor had become one of the team's greatest assets in the locker room.

He was the kind of guy who could defuse tension with a single joke, which made him invaluable in a job as stressful as mine. I was going to miss him at the end of the season.

"And then there's Coach," Nico said, capping his bottle and leaning against the counter. "You want a story? He's got one."

Whitney raised an eyebrow. "Oh?"

"I do?" This was news to me.

"Yeah," he said, his grin turning roguish as he looked at me. "You should talk to my sister. She's a sportswriter—just moved back to Atlanta. She could do a piece on the team and you and me. You know, 'hometown hero in his final season' kind of thing, while also showcasing the rest of the team and how you turned us around and got us on the right track. It'd be perfect."

I blinked, surprised by the suggestion. "Your sister's a journalist?"

"*Sportswriter*," Nico corrected me. "She's worked for some big names out in L.A., but she just took a job here. I think she'd kill it. And Whitney, aren't you always saying earned media is better than paid media? This is that, right?"

Whitney looked intrigued, but hesitation sat on my shoulders. I'd seen what the media could do when they decided to dig their claws in. Luke's name had been dragged through the mud for months, and while he'd brought some of it upon himself, the rest had been pure sensationalism. He had made the mistake of dating a married woman. He hadn't known it but the media had a field day with him.

And then there was the ex-girlfriend who set his car on fire, but that wasn't his fault. Or so he said.

Whitney said, "It's not a bad idea, Casey. What do you think?"

"I don't know," I said slowly. "I'm not sure it's a good idea to invite the press in like that. It could backfire."

Nico waved me off. "Nah, Gemma's not like that. She's not looking for dirt. She's smart, professional, and, honestly, this would be more about the team than just me. A breezy puff piece. Feel-good stuff. No gotchas, nothing hard-hitting."

Whitney leaned forward, clearly considering it. "A feature like that could be huge for us, especially if it's done by someone who knows the game. It would humanize the team, show people the heart behind the sport."

"I still think it's risky," I said, glancing between the two of them. "We've worked hard to keep things steady after last year. I don't want to stir up trouble."

"Coach," Nico said, his tone serious now. "Trust me. Gemma wouldn't do anything to hurt the team—or me. She's my sister. I'll vouch for her."

I hesitated, weighing his words. Nico had always been one of the most dependable guys on the team, both on and off the ice. If he said his sister could handle this, then I owed it to him to listen.

"I know she's your sister, but do you think she'll come here with the sister hat on or the journalist hat?"

"Sister. Totally sister. She won't screw us over, Coach. I know her."

Whitney gave me a pointed look. "This wasn't in my PR

plan but it could certainly help. Something positive to start the new season."

I sighed, running a hand through my hair. "All right. Set it up."

Nico grinned, clapping me on the shoulder. "You won't regret it, Coach. Gemma's the real deal."

Whitney smiled, her shoulders relaxing for the first time all morning. "Good call. I'll coordinate with her and figure out the details."

As they started discussing logistics, I leaned back in my chair. I didn't know much about Gemma Grimaldi, but if she was anything like her brother, this might just work out.

Or it could blow up in our faces. Only time would tell.

Chapter 6

Gemma

His office was smaller than I had expected. The walls were painted an uninspired shade of beige, and the shelves were crammed with binders, framed photos, and a few trophies that seemed to have been tucked between strategy books as an afterthought.

The air was chilly enough to raise goosebumps on my arms, and I resisted the urge to tug my jacket tighter around myself. A desk sat in the middle of the room, papers strewn across its surface in an organized chaos that somehow fit the man sitting behind it.

Coach Casey McConnell.

I recognized him from his pictures online when he stood to greet me, though this was the first time we'd officially met.

He wasn't what I'd expected, either—less intimidating than I'd imagined for someone who managed a team of grown men who made their living by crashing into one another on the ice.

But there was a quiet authority in the way he carried himself, from the straight set of his shoulders to the firm grip of his handshake.

"Gemma," he said, his voice steady but low. "Thanks for coming in."

"Thanks for having me," I replied, offering a smile as I sat in the chair across from him.

As I settled in, I couldn't help noticing his outfit. Despite the chill in the room, he was wearing athletic shorts and a thin, short-sleeved polo that clung to his broad frame. He was strikingly handsome in the classical sense. He had a jaw made of granite and a body made in the gym.

He also had that silver fox thing happening—his gray hair making him look older than his listed age on the team's website. He was only forty-eight according to it, but he must have gone prematurely gray years ago.

His team picture was from when they'd hired him, and he was gray even then. His posture was surprisingly relaxed —until I noticed the way his fingers tapped lightly against the arm of his chair.

He was nervous.

The thought made me smile. Here was a man who could yell at a room full of huge sweaty athletes without batting an eye, yet he looked like he'd rather face off against the league's best enforcer than sit through a puff-piece interview.

It was kinda cute.

"You look comfortable," I said, gesturing to his shorts. "Most people would've dressed up for this."

He glanced down at himself and gave a half-shrug. "I

don't wear what I'd call dress-up clothes when we're training."

I laughed, and the sound seemed to put him at ease. "Fair enough."

This wasn't my first interview, not by a long shot, but it felt different. The stakes were lower—or at least they should've been.

My job was simple. Write a feel-good story about the Atlanta Fire and their veteran center, Nico, whose career was nearing its end.

The team's PR manager had made it clear that this wasn't an exposé or a deep dive. It was a fluff piece, plain and simple. And I was fine with that. I didn't have the energy for drama these days.

But as I pulled my notebook and recorder from my bag, I couldn't shake the strange sense of familiarity that had crept in the moment I walked into his office.

There was something about Casey McConnell—his voice, the way he held himself, the sparkling blue of his eyes—that tugged at the edge of my memory.

It was odd.

I pushed the thought aside and hit record. "So, let's start with the basics. What's it like coaching a team like the Fire?"

His lips twitched into a small smile, though it didn't quite reach his eyes. "It's a challenge, but a good one. We've got a mix of veterans and younger guys, so it's about finding that balance and helping them grow while keeping everyone focused on the same goal."

"And what's that goal?"

He raised an eyebrow, as if the answer was obvious. "Winning."

I laughed again, and this time, his smile softened. "Of course," I said. "But it's more than that, isn't it? There's a culture to build, a legacy to uphold. Do you think the younger players understand that?"

His expression shifted, his gaze thoughtful. "You're right. It's about more than just what happens on the ice. These guys are part of something bigger than themselves. They represent the team, the city, the fans. That comes with responsibility."

"And you're the one who makes sure they don't forget it."

"Try to," he said, leaning back in his chair. "Doesn't always work. But they're good guys. One of the things we focus on is community service to keep us engaged with the city and remind our neighbors we're here for them. When Hurricane Velma came through three years ago, we took the team to the coast to help with relief efforts there and held a fundraiser. Our guys volunteer in the city, each devoting ten hours a week during the season and twenty hours a week in the off-season. The legacy of the Fire is one of service above everything else."

I nodded, scribbling notes as I spoke. I'd forgotten about the hurricane—that was a good note to add for the story. Remind readers what their team has done for them. I shifted gears from the fluffy stuff so I could say the interview was more than just puff. "What's the toughest part of the job?"

"Depends on the day," he said. "Sometimes it's

managing personalities. No one gets into hockey by being a shrinking violet."

"I imagine it's a lot of big egos, that kind of thing?"

"It can be."

A careful answer, sure to not irritate anyone. Was he hiding something? "Coach McConnell, what other challenges do you face with the team?'

He gave a short shrug, and if I wasn't mistaken, there was a hint of a smirk. "Sometimes it's dealing with the media."

He's not going to give me anything juicy. Which was fine. This was, after all, a puff piece. I couldn't blame him for being guarded around me. "Touché. So, what's the easiest part?"

"The game," he said without hesitation. "That's the part I love. Always have. There's nothing like it."

His earnestness caught me off guard, and I found myself smiling again. There was nothing phony about the coach. He wasn't polished or rehearsed the way some people could be during interviews. I detected no media training whatsoever. He was direct, almost blunt, but there was a warmth beneath his professionalism that made me want to keep asking questions.

"Readers will want to know more about you personally. I hope that's all right."

"I'm an open book."

I had interviewed hundreds of people, and of them, a few had made that same declaration. I'd never believed it until now. During my Q&A, I kept it professional, but the truth was, "readers" was me. I wanted to know more about him personally.

The longer we spoke, the more his nervousness seemed to fade, replaced by a quiet confidence that reminded me of why he'd been such a successful coach.

He was passionate about his players, fiercely protective of the team, and deeply invested in the game. And yet, there was an unguardedness about him that I hadn't expected.

It wasn't long before I realized I'd stopped thinking about the story altogether. The questions were flowing easily, naturally, and I wasn't just interviewing him anymore—I was talking to him.

"So," he said, his voice cutting through my thoughts, "what about you?"

"Me?" I asked, caught off guard.

"Yeah," he said, leaning forward slightly. "You're writing about us, but you don't seem like the typical sports-writer. What's your story?"

I hesitated, unsure how much to share. I wasn't used to answering questions. When people got interviewed, they were usually on the defensive or just bragging.

Few ever asked me about me.

I shrugged. "Not much to tell. I grew up in Atlanta, moved to L.A. after college. I've been writing about sports for a few years now."

"And you came back to Atlanta for...?"

"My daughter," I said, the words slipping out before I could think twice. "She's starting school soon, and I wanted to be closer to family."

He nodded, his gaze steady. "That's a big move."

"It is," I admitted. "But it's going well so far."

For a moment, there was silence, the kind that felt heavier than it should have. I couldn't explain why, but something about the way he looked at me made my pulse quicken.

He wasn't just waiting for me to stop talking so he could start talking about himself more. He was studying me, like he was trying to piece together a puzzle.

"You're impressive," he said suddenly, his voice quiet but firm.

The compliment caught me completely off guard. "What?"

"You've got this...calm about you," he said, searching for the words. "But there's strength under it. I can see why Nico speaks so highly of you."

I felt my cheeks warm, and I glanced down at my notebook, trying to regain my composure. "Well, I think Nico might be a little biased."

"Maybe. But I don't think he's wrong."

The air in the room shifted then, charged with something I couldn't pin down. This wasn't an interview anymore. It wasn't just two people talking about hockey.

There was something else, something unspoken, and it set my heart racing. "That's kind of you to say."

"Not kind. Just honest."

"Whatever you want to call it, thank you."

"Would you let me take you out sometime?" he said, his tone careful but direct.

The question hung in the air, heavy with possibility. My brain scrambled for a response, caught between surprise and...something else. Excitement? Nerves? "You went from nervous to bold pretty quickly," I teased, stalling for time to think of an answer.

He chuckled softly, leaning back in his chair. "I've spent

enough time regretting the things I didn't do. Not making that mistake again."

I studied him, my mind spinning. He wasn't what I had expected—at all. But there was something about him that drew me in, something I couldn't ignore.

"Yeah," I said finally, the word slipping out before I could second-guess myself. "I'll go out with you."

His smile widened, and for the first time, I saw the tension in his shoulders ease. He simply said, "Good."

As I packed up my things and headed for the door, I couldn't help but wonder what I'd just gotten myself into.

Saying yes was the easy part. Now, I had to figure out how to make it work—especially with a four-year-old at home and no babysitter lined up. I made a mental note to text Megan as soon as I left. If anyone could help me juggle this new chapter of my life, it was her.

But as I walked out of Casey McConnell's office, my heart still racing, I couldn't help but feel like I'd made the right choice. For once, I wasn't overthinking things. For once lately, I was doing something for me.

Chapter 7

Casey

I was finding it hard to keep in control.

It had been years since I'd been on a real date. Coaching schedules didn't leave much time for romance, and when I'd been in a relationship, I didn't have to worry about dates.

As I sat at a table in one of Atlanta's nicer restaurants, fiddling with the edge of my napkin and waiting for Gemma to arrive, I felt utterly unprepared.

The restaurant was everything I thought a first date required: quiet, classy, and intimate enough to let us actually talk.

I adjusted the cuffs of my shirt, glancing at the door for the hundredth time. My palms were damp, and my heart was doing something that felt suspiciously like a slap shot in my chest. Or a heart attack.

What the hell was wrong with me? I ordered around a team of professional athletes on a daily basis without breaking a sweat, but the thought of spending an evening with Gemma had me tied in knots.

When she finally walked in, I almost forgot how to breathe.

She was wearing a simple black dress that hugged her curves in all the right ways, her red hair cascading over one shoulder like fire against the cool, muted tones of the restaurant.

She looked both elegant and effortlessly herself, and the sight of her sent a wave of heat through me that I hadn't felt in years.

"Sorry I'm late," she said as she approached, her voice light and easy. "Winnie insisted on showing me every single drawing she's ever done before I left."

"You're not late," I said, standing to pull out her chair. "And even if you were, I wouldn't blame you. Sounds like important business."

She smiled as she sat, her brown eyes shining. "It really is. Four-year-olds don't mess around when it comes to their art. Her teddy bear era has ended and we've gotten into drawing food for some reason."

I laughed, settling back into my seat as the waiter appeared to take our drink orders. I opted for a glass of wine, though I was tempted to ask for something stronger to calm my nerves.

Gemma ordered sparkling water, and the way she smiled at the waiter—warm but not flirtatious—made me think she was as naturally kind as her brother always claimed.

"So, do you think she'll be an artist one day?"

"I try very hard not to project onto her what I want for her that way. My only goal is for my girl to be safe and happy. What she does with that is up to her."

"That sounds very open minded of you."

Gemma smiled and shrugged. She did that a lot when I complimented her, and it left me with the impression that she wasn't used to compliments, which was a damn shame. She said, "When you have the safety and happiness stuff taken care of, it's easier to become who you're meant to be, don't you think?"

"I'd have to imagine so. But I don't have any kids, so I'm out of my depth on that end of it, and I'd never presume to know how to raise one."

"It's a lot, but a lot of it you make up on the fly. Reminds me of the one improv class I took in college."

"I bet you were great at it," I said.

She laughed once. "I was awful at it. Nearly failed."

"Can't picture you failing at anything."

"There you go again, being kind."

I shook my head, smiling. "Just honest."

Our drinks came and she went on, "The improv class was stressful. Constantly stressful. I never knew what to expect. But by the end of the class, I had a C to pass it and an understanding of how to deal with people better. It's probably the class I use the most in my day to day routine, and not just with Winnie, but with interviews, too."

"Because you never know what someone will say?"

She nodded once. "For instance, I didn't know you were going to ask me out."

"Neither did I," I confessed. "It just sort of slipped out."

"Is that how you get your dates, Coach McConnell? Accidentally?"

I snorted. "Call me Casey, and usually, no. It takes a lot

of working up the courage and hoping I don't fall flat on my face."

"Am I not intimidating enough to warrant all that effort?" she teased.

"You scare the panties off me."

Gemma laughed far too loudly for the decorum of the restaurant, and I loved to see it. She slapped her hand over her mouth, but her shoulders heaved with residual giggles until she calmed down. "Sorry about that."

"I'm not."

"How precisely do I scare the panties off of you, and yet you were able to ask me out so easily?"

"Because when it came to you, I couldn't help myself."

Her cheeks flushed red from that, but before she could respond, the food came out. After a few initial bites, she asked, "Do you mind if I ask a few work questions?"

"Shoot."

"Not the thing to say to a sharpshooter," she said with a gleam in her eyes.

"Seriously?"

"My dad used to take us to the range when we were kids. I've always had a knack for it."

"See? I knew you were impressive. Does Atlanta still feel like your hometown, or have we changed enough in the past few years to make it different for you?"

She sat back, thinking. "It's still home, but a few of my old haunts are different now. Bing's Books is now a tattoo parlor, that kind of thing. But it still has my favorite people, so it's home."

The moment felt easy, natural—until the waiter returned to deliver our second round of drinks, and in the process, managed to knock over my glass of wine. Red liquid spread across the tablecloth like a bloodstain, soaking through the edge of my shirt and dripping onto my lap.

"Oh, no!" the waiter said, his face going pale as he scrambled to clean up the mess. "I'm so sorry, sir."

"It's fine," I said quickly, though I could feel the heat creeping up my neck because everyone else was staring. I was used to attention in my professional life, but when I was off the clock, I wasn't a fan of it. "Don't worry about it."

Gemma bit her lip, her eyes wide, and for a second, I thought she might be embarrassed and leave. But then she started laughing—softly at first, and then harder, until she was shaking her head and wiping tears from her eyes.

"You're taking this well," I said, trying not to feel like a complete idiot.

"I have a kindergartener," she said, still laughing. "This is nothing. You should see my dining table after spaghetti night."

Her humor was infectious, and before I knew it, I was laughing too. The waiter looked relieved as he cleaned up the mess, and when Gemma reached across the table to squeeze my hand, I felt a warmth that had nothing to do with embarrassment.

The rest of the night didn't go much better.

Her steak came out cold. To my surprise, she still ate it. "I haven't had a hot meal in years. You get used to it."

When my credit card was briefly declined because I'd forgotten to activate the new one my bank sent, I had a small internal panic attack until things got settled.

As we waited for that to be handled, a small child from another table ran up and stole her purse. She laughed as his mother returned the bag, brushing it off with an ease that made me feel like none of it really mattered. "As long as everything's inside, no harm, no foul play."

The mother sighed. "Thank you. He's done this twice in the past month. I don't know what's gotten into him."

"Mine's the same way with the fall leaves since we moved back. I've found a pile under her pillow. You just never know with kids."

"Good luck, hon."

"You, too."

I couldn't believe her. Every woman I'd dated would have lost their shit if a kid stole their purse. "You're hard to rattle."

"I could stress out about the little things or roll with the punches. That kind of stress is a choice, and I choose not to worry about it. The kid was just being a kid, and everything is in my bag."

After we finished at the restaurant, we walked out into the cool night air of an Atlanta autumn. "It's refreshing to spend time with someone who has such a positive outlook on life."

"I didn't always. It took practice and sometimes, it still does," she said, holding up her phone, which was now tethered to a small portable charger. "Case in point, I forgot to charge my phone before I left, so this thing is my lifeline. Most problems have easy solutions. You just have to know where to look."

I grinned, shaking my head. "You're something else, you know that?"

She laughed, nudging me with her shoulder as we walked. "I'll take that as a compliment."

We strolled in companionable silence for a while, wandering toward a nearby park. The city lights glittered in the distance, and the sound of crickets filled the air. It felt strangely intimate, like we'd stepped into a world that belonged only to us.

"Can I ask you something?" I said as we reached a bench near a small fountain.

"Of course."

"Why are you here?" I asked, my voice quieter now. "With me, I mean. I'm so much older than you, and..."

"And what?" she asked, tilting her head.

"I guess I just don't understand why you'd be interested. You could be out with any guy. But you're not."

She studied me for a moment, her expression softening. "Do you really not see it?"

"See what?"

She smiled, reaching up to brush a stray piece of hair out of her face. "You're kind, Casey. And thoughtful. And maybe you don't realize it, but you have this way of making people feel safe. And you've got a great ass."

I laughed because her words caught me off guard. There was something about this woman that I couldn't figure out. I felt a flicker of something I couldn't quite name. Whatever it was, it settled deep in my chest, warming me from the inside out. Gemma saw me as a man. Not just Coach. It had been a long time since someone saw me that way.

"I'm glad you think so," I said finally. "Because I don't think I could stop being interested in your ass even if I tried."

She laughed and I moved in. I kissed her, her hands on

my shoulders and mine cradling her face. Her lips were soft and warm, and the world around us seemed to fade into nothing.

And then it started to rain.

At first, it was just a light drizzle, but within seconds, it turned into a full downpour. Gemma laughed against my lips, and I couldn't help but laugh too, pulling her closer as the rain soaked through our clothes.

"Guess this date isn't done going wrong," I said, grinning.

"Depends on how you look at it," she said, her eyes sparkling with mischief.

"We should find someplace to lay low until the rain passes—"

"Why would we do that? You'll keep me warm, won't you, Casey?"

I answered without words, slanting my mouth over hers as I backed her against a nearby tree that stood in a cluster of them. It was the most privacy we could find in the moment, and since no one had been around before the storm, I wasn't too concerned with propriety.

The rain on her lips, the way it soaked through her dress so it clung tighter to her body, I was lost in my senses and all of them pointed to Gemma.

She wasn't shy about what she wanted, either. Her hands wandered down over my pants, and I hadn't planned on that, but I wasn't about to turn it down.

I wanted Gemma. It wasn't right of me—consorting with a player's family was strictly forbidden for a number of reasons. But I couldn't remember a single one of them at the moment. She had me, and I couldn't help myself.

I reached beneath her dress, my hand sliding between her thighs. She groaned in my mouth, and it was a sound I wanted to hear over and over. Blood was pouring into my cock. "You like this, don't you."

"Don't stop!"

I couldn't help but smile hearing that. When I slipped my hand into her underwear, she was wet already, and her body jolted when I played with her. She was tight on my fingers, and her whimpers only grew when I worked her over.

She rode my hand, bucking between me and the tree with her arms around my neck for balance. We kissed, but it was more than that.

It was everything.

As she came, she cried out, the rain drowning out the sound. I gentled my fingers out of her, and she gasped, "I want more."

Thank God.

I pressed my forehead to hers. "Tell me what you want, Gemma."

"I want you inside of me."

No sweeter words in the English language. Unfortunately, I was unprepared. "I don't have a condom."

She pulled one from her purse. "I do."

I put it on, and with a furtive glance around the park, asked one more time, "How do you want me?"

"Bad." She giggled.

"I mean, what angle?" But I didn't wait for an answer.

I kissed her and picked her up, so her back was against the tree and her legs belted my waist.

I slid inside of her and the deeper I went, the more her

head tipped back to the tree as she moaned. Her exposed throat begged to be licked and bitten, and I obliged, tasting every raindrop that dared to touch her.

I pumped deep into her and relished the feel of her tight heat. It was addictive, this feeling. I should have been scared to death, unable to perform. We were in public. She was too young for me. She was one of my player's sisters.

But none of that mattered. Or maybe the forbidden aspect added an edge that I didn't want to acknowledge.

Gemma rode me rough, bouncing on my cock like it belonged to her. And in the moment, it did.

She gripped my shoulders, her thighs squeezed my waist, and all I wanted in the world was to see her come. None of that other stuff was on my radar.

When she came, I felt it, too. That rhythmic pulse. It drove me to my own edge, and just moments later, a surge shot through my spine and my balls as it hit, taking my breath away.

I leaned on the tree to stop from collapsing. My heart pounded in ways it hadn't in years.

When it was over, we stood there for a moment, the rain cooling the heat between us. I turned my head to look at her, and she smiled, her hair plastered to her neck and her eyes bright with something I couldn't quite name.

"You're incredible," I said softly, brushing a piece of hair out of her face.

"So are you," she said, her voice just as soft.

As we cleaned up and headed back toward the street, I reached for her hand, lacing my fingers through hers.

I didn't know what would come next, but I wasn't going to let it slip through my fingers.

Not this time.

I walked her to her car. "I'll call you."

"You better," she said, her smile teasing but sincere.

And as I watched her drive away, I couldn't help but feel like my world had tilted on its axis. And I couldn't have been happier about it.

Chapter 8

Gemma

The sound of my phone vibrating against the desk startled me out of the trance I'd been in while reading the comments section on my latest article.

Normally, I avoided the comments like the plague, but today, I couldn't help myself.

The piece—an in-depth interview with Coach Casey McConnell about his coaching philosophy and the culture of the Atlanta Fire—had been up for less than a day, and it was already blowing up.

"Smart, insightful, and a great read," one commenter had written.

"Finally, something positive about the Fire in the press!" said another.

Admittedly, I might have slanted the puff piece a little more in his favor than a reputable journalist should have, but I didn't care. I wanted the city to see him the way I saw him.

The man who had fixed the Fire.

I clicked out of the page and leaned back in my chair, letting out a breath I hadn't realized I was holding. It was good press for the team, yes, but it was also good for me.

My editor had already sent a gushing email that morning, asking if I had any other ideas for Fire-related pieces. I could practically hear the excitement in his voice when he mentioned the spike in web traffic.

"I knew you'd be a great fit here," he'd written. "More interviews like this, Gemma. Keep them coming."

It was exactly the kind of validation I'd been hoping for when I'd taken this job, but it left me feeling conflicted. I wanted to succeed, yes, but my budding...whatever-it-was with Casey complicated things.

I didn't want to use him for clicks. According to Nico, he'd been hesitant to agree to the interview in the first place, and while it had turned out well, I didn't want him to feel like I was exploiting our connection for my career.

Then there was the other issue: Nico.

My brother was protective on a good day and downright territorial when it came to the people he cared about.

If he found out I was seeing his coach he'd lose his mind.

There was an unspoken code about sisters being off-limits, and while I wasn't about to let my brother dictate my love life, I also didn't want to make things harder for Nico or Casey at work.

"Gemma," Megan's voice broke through my thoughts. She leaned against the doorway to my home office, holding a steaming mug of tea. "Why are you smiling like that? Did someone send you another email about how brilliant you are?"

"No," I said quickly, though my cheeks heated. "I was just thinking."

"Thinking about what?" she asked, setting the mug on my desk and settling into the chair opposite me.

I hesitated for half a second before deciding to tell her the truth. Megan was my best friend. She knew everything about me, and there was no way I could keep this from her any longer. Besides, if I didn't spill, she'd probably drag it out of me eventually.

"Okay," I said, sitting up straighter. "The other night when I told you I had a work thing that I needed you to babysit Winnie for—"

"It was really a date, right?"

I gulped. "How did you know?

"Because you came back giddy like you used to when you got laid in high school," she said, her eyebrows arching.

I'd forgotten all about that. "Wait—so you knew?"

"Duh. I've only known you since we were assigned seats in Mrs. Wilson's class in third grade. Of course I knew. Stop beating around the bush and tell me what you're building up to."

"I wanted to tell you about the date, actually. It—"

"Was a perfect fairytale?"

I snickered. "Actually, no. It went terribly wrong. The waiter spilled wine on him, the food was awful, a kid stole my purse, his credit card got declined, and we ended up soaked in the rain."

Megan looked horrified. "Then why are you smiling while telling me about it?"

"Because he called me this morning to ask me out on another date."

"Wait, wait, wait," Megan said, holding up a hand. "He *called* you? Like, on the phone? Who does that?"

"Apparently, older guys," I said, laughing.

"How much older are we talking?"

I took a breath, hoping she wouldn't judge me for it. "He's forty-eight."

"That's...nineteen years older than us."

"Trust me, I've done the math." Too many times. "Is that weird?"

She frowned and thought about it. "It's not normal, and is therefore weird, but do I think it's bad? Not really. You're both adults. I'm pretty much of the opinion that as long as everyone involved is over twenty-five, do whatever you want."

Thinking about that night, I couldn't help but sigh. "I did. I really, really did."

"The sex was that good?"

"Good is an insufficient word for it. The man knows his way around a woman's body."

"Well he should. He was there when Eve was made from Adam's rib."

I smacked her shoulder. "Hey."

She only grinned. "Oh, come on. You're dating a fossil and I can't say anything about it?"

"He's not that old."

"Okay, sure. But seriously, you think this might go somewhere?"

"Maybe." I thought about it. In fact, it was all I'd been thinking about. Looking at my comment section had been a distraction from it, but in the back of my mind, the question had lingered. "He isn't like anyone I've ever dated before,

Meg."

"How so?"

"There's no games, no guessing. He's...direct."

"Well, yeah. He used his phone for a phone call." She wrinkled her nose. "I don't know if I like that. It's weird. I mean, what's wrong with texting?"

"Nothing," I said, shrugging. "But there's something charming about a guy who knows what he wants and isn't afraid to say it to you."

Megan stared at me for a moment, then leaned back in her chair, crossing her arms. "You're really into him, aren't you?"

"I think I am."

She let out a dramatic sigh, shaking her head. "I don't know how to process this. You're dating a guy old enough to have a landline."

I tossed a pen at her. "Stop. He's not *that* old."

"Okay, okay," she said, her tone more serious now. "So, are you going to tell me who he is?"

My stomach sank. But if I couldn't trust Megan, I couldn't trust anyone. "The coach of the Atlanta Fire."

Her mouth dropped open. "The guy you interviewed? The guy who coaches your brother's team? *That* coach?"

"Yeah."

She blew out a breath. "Are you sure this is a good idea? That could get messy."

"I know," I said, my smile fading. "But we're keeping it quiet for now. Just until we figure out what this is."

She nodded slowly, though she still looked skeptical. "Okay. But if Nico finds out and loses his mind, don't say I didn't warn you."

"Noted." But the memory of our rainy night sex hit me hard. "Meg, this is bad. I can't stop thinking about the sex."

"Need me to distract you or do you want to talk about it some more?"

"He just...the way he kisses, the way he touches me, it's electric. It took all the strength I had to leave him that night, and after the sex, I had almost none to speak of."

"Sounds dangerous."

"Well—"

"No, I meant in a good way."

I laughed. "Yeah. Definitely."

Just then, my phone buzzed on the desk, and my heart skipped a beat when I saw Casey's name on the screen.

"Speak of the devil," Megan said, smirking. "Are you going to answer?"

"Of course," I said, picking up the phone. "Hello?"

"Hey," Casey said, his voice warm and steady. "Did I catch you at a bad time?"

"No, not at all," I said, leaning back in my chair. "What's up?"

"I was thinking about our next date," he said. "Maybe this time we try something a little less...disastrous."

I laughed, glancing at Megan, who was now pretending to type furiously on her phone to give me some privacy. But I knew she could hear everything. "I'd like that," I said. "What did you have in mind?"

"There's a rib joint downtown I've been meaning to check out," he said. "It's laid-back, good music, good drinks. I think you'd like it."

"That sounds perfect."

"Great," he said, and I could hear the smile in his voice. "How's Friday?"

I mouthed the question to Megan, and she nodded, my babysitter guaranteed. "Friday works."

"Looking forward to it," he said. "And, Gemma?"

"Yeah?"

"I'm glad you said yes."

The line went quiet, and I stared at my phone for a moment, a stupid grin plastered across my face.

"Okay, I take it back," Megan said, leaning forward. "That was kind of adorable."

"Told you."

But as the excitement settled into something quieter, I couldn't help but wonder where this was all heading. Casey was unlike anyone I'd ever dated—older, steadier, and completely uninterested in playing games. It scared me a little. In a good way.

Chapter 9

Casey

I hadn't felt this nervous about a date in forever.

I'd spent the better part of the day trying to keep my focus on work—practice schedules, player drills, game plans—but every time I had a free moment, my mind drifted back to Gemma. Her laugh, her smile, the way she made me feel like I wasn't just some old geezer she was humoring for a story. I couldn't put my finger on it, but there was something about her that was starting to pull me in deeper than I'd thought possible.

It scared the hell out of me.

By the time the evening rolled around, I had a plan—a simple one, because I didn't want this to feel like a production. I wanted her to know that I liked her. Not just because of what happened in the park, though that had been incredible, but because of who she was. I was entranced by her humor, her honesty, the way she looked at life with a kind of calmness I hadn't realized I'd been missing until she walked into my office.

Normally, I was all work, no play. The team was my

focus, and that was enough for me. It was also the reason I was single. Hard to maintain a relationship when your attention was divided. I was always coming up with new plays in the back of my mind, so when a woman asked the usual, "What're you thinking?" type of question, I told them.

As it turns out, no woman likes it when you tell her you're thinking about work while you're in the shower together.

But when it came to Gemma, all that noise went away. I wasn't focused on work around her. I was focused on her. What she might say in the next moment or how I could make her smile. The way she laughed when things went sideways. She was a breath of fresh air in every sense of the phrase.

So, tonight, I'd do my best to show Gemma who I was outside of the arena. I was determined not to make the same mistakes I had in the past. I decided to take her to my favorite barbecue spot—a no-frills place tucked into a corner of downtown Atlanta that served the best ribs I'd ever had. It wasn't fancy, and it wasn't romantic, but it was real. And for some reason, I felt like Gemma would appreciate that.

When I pulled up to her house to pick her up, she stepped out wearing a casual pair of jeans and a simple blouse, her red hair loose around her shoulders. She looked effortlessly beautiful, and when she smiled at me, the tension in my chest eased.

"You look great," she said, glancing at my jeans and polo.

"Thanks," I said, opening the passenger door for her. "I hope you're up for the best ribs in Atlanta."

Her eyes lit up, and I knew I'd made the right call. "That's a hell of a claim."

"You'll see."

The restaurant was just as I remembered it—dimly lit, the scent of smoked meat wafting through the air, and hip hop playing low in the background. The place was mostly booths with a few tables in the middle, each one covered by a checkered plastic tablecloth topped by a full napkin dispenser. A cooler sat near the entrance so we grabbed some sodas and sat in a booth near the cash register. The place was half full, and no one was in a hurry.

When the waiter came to take our order, Gemma didn't hesitate. "Full rack of ribs," she said, her tone decisive. "And fries. And extra wet wipes, if you've got 'em."

I laughed, raising an eyebrow. "Not holding back, huh?"

"It's been five years since I've had good southern ribs," she said, practically bouncing in her seat. "I'm not wasting the opportunity."

I ordered the same thing and after he left, I asked, "Five years? How come?"

"Los Angeles," she said, rolling her eyes. "They don't do barbecue like this out there. Everything's kale and quinoa. No offense to kale and quinoa, but it's not the same. Not even if you drown it in barbecue sauce."

I chuckled, watching as her enthusiasm bubbled over. "So you're happy to be back in Atlanta?"

"I didn't realize how much I missed it until I came back. The food, the people, the way the air feels...it's just different. This is home."

Something in her tone tugged at my chest. I wasn't sure if it was the way she said the word *home* or the way she looked at me when she said it, but it made me want to reach across the table and hold her hand. But I worried that'd be forward. Weird, that.

We'd had sex, but holding her hand right now felt too intimate. So, instead, I settled for a smile. "I, for one, am glad you're back."

Her gaze lingered on mine for a moment, and I thought I saw the faintest hint of color rise to her cheeks before the waiter arrived with our food. "Me too."

I wasn't prepared for how thoroughly Gemma would tackle her ribs. By the time she was halfway through her full rack, her hands were covered in sauce, her face wasn't much better, and there was a small pile of used napkins accumulating on her side of the table. She didn't seem to care, though—in fact, she looked like she was having the time of her life.

"These are incredible," she said, licking a bit of sauce off her thumb. "I don't think I've ever been this happy."

I laughed, shaking my head. "You're a mess."

"I know," she said unapologetically. "Totally worth it."

Watching her was exhilarating in a way I couldn't explain. She wasn't self-conscious, wasn't trying to be anything other than exactly who she was. That kind of confidence was rare, and I couldn't get enough of it.

"Five years," I said, leaning back in my seat. "That's a long time to go without good ribs."

"It's not just the food, though the food here is far and away better than Los Angeles," she said, reaching for another napkin. "Minus the tacos. That's where they have Atlanta beat."

"I'll have to take you to my favorite taco shop some time. We'll see how they compare."

"Oh, yes please." She excused herself to the bathroom to wash up, so I did the same. When we came back, she said, "I didn't realize how much I'd missed Atlanta until I came back. It's good to feel like I belong somewhere again."

Her words hit me harder than I expected, and I found myself nodding. "I get that. Sometimes it takes leaving to figure out where you're supposed to be."

"How so?"

"My family is from Maryland, and I visit now and then, but after living in Atlanta, Maryland doesn't feel like home anymore. This is home."

She looked at me then, her green eyes locking onto mine, and for a moment, the world felt quieter. I wanted to say more, to tell her how much I was starting to feel like she might be where I was supposed to be. But the words felt too big, too soon, too crazy, so I let the moment pass.

After dinner, I asked if she wanted to come back to my place to watch a movie. She agreed without hesitation, and as we drove, I was nervous again. Funny. No other woman had ever made me nervous the way Gemma did.

I was stuck somewhere between wanting to impress her and wanting to show her the real me. I'd been looking forward to showing her my favorite movie all week—not because I thought she'd love it, but because it felt like letting her into a part of my world.

When we got to my house, I led her into the living room and grabbed the DVD off the shelf. She laughed when she saw the cover.

"*Casablanca*?" she asked, raising an eyebrow. "How old are you again?"

"It's a classic!" I said, grinning.

"I'll be the judge of that."

She settled onto the couch, tucking her legs beneath her as I started the movie. I sat next to her, leaving a polite amount of space between us at first, but it wasn't long before she leaned into me, resting her head on my shoulder. The simple intimacy of it set me at ease, and I wrapped an arm around her, pulling her closer.

As the movie played, I felt myself relaxing into the moment. The plot was as familiar as an old friend, but having Gemma there made it feel new. She asked questions about the story and gasped when the tension ramped up. Watching her react to something I loved made me see it through fresh eyes, and I couldn't remember the last time I'd felt so content.

About halfway through, she turned to me with an apologetic smile. "I hate to say this, but I'm not up for fooling around tonight. I think I'm slipping into a food coma from those ribs."

I laughed, shaking my head. "Neither am I. I just wanted to watch the movie with you."

Her smile softened, and she nestled closer, her back pressing onto my chest as we spooned on the couch. "You're full of surprises, Casey."

"So are you," I said, brushing a strand of hair away from her face.

"I hope you like surprises."

"Most of the time. You?"

She yawned. "Yeah. Especially from you."

She fell asleep not long after, her breathing evening out as her body relaxed against mine. I stayed where I was, not wanting to wake her, and let my thoughts wander.

I'd been in love before. I knew the symptoms. Or at least, I thought I did. Feelings for different women were always unique in their depth and breadth. But this thing with Gemma was something else entirely.

The other times I'd been in love, it was this grown-up, mature kind of thing. It lacked the magnetic pull I felt with her. It was more cerebral—go to her house, bring her flowers, take her to the nicest places in town, keep things formal so she knew I took her seriously, all that stuff adults were supposed to do to show that they cared.

But how much of that was something I wanted to do? Was I just using plays from someone else's playbook this whole time? I had never felt like my exes knew me. Or maybe that was how I kept from getting too involved. My way of keeping them at a distance.

Had I ever watched *Casablanca* with any of them?

The truth was, what I felt with Gemma was completely unique. I hadn't felt this way about anyone before—not even in my longest relationship. There was something about her that made me feel like I was seeing the world differently, like I was finally waking up after years of sleepwalking.

As I held her, her warmth pressing against me, I felt a stir of desire that had nothing to do with sex and everything to do with her. She was messy, unfiltered, and completely herself, and I couldn't get enough of it.

I couldn't tell her now or anytime soon, but there was

something about Gemma Grimaldi that felt like home. Like she was the person I could be myself with and she wouldn't run screaming for the hills.

Chapter 10

Gemma

The faint light of morning seeped through the windows when I woke up on the couch. For a moment, I wasn't entirely sure where I was, the unfamiliar surroundings catching me off guard. Not in LA anymore, genius.

But this wasn't my place.

Then, everything flooded back—the relocation, the date, the ribs, the movie, and the way I'd fallen asleep spooned against him, his arm wrapped protectively around me. What the hell was in those ribs? I hadn't slept that deeply in years. If ever.

Careful not to disturb him, I shifted slightly, my limbs stiff from sleeping in the same position for hours. Casey was still asleep, his breathing deep and steady. His hair was slightly mussed, and his lips were parted just enough to let out the faintest hint of a snore. The sight made my chest ache in a way I wasn't sure how to describe.

But nature was calling, and I didn't want to risk waking him, so I slipped out from under his arm and padded toward the bathroom. The cool tile under my feet helped shake off the lingering grogginess as I splashed water on my face and stared at my reflection. My cheeks were flushed, my hair a bit of a mess, but I couldn't help the smile on my lips.

We'd had a completely nonsexual date, and somehow, I felt even closer to him. First his favorite rib place, followed by his favorite movie. And when I told him there'd be no sex for the night, he was relieved. I saw it on his face. We were simpatico in a way that I didn't quite understand, like we shared a vibe or something.

Megan was going to have a field day with this one. She'd probably demand to know his birth date so she could do his astrology chart and see if we're destined or something.

I didn't know what the future held for us, but I was eager to find out.

After a few minutes, I made my way back into the living room, ready to finish that nap. When I was gone, Casey had rearranged himself in his sleep, sprawling out on the couch. His shirt had shifted to the side, exposing a sliver of tanned skin and the curve of his shoulder.

That's when I saw it.

The birthmark.

It wasn't a subtle mark—it was shaped unmistakably like Italy, stretching along his shoulder.

I froze, my breath catching in my throat as my heart pounded against my ribs.

I knew that birthmark.

It was burned into my memory, as clear as the night I'd first seen it. That masquerade ball, five years ago. The man I'd called *Red,* the man whose face I'd never seen but whose warmth, whose voice, and whose body had stayed with me long after I'd left him.

Casey McConnell was Red.

No, no, no...

A wave of dizziness washed over me as the realization hit.

This man wasn't just a stranger I'd hooked up with years ago.

He was Winnie's father.

There had been no one else around that time. Just him.

My first instinct was to wake Casey up, to blurt out the truth and tell him everything. He deserved to know the truth. But as I stared at him, his peaceful face free of worry and the faintest smile playing on his lips even in sleep, a knot of fear twisted in my stomach.

What would he say?

How would anyone react to being woken out of a sound slumber by life-changing news? Would he be angry with me for not tracking him down? For not telling him he had a daughter? Would he hate me for making the decision to keep her without involving him?

I'd convinced myself all those years ago that I was sparing both of us by not reaching out. I hadn't wanted to burden him with the responsibility of a child, especially when he'd never asked for one. And if I was honest, I hadn't been ready to give up my dream job or the life I'd been building for myself in L.A.

And I didn't know how to contact him. Not really. No name, no number.

I would have had to ask Nico to help him narrow the search down, and that wasn't happening. As much as my brother understood I was an adult with a life of her own, if I'd asked him to track down the man I'd had my one and only one night stand with, he might have exploded.

But now... now everything was different.

Now, her father was in my life in a way I hadn't expected.

And he was already starting to mean something to me—not just as Winnie's father, but as a man I cared about.

I stood there for what felt like an eternity, my mind spinning with questions and doubts. I stared and stared, not sure what to do. Every possibility swirled into muck in my head, and I wanted to run away or tell him or beg him to forgive me or all three.

When Casey stirred and opened his eyes, I quickly wiped the panic off my face, replacing it with a forced smile. "Hey there."

"Hey," he said groggily, his voice low and warm. "You're up early."

"Yeah," I said, my voice too bright. Old habits crept in, knowing exactly how to get me out of here. "Um, the ribs didn't sit well with me. I think I need to head home."

Concern flashed across his face, and he sat up, his hair adorably disheveled. "Are you okay? Do you want me to drive you?"

"No, no," I said quickly, grabbing my purse. "I'll be fine. I didn't want to wake you, so I called a ride share. I think I just need to rest a bit."

He hesitated, clearly reluctant to let me leave like this, but he didn't press. "All right. Text me when you get home, okay? Just so I know you're okay."

"I will," I promised, my chest tightening at the worry in his voice. "Thanks for understanding."

He walked me to the door, his hand brushing mine briefly as I stepped outside. For a moment, I almost turned back, almost told him everything. But the words caught in my throat, and I gave him a weak smile instead.

"Bye, Casey," I said, my voice barely above a whisper.

"Take care, Gemma."

Thankfully, the rideshare came quickly, and my driver was a woman. She knew enough not to ask too many questions as she drove me home. Picking up a woman in last night's clothes probably meant she didn't want to answer a bunch of questions.

I replayed the memories of the night at the masquerade, checking and rechecking them over and over, and each time, the realization hit harder.

As I got out of the car, I made sure to give the driver all the stars and a hefty tip.

When I got home, Megan was sitting on the couch with Winnie, the two of them engrossed in a coloring book. Winnie's bright red hair was pulled into two messy pigtails, and she was babbling excitedly about the food she'd drawn, her crayons scattered across the coffee table.

"Mommy!" she exclaimed when she saw me, running over to wrap her arms around my legs. "Look what I made!"

"That's amazing, sweetie," I said, ruffling her hair and planting a kiss on her cheek.

As Winnie ran back to her coloring, Megan raised an eyebrow at me, her expression equal parts curious and concerned. I followed her into the kitchen so we could talk privately. "You're back early. Though, I guess technically, it's late. What happened?"

I leaned against my fridge, my hands trembling slightly as I tried to find the words. "Megan," I said, my voice shaky. "I think Casey is Red."

Her eyes widened. "Who's—wait. *Red*? From the masquerade? Are you sure?"

"He has the birthmark, the one that looks like Italy that I told you about. The same gray hair. The same blue eyes. He's been coaching the team for seven years, so he would have been there. It's him."

She leaned back on the counter, clearly stunned. "You're sure?"

"One hundred percent," I said.

Megan stared at me for a long moment before finally speaking. "Okay. Wow. So...what now?"

"I don't know," I admitted, burying my face in my hands. "What am I supposed to do? Just blurt out, 'Hey, by the way, you're my daughter's father'? What if he hates me for not telling him sooner?"

"I mean, you had your reasons," Megan said carefully. "You were trying to protect him—and yourself. And Winnie. It's not like you knew him or whether he'd be a good father. You didn't do anything malicious."

"But will he see it that way?" I asked, my voice cracking. "Or will he think I kept him out of Winnie's life on purpose?"

Megan didn't have an answer for that, and the weight of the situation pressed down on me like a boulder. She paused before asking, "What do you even want from him? Do you want him to be part of

Winnie's life? Or is this about your relationship with him?"

"I don't know. I just...I don't want to lose him. But I don't want to blindside him, either."

Megan reached across the gap between us, squeezing my hand. "Maybe you don't have to figure it out right this second. Keep seeing him, get to know him better. Maybe that'll help you decide what to do."

Her words made sense, but they didn't make the fear go away. "The longer I date him without telling him, the more he'll hate me when he finds out."

"*If* he finds out. Gem, this is huge. You don't have to tell him anything you don't want to tell him."

My voice shook. "But I want to tell him, Meg. I want to tell him everything right now. No more secrets."

"Then tell him."

"I...I don't think I can."

She gulped. "Do you want me to tell him?"

"Oh God, no! Wait, are you serious? You'd do that?"

"Don't insult me with questions like that. I'd do anything for you, and you know it."

"Right, I know, it's just..."

"This is huge and it's related to Winnie, so you're freaking out extra?"

"Yeah."

She pulled me in for a hug, and it broke me. I crumbled in her arms, weeping for the cruelty of the situation.

How could I tell him? How could I not? I was screwed either way.

Telling him might mean anything from him being overjoyed to learn he has a daughter, to an ugly court case over custody. Not telling him felt like hell, and it'd only been an hour since I'd figured it out.

I glanced over at Winnie through the pass-thru, who was now singing softly to herself as she colored. She was my whole world, and I'd done everything in my power to give her the best life I could.

But now, with this hanging over me, I couldn't shake the feeling that my choices were about to catch up with me.

For better or worse, Casey McConnell was in our lives now.

And I had no idea what to do about it.

Chapter 11

Casey

The door slammed open, and Whitney strode into my office, looking like a general charging into battle.

I barely had time to look up from the practice schedules scattered across my desk before she dropped a thick folder in front of me with an audible thud. "What's all this?"

"Good morning, Casey," she said briskly, not bothering to wait for an invitation to sit. She plopped herself into the chair across from me, her energy buzzing like she'd just downed three espressos. Knowing Whitney, she had.

"Morning, Whit," I said, pushing aside the coffee I'd been nursing. "What's got you so fired up?"

"This," she said, flipping open the folder. "The interview with Gemma? It's a hit. No, scratch that—it's a home run. The press is eating it up."

"Good," I said cautiously, not quite ready to match her enthusiasm. I wasn't sure if I ever could. She was younger than me and naturally intense. Everything Whitney did was done to the fullest. I admired that about her, but I also wondered whether she ever slept.

I scratched my head. "What kind of numbers are we talking about?"

"Big ones," she said, her grin widening. "Website traffic is up nearly forty percent since the piece went live. Social media engagement? Through the roof. We're even seeing a bump in ticket sales and merch. That woman is a miracle worker."

"That's great news." The Fire had been slogging through a rough patch with the press for the past year, and any positive attention was a win.

"It's not just great—it's game-changing," Whitney said, leaning forward, her elbows on my desk. "For the first time in a long time, people are excited about this team. They're talking about us in a good way. We're not a joke. They're taking us seriously again. And it's all thanks to that interview."

I nodded, letting her words sink in. The piece had been good—Gemma had done a fantastic job capturing the heart of what we were trying to build here. But Whitney's energy suggested there was more to this conversation than just a pat on the back.

"What else?" I asked, crossing my arms.

Whitney's grin turned sharper like she'd been waiting for me to ask. "We need more."

"More?"

"More Gemma," she said bluntly. "She's got a knack for this kind of storytelling, and the fans love it. I want her to have full access to the team."

I didn't like the sound of that. I frowned, my arms tightening across my chest. "What exactly does 'full access' mean?"

"It means she spends time with the players," Whitney explained. "Individual interviews, behind-the-scenes features, personal profiles. Anything that keeps fans engaged and invested. They need to see us as a draw to Atlanta, something to be proud of. They need more."

I tried to keep my face neutral, but the thought of Gemma hanging around the locker room or chatting with the guys during downtime made my stomach twist.

I trusted her—of course, I did—but the idea of someone like Simon or Leo turning on the charm around her? It bugged me more than it should have. And they weren't the only ones to worry about.

No one else knew about what was going on between me and Gemma, and dating her was playing with fire. It was so against the rules that I could lose my job over it. But how could I stop now?

The players would never hit on a woman who was involved. That was not the concern. My guys were completely ignorant of what was happening, which meant they'd have no reason not to hit on her.

And that was a problem.

They were all younger than me.

Simon and Leo were charmers, but they weren't the only ones. The team was full of them. Handsome, younger men who made more money than me. Who had a bigger spotlight on them than me. I didn't hold any of that against them. But in our circumstances, I didn't like the thought of Gemma spending one-on-one time with any of them.

Especially Patrick. He was the unofficial team dad, one

of the few guys they turned to (aside from myself) when it came to knowing how the world worked. At thirty-eight, he was ancient in the world of hockey. But Gemma had shown a predilection for older men by dating me. What would happen when she met another me, but younger, more handsome, and richer?

No. There was no way in hell I was going to let any one of my players within five feet of her.

"You really think this is a good idea?"

"I wouldn't have brought it to you otherwise."

I knew that. Mostly, I was just stalling. We both knew I'd give in to this. It was for the betterment of the team, no matter how I felt about Gemma. I sighed. "For how long?"

"As long as it takes," Whitney said. "Look, I know this isn't ideal. But if we're serious about rebuilding this team's reputation, we need to strike while the iron's hot. Gemma can help us do that. The woman knows how to craft a story with heart and humanity, two things the press has been willfully ignoring about us for too long. We need her."

She wasn't wrong. We were still working to claw our way back into the good graces of the fans. But I still didn't like Gemma hanging around the team like this.

Then again, what I wanted didn't matter.

"I'll talk to the guys," I said finally, forcing a nod. "We'll make it work."

Whitney grinned, standing and gathering the folder. "Knew I could count on you, Casey. I always can."

She swept out of the office as quickly as she'd entered. I leaned back in my chair, running a hand through my hair as I stared at the practice schedules in front of me. But the numbers and letters blurred together, and I couldn't make heads or tails of them.

This was for the team, I reminded myself. For the fans. That was all that mattered. I shook it off and started again.

I hadn't even had time to clear my head when there was a soft knock at the door. This time, the interruption was less forceful but no less disruptive. I looked up to see Matthew Edwards, the team's seventy-nine-year-old owner, peeking his head inside with a mischievous grin.

"Got a minute, Casey?" he asked, his cane tapping lightly on the floor.

"Of course," I said, standing as he entered.

Matthew was, without a doubt, the most eccentric person I'd ever worked for. With his tailored suits, perpetually twinkling eyes, and a seemingly endless supply of bizarre anecdotes, he was equal parts entertaining and exhausting. But he loved the Fire, and he'd poured a fortune into the team over the years, so his quirks were just part of the package.

He waved a hand at me as he settled into the chair across from my desk. "Sit, sit. No need to stand on my account."

I lowered myself back into my seat, bracing for whatever tangent he was about to launch into. There was always a tangent or ten when he visited. I gulped down some coffee so I might have a chance to keep up with him. "What can I do for you, Matthew?"

He leaned forward, his expression suddenly serious. "How's the team shaping up this year?"

"Solid. We've got a good mix of veterans and younger guys. I think we'll surprise some people."

"Good, good," he said, nodding. "But I've been thinking..."

The way he trailed off made the hairs on the back of my neck stand up. Whenever Matthew started a sentence like that, it meant trouble. He could be thinking of telling concessions to change out their plastic cups for metal beer steins or talk about how we need pyrotechnics to burst each time a goal was scored.

I liked that he was creative, but he usually needed that creativity reined in.

"Thinking about what?" I asked cautiously.

"You," he said, pointing his cane at me. "You've done a hell of a job with this team, Casey. Turned them around, made them contenders. But..."

There was always a but.

"But?" I prompted.

"You've gotten too comfortable," he said bluntly. "Too predictable. And predictable doesn't win championships, does it?"

I stiffened in my seat. "Predictable?"

He nodded, leaning back in his chair. "Don't get me wrong—you're a damn fine coach. One of the best. That's why I've kept you on this long. But hockey isn't just about systems and strategies. It's about passion. Fire. Hence the name. And right now, I'm not seeing enough of that from this team—or from you."

I opened my mouth to argue, but he held up a hand. "Now, I know what you're going to say. You're steady, reliable, consistent. And those are good things. But you can't lean on them forever. The Fire needs to evolve. And so do you. Or else."

The sting of his words settled in my chest, and I forced myself to nod. This wasn't personal. It was business. If I needed to evolve, whatever that meant, I could do that. "What do you want from me?"

"I want you to shake things up. Try new plays, new strategies. Remind the fans why they love this team. Bring some excitement back to the ice."

"All right. I'll work on it."

"Good man," Matthew said, clapping his hands together. "Now, on to more important matters."

I raised an eyebrow, bracing myself. "More important than the Fire?"

"The Penguins," he said.

I blinked, certain I'd misheard. I did just hear him say penguins, didn't I? "Come again?"

"The Penguins," he repeated, his grin widening. "I've been thinking about rebranding the team. The Atlanta Penguins has a nice ring to it, don't you think?"

I stared at him, trying to gauge whether he was serious. I smiled to let him know I thought he was funny. Half the time, all he wanted in the world was someone else to be in on all his jokes. "You're funny today, huh?"

"Not at all," he said cheerfully. "Penguins are charismatic, resilient, and universally beloved. We will buy the name from Pittsburgh, paint penguins all over the city, add a penguin exhibit to the aquarium—"

"Matthew," I interrupted, struggling to keep my voice calm. "Atlanta is known for its heat and passion. That's why we're the Fire. Penguins have nothing to do with Atlanta."

"They will if I say they do," he said with a wink. "I can

sell anything to anyone, Casey. And I've got the money to back it up."

I rubbed my temples, trying to process the absurdity of the conversation. "Atlanta won't accept Penguins in exchange for Fire. We are all about heat and passion here—"

"Precisely." He smiled, and his eyes narrowed on me. "So, show me some of that heat and passion on the ice this year, and I'll drop the Penguin idea. Otherwise, you're out. Deal?"

So not only the team's name, but my job was on the line as well. Fan-fucking-tastic. But I had no other choice than to accept his terms. He was the boss, and even though I was under contract, Matthew would happily buy it out if he wanted a new coach to come on.

I gave him the only answer I had to give. "Deal."

He stood up with a grunt. "Stop living at the arena, Casey. Get out there and find your fire."

With that, he was gone, leaving me alone with a head full of questions with no answers. When I thought of my fire, Gemma's perfect face came to mind. Maybe that was my answer.

As absurd as Matthew's penguin pitch had been, his words about passion lingered long after he'd left. I leaned back in my chair, staring at the ceiling as I let my thoughts spiral. Had I really gotten too comfortable? Had I let my methods—and my love for the game—stagnate?

My thoughts drifted, unbidden, again to Gemma. There was something about her that reminded me why I'd fallen in love with hockey in the first place—something about her warmth, her curiosity, her way of seeing the world that made me feel alive again. Maybe Matthew wasn't entirely wrong. Maybe it was time to stop playing it safe and start rediscovering the fire.

Maybe she could help me. There was only one way to find out.

Chapter 12

Gemma

The park was quiet for a Saturday afternoon, the crisp autumn air keeping most people inside. Leaves swirled in lazy spirals across the grass, and the distant sound of children laughing floated over from the playground. I tightened my scarf around my neck, glancing at Winnie, who was busy organizing her crayons into a rainbow on the picnic table next to me.

I'd spent the entire morning second-guessing my plan. Introducing Casey to Winnie was a big step—the step, really—and I wasn't sure I was ready. But I also knew I couldn't keep putting it off. If Casey was who I thought he was—if he was Red—then this meeting would tell me everything I needed to know.

Was he the kind of man who could be a father to my daughter? Did I want him to be? I hoped I was doing the right thing. But does anyone really ever know when it's the right time to introduce their daughter to her father when he doesn't even know that he is?

When did my life get so complicated?

"Mommy, I'm done!" Winnie called, holding up her drawing with a triumphant grin. It was a scribbly masterpiece of trees, a sun, and what I assumed was me holding her hand.

"It's beautiful, sweetheart," I said, leaning down to kiss the top of her head. "You're such a good artist."

"Do you think Casey will like it?" she asked, her eyes wide and hopeful.

My heart twisted in my chest. Winnie didn't know why we were meeting Casey, didn't know anything about the thunderous storm of questions in my head. That was my job. Not hers. To her, he was just the nice man I'd mentioned once or twice—the man who made me smile in a way she hadn't seen before.

"I think he'll love it," I said, brushing a stray curl out of her face.

I spotted Casey before Winnie did. He was walking toward us, his hands tucked into his pockets and his breath visible in the cool air. His eyes found mine almost immediately, and he smiled, the kind of smile that made me forget the world for a second. My nerves eased, just a little. Whatever happened today, at least I knew Casey cared about me. That much was clear.

"Hey, Gemma," he said as he approached, his voice warm and steady. His gaze shifted to Winnie, and he crouched slightly, lowering himself to her level. "And who's this?"

"This is Winnie," I said, my voice catching slightly. "Winnie, this is Casey."

"Hi," she said shyly, clutching her drawing to her chest.

"Hi, Winnie," Casey said, his tone gentle. "What's that you've got there?"

She hesitated for a moment, then held out her drawing. "It's a picture. Do you like it?"

Casey studied it like it was a priceless piece of art, his brow furrowing in concentration. "Are you kidding? This is amazing. You've got real talent."

Winnie beamed, her shyness evaporating. "Really?"

"Really. You know, I've always wished I could draw, but I'm terrible at it. My stick figures look like trees." When she giggled at that, I would have sworn he gulped. He was nervous, too, and that made me like him even more. He went on, "You'll have to give me some tips."

She giggled again, and my chest tightened. Watching them interact was almost too much. Casey was natural with her—kind, patient, and genuinely interested in what she had to say. I wasn't sure what to expect, but it was not this.

"All right, kiddo," Casey said, standing up and clapping his hands together. "What's next? Swings? Jungle gym? Monkey bars?"

"Swings!" Winnie shouted, already running toward them.

Casey grinned at me, shrugging out of his jacket. "Looks like I've got my orders."

"Wait. She forgot her jacket again. Winnie, your—"

"I've always been like that too. Hated wearing a hat or a jacket as a kid and gloves? Forget about it. Bet she doesn't like it when you slather sunblock on her either, right?"

I snorted at that. A memory of the last beach trip before we left LA sprang to mind. "She hates it. Squirms away."

He smiled. "I'll keep an eye on her. Can you keep an eye on this for me?" He passed me a ring he always wore on his thumb. "It was my dad's, and I don't think I can climb monkey bars wearing it, and if we hang upside down, it'll fall out of my pocket."

"I'd be happy to." I tucked the ring into my purse.

Then he was off, jogging after Winnie with a lightness I hadn't expected. I watched as he caught up with her, lifting her effortlessly onto the swing and giving her a gentle push. Her laughter echoed across the park, clear and bright, and something deep inside me started to crack.

For the next hour, Casey and Winnie were inseparable. He chased her around the jungle gym, caught her at the bottom of the slide, and even climbed the monkey bars with her, his grin never fading.

For every activity, he made a big show of her being better at it than him, and she ate it up. By the time they returned to the picnic bench, Winnie was practically glowing, her cheeks flushed from the cold and her energy spent.

"Mommy, Casey's the best," she said, flopping onto the bench next to me. "Can we play with him again tomorrow?"

I swallowed hard, nodding. "We'll see, sweetheart."

"I can make time to play with you again. Your mom will help us out.""

She beamed. "Okay, Casey."

It was less emotionally fraught than calling him Dad.

He sat across from me, his thick gray hair slightly disheveled and his face lit with the kind of joy that was impossible to fake. I couldn't tell who had had a better time. "She's got a lot of energy."

"She wears me out most days," I admitted, brushing a strand of hair out of Winnie's face. "But it looks like you kept up pretty well."

"I've still got some gas left in the tank." He smiled at her. "Think you can beat me to that tree?"

"No," Winnie said in a sing-song voice. Then she yawned. "I'm tired."

"It's just as well," he said with a shrug. "Pretty sure you'd win."

"Nuh-uh. Your legs are bigger."

"Well, we could try to find out, but you said you're tired."

"Okay, one more game." She said it as though she was doing him a big favor, but really, there was a sly smile hidden on her face that she showed only to me.

She was loving this.

They bolted for the tree on the other side of the park, and I was grateful for the few minutes of silence. My mind was racing. Watching Casey with Winnie had been both a relief and a heartbreak. He was everything I could've hoped for in a father figure for her—kind, patient, fun—and I wanted all of that for her.

But the reality of what that meant was overwhelming. There was no easy way out of this relationship. I would have dumped him if he and Winnie didn't get along, and he was a reasonable person, so he would have understood that. It would have been awful, but I'd never stay with someone my child didn't like.

But now, I owed him the truth, and if I told him he was her biological father, what would happen next? Would he want to be part of her life? Part of mine? Or would he feel betrayed, blindsided by a truth he'd never asked for? Would he hate me for what I'd done?

There was no Hallmark card for that to smooth things over. I had looked for one.

Worse still, what if he was on his best behavior right now, and the real him was somewhere beneath the surface? What if he was secretly a jerk, only lying to me for sex? What would a bad person say to, "Hey, you're actually her father?"

Things were still too up in the air. I couldn't tell him, and I couldn't not tell him.

By the time we got back to my house, Winnie was fast asleep in the back seat. Her head was tilted at an awkward angle, and her tiny snores filled the car. I turned to Casey as I unbuckled her seatbelt.

"Thanks for today," I said quietly. "She had a blast."

"So did I," he said, his voice just as soft.

He carried Winnie inside for me, her small frame cradled against his shoulder as she stirred slightly but didn't wake. Megan was already waiting for us, her arms crossed and a knowing smile on her face.

"Looks like someone had a good time," she said, nodding toward Winnie.

"Can you watch her for a while?" I asked, glancing at Casey. "She's already out."

"Of course," Megan said, taking her from him with practiced ease. "Take your time. Let me know when you're ready for her—when she wakes up, we have several princess sequels to watch, so take your time."

"You're the best. Thank you."

She carried Winnie to her car and drove the two blocks to her house, leaving us alone. Casey and I retreated to the living room after I grabbed a bottle of wine and two glasses from the kitchen. My nerves were still humming from the day, but as I poured the wine and handed him a glass, I started to relax.

"To a successful first playdate," he said, raising his glass.

I laughed, clinking mine against his. "Cheers."

The wine helped me unwind the tangle of thoughts in my head. Right now, I didn't have to sort any of that out. I could just breathe easy, knowing that I had a night to spend with the man I liked.

I shoved his impending fatherhood out of my head.

"What's on your mind? You looked like you went somewhere else just now."

Crap. I smiled. "Long day. So," I screwed up my courage with more wine, "still thinking of dating the single mom?"

He laughed. "Well, her daughter is the cutest kid I've ever seen, so yeah, I think so."

A good start. I filled my glass before asking the next question. "Have you ever thought about having kids of your own? One day, I mean."

"Yeah. Definitely. I get a slight taste of it with my job—being coach means you have to rally the team, get them to listen to you, tell them what to do, show them how to do it—it's a lot like parenting, I would imagine."

I nodded. "That's a lot of what I do each day, actually."

"And my cousins all have kids of their own, so when we hang out, I love seeing the world from their perspective.

Kids are pure, you know? They see things other people don't. They're brutally honest without meaning to be, and I like that. Adults...we lose that innocence somewhere along the way to adulthood. Honesty becomes a scarce resource."

I swallowed too big of a gulp. "True."

"I require honesty in a relationship, Gemma. It's fundamental to the health of it. So, cards on the table, if there's ever anything you need to tell me, I want you to just tell me. No bullshit, no games. If we're going to make this work, that's what I need. That make sense?"

My heart weighed too much. It squeezed the air from my lungs. "Yeah."

"What do you need from me to make this work?"

I couldn't say it. Not now, though. Not when my tongue was tied in knots.

I went another way. Hooking my hand into his collar, I pulled him close and slanted my mouth over his wine-flavored lips. He clutched at my waist to pull me into his lap, and once I straddled him and felt his hardness through our clothes, all sense of the world fell away.

The kiss deepened, heady and firm, and before I knew it, our clothes had peeled away almost of their own accord. His hands traced the curve of my back as my fingers tangled in his hair.

"Are you sure?" he asked, his voice low and rough.

"Yes," I whispered, pulling him closer.

This time, he produced a condom from his pocket and slid it on without another word. I was practically panting for him, and the moment I took him into me, we both let out a breath of relief. This was what we needed, honesty be damned.

His every inch fit perfectly inside of me, leaving me shaking. Riding him, I drove my nails into his shoulders as he grabbed my ass and pumped me up and down his length. "That's it, baby, you're doing so good, taking my cock like that." His hands slid around my hips and down my thighs as he leaned back to watch me. "Let me see you."

I slowed to a stop. My words shuddered out, "What do you mean?"

A sly smile spread across his mouth. "Give me a show."

He wanted a show? I'd give him one. I pulled up off of him and stood, his eyes at hip level, clearly enamored of me naked in front of him. I turned around and carefully aimed him back inside as I sat facing away from his hungry eyes. The fit was different, hitting new spots that made me tremble harder.

As I started to ride him again, he groaned, "Fuck." His hands gripped my ass, squeezing tight.

"Liking the show?"

"Too much."

I glanced over my shoulder at him. "No such thing." I rolled my body against his, taking everything he had to give me. Bouncing on him, my own climax threatened me with a good time. But when he reached around my hip and played my clit, I lost myself to it. My head whipped back against his shoulder, and I was utterly helpless in his hands as I came.

He growled in my ear, "That's a good girl, mm, fuck, baby just like that. Come on my cock."

"I am," I whimpered.

He grabbed my hips harder this time and lifted himself up, turning us until I was bent over the couch armrest, and he was behind me. The movement stretched me in the strangest way, and it made me ache from my orgasm. Our bodies slapped together hard, over and over, while he made me erupt all over again.

But when it was done, he wrapped his arms around me, still bent over my body. He planted kisses along the back of my neck as he murmured, "Next time, I'm getting you in a bed."

"Huh?"

"We haven't had enough room to stretch out just yet, and I want to find out just how flexible you are. I think you're a human pretzel." He licked the sweat from my neck, making me shiver. "Would you like to test that theory?"

What else could I say but "Yes?"

"Good girl." He slammed deep and started up again, this time fisting my hair as he worked me over. I couldn't do anything but let him have at me, and right now, that was the only thing stopping me from telling him we'd had a bed our first time.

I couldn't say that. He didn't know.

Casey cupped my pussy as he pounded me harder and harder, toying with me there while I took it all. The build-up was almost as good as the orgasm, and I cried out so loudly I worried I'd hurt his ears. But I had a feeling he'd happily live with that.

He came, gasping and almost laughing. "Damn, woman. You're gonna be the death of me."

"I sure hope not."

After we cleaned up, we lay tangled together in the quiet glow of the living room, and I rested my head on his chest, listening to the steady rhythm of his heartbeat. I knew I couldn't keep the truth from him forever.

But for now, in this moment, I let myself believe that everything would work out. For me. For Winnie. And maybe, just maybe, for Casey too.

I just had to figure out how.

Chapter 13

Casey

Love had always seemed like a far-off concept to me, something that other people talked about, something you saw in movies. If I was entirely honest about it, I wasn't sure I believed in it at all.

I'd loved women in my past, or I thought I had. But what I felt for Gemma dwarfed all of that.

I wanted to know everything about her. I wanted to see her at her worst, to be there to comfort her through things, to help her laugh again. I wanted to see her at her best and help her reach new heights. More than any of that, I wanted her.

Every day. All the time.

She had single-handedly ruined everything I thought I knew about love, and I was grateful. At first, it was her smile, the way it lit up her face and made me feel like the only person in the room. Then it was her laugh—genuine, unpolished, the kind that tugged a grin out of me no matter how bad my day had been.

But after meeting Winnie, the feeling deepened into

something that scared the hell out of me in the best way. It wasn't just about Gemma anymore. It was the two of them —this incredible woman and her equally incredible daughter. And somehow, I'd stumbled into their lives, feeling completely unworthy of the space I was starting to occupy.

How could I be? I was ancient in comparison to Gemma. I tried to brush that aside, but it was hard. Lying next to her in the morning, seeing her firm body, something like guilt hit me. My hand rested on her bare hip, and the contrast was stark. My skin was not unlined like hers, not smooth and unblemished. I wasn't quite old enough to have age spots, but they'd hit me a lot faster than her.

How could I let her waste her youth on my old ass?

The morning sunlight spilled into the kitchen, casting a pale yellow glow over the small space. Gemma was curled up in one of the chairs at the table, her oversized sweater slipping off one shoulder as she cradled a steaming mug of coffee. Her hair was pulled into a messy bun, and her bare feet were tucked under her, the picture of effortless beauty.

I leaned against the counter, watching her for a moment before I spoke. There was no sense in workshopping this. I had to know. "I've been thinking about dyeing my hair."

She looked up, her eyebrows raised in surprise. "Why?"

I shrugged, running a hand through the silver strands that dominated my head. "I don't know. Maybe it's the age thing. The difference between us, I mean. The gray makes it obvious."

"Obvious that you're a grown man who has his life together?"

"Obvious that I'm older than you," I said, my tone softer.

Gemma set her mug down, tilting her head as she studied me, her pretty eyes settling on my head. "Casey, it's your hair. If you want to dye it, go ahead. But if you want my opinion, I think the silvery look is incredibly sexy."

"You're not just saying that?"

"No," she said, her smirk widening. "You're a silver fox. Distinguished. Rugged. Very hot."

I laughed, shaking my head. "Distinguished, huh?"

She nodded. "Absolutely."

I took a sip of my coffee, letting her words clink around the old brain pan. I wasn't sure I believed her—I'd been self-conscious about the age gap between us since the start of things—but hearing her say it made me feel lighter, like maybe it didn't matter as much as I thought it did.

I might actually believe that one day.

We sat in comfortable silence for a while, the sounds of the morning filling the air around us. She had put on some music, but it was soothing lo-fi, nothing too heavy. Kind of perfect, actually.

It set the mood for more conversation instead of wanting to dance. I wanted to ask her something meaningful that would bring us closer, and before I could stop myself, the words spilled out.

"What's your relationship with your dad like?" I had to know. If our thing was some warped Daddy Issues thing, I couldn't keep getting attached to her.

Gemma stilled for a moment, her mug halfway to her lips. I regretted the question immediately, remembering too late what Nico had mentioned about her dad's health. This was it. I was officially the world's worst boyfriend.

"It was great," she said finally, her voice steady. "Before his stroke."

"I'm sorry," I said, setting my coffee down. "I forgot Nico told me about that."

"It's okay," she said, waving me off. "It's just part of life. My dad's in a nursing home now. He doesn't recognize us much anymore, but he knows he's a dad. He calls Winnie by my name sometimes, so he's close. Just...not quite there most of the time. The moments of lucidity are nice until they fade away, and you're left explaining who you are to your own father."

My heart clenched at that. I could not imagine how hard it was. "That must be rough, having your own dad not recognize you."

Her eyes flickered with something—pain, maybe—but she nodded. "It is. But now that I'm back in town, I visit him every week. It helps. Most of the time."

"That's admirable," I said, meaning it. "I think it's amazing that you do that."

She smiled faintly. "It's hard. Especially since my mom passed when I was a teenager. Our dad's all I have left, even if he's not fully himself anymore. He got to see me graduate high school, but his stroke hit when I was in college, and I hate that he didn't remember seeing me walk across the stage for my college graduation." Her smile died, replaced by a wistfulness that killed me. "If I hadn't...if I hadn't fucked around in high school and had gone straight to college right after, then he would have that memory, too."

"Oh, Gem, you can't think like that."

She gave a tiny shrug. "It's impossible not to. But I cheer

myself up by remembering how proud he was when I graduated high school, and it has to be enough."

"Does that have anything to do with Los Angeles?"

"Yeah, definitely. The opportunity was huge, but it wasn't the only one. I could have stayed here. But Nico encouraged me to leave Atlanta for a while. See the world, that kind of thing. He said he'd watch out for Dad and stick around here." She took a steadying breath and finished her coffee, refilling both our mugs for a second go-round. "I was lucky to get that break from Dad's situation, and I'm lucky he's still alive for me to get to know this new version of him."

I reached across the table, brushing her hand with mine. "You're stronger than you give yourself credit for."

Her smile widened slightly, but I could tell the conversation was starting to weigh on her. I wanted to ask more, but I also didn't want to push too far. Instead, I decided to shift gears.

"What about Winnie's dad?" I asked cautiously, keeping my tone light. "What's his deal?"

Her entire demeanor changed. The warmth in her eyes dimmed, her expression tightening as if I'd struck a nerve. "It's not something I talk about."

The wall she'd put up was immediate, and I backed off without pressing. "Got it. Sorry I asked."

"What about your family?" she asked, kindly changing the topic.

"The team is my family," I said honestly. "My dad passed from cancer when I was in my twenties. My mom had a heart attack a few years later. I was an only child, so... that was that."

Gemma's expression softened, her hand resting lightly on mine. "I'm sorry. That must've been hard."

"It was," I admitted. "I have an uncle in Maryland and the cousins I mentioned, but we were never close. Hockey's always been my constant. The team is what keeps me grounded."

She nodded thoughtfully, and for a moment, it looked like she was about to say something. But before she could, keys jingled in the door. Megan appeared in the doorway, carrying a sleepy Winnie in her arms.

Winnie's head was resting against Megan's shoulder, her tiny arms hanging limply at her sides. She was wearing a tank top despite the cool weather, and her soft snores filled the room as Megan carried her closer.

"Sorry to interrupt," Megan said with a grin. "But I think someone's ready to come home."

I stepped forward, reaching out instinctively to take Winnie from her. She stirred slightly but didn't wake, her small body relaxing against my chest as I held her.

Megan smiled. "We had a hell of a slumber party."

"Did she stay up late or something?"

Megan nodded vigorously but said, "No, of course not. I'm a responsible auntie."

Gemma snickered. "And I'm sure dinner was a plate of broccoli and carrots."

"She asked for seconds," Megan baldly lied as she passed Gemma a small bag. "Right now, I think she's out for the count."

Gemma smiled, brushing a strand of hair from Winnie's face. "Thanks, Megan. I owe you."

"Don't even play like that," Megan said, waving her off. As her best friend left, I shifted Winnie slightly, my gaze falling on her bare shoulder. My breath caught in my throat.

There was a faint café-au-lait birthmark. It wasn't an exact match for mine—it wasn't shaped like Italy -but it was long, thin, and oddly familiar. What a weird coincidence.

"Casey?" Gemma's voice pulled me out of my thoughts. "You okay?"

"Yeah. Just...thinking."

She didn't press, but her eyes lingered on mine for a moment before she turned her attention back to Winnie. "Would you mind carrying her to bed for me?"

"Of course not. Lead the way." I followed behind, happy for the view of her ass, but that felt wrong to think about while carrying Winnie. Once I tucked her into her princess bed, Gemma drew the curtains to let her sleep. "Slumber party hangovers are the worst. She'll be out for another few hours."

"What makes them so bad?"

"Because at some point, you had to choose sleep over fun. What kid wants to do that?"

I chuckled, and as we left her bedroom, the sheer domesticity of tucking a child in struck me in the chest. That birthmark, her propensity for not wearing a jacket in the cold, her great big heart, it was almost enough for me to slide Winnie into that daughter-shaped hole in my heart.

I had always wanted a daughter. And a son. And a few more. A team of my own, so to speak. And Gemma would make the perfect mom to a fleet of kids. The way she didn't stress the small stuff, the way she loved her family, I knew she'd knock it out of the park. I wondered whether I could convince her of that, too.

Chapter 14

Gemma

Work had been amazing lately. No, amazing didn't even cover it—it was transformative. Every day felt like I was finally doing what I was meant to do. My articles about the Atlanta Fire had resonated with readers, and my editor was practically glowing with every new piece I submitted.

I was on Fire.

Okay, terrible pun, but it was true. Today, I was on the ice for interviews. The players were coming off a grueling practice, their jerseys soaked with sweat and their faces flushed from exertion. The air inside the rink was cold enough to sting my cheeks, but the energy from the team warmed the space. It was the kind of scene sportswriters dream of—easy camaraderie, great quotes, and just enough chaos to make things interesting.

Hudson, center, had pulled some ridiculously skilled moves on the ice, and no one was sure how he accomplished them. How he did backflips on hockey skates was beyond me. It was one thing to do them on figure skating skates. They had toe picks that made stunts a lot less dangerous because they offered more control. Hockey skates were made for speed and hard stops, not acrobatic moves. As I was pondering this, he jumped and spun almost horizontally in the air to avoid a player charging at him, and I laughed out loud in shock. I wasn't the only one.

"That is not regulation," Sergei said, his Russian accent drawing my attention.

Hudson laughed easily. "No, it's not. But it looked cool, right?"

Sergei grumbled, and he and the team's other Russians huddled off together to gripe in their mother tongue.

Jesper high-fived Hudson as they both skated toward me on the bench. "Dude, how come you never do that shit when we're playing for real?"

"Ees not regulation," Hudson said in a mock Russian accent.

"Yeah, sure, but they'll never see it coming."

I interjected, "So, what was that? Were you a figure skater before coming onto the Fire?"

Hudson smiled at me and gently elbowed Jesper to pay attention. "Before making it onto the Fire, I was a choreographer."

"Who did you train?"

The unmistakable look of pride filled his deep, dark eyes. "Probably half of your workout playlists."

I blinked, unsure what he meant by that. "Um—"

"I was a hip-hop dance choreographer and professional dancer. I worked with some of the greats. Now, I'm stuck working with these dickheads—"

Jesper playfully shoved him, and a few of the other guys joined us, carrying on amongst themselves until they closed in. "You're the dickhead, dickhead."

Hudson laughed. "Yeah, maybe I am." Then he turned to me, looking me over. "You're the reporter we're all supposed to talk to, right?"

"Gemma Grimaldi," I said, extending my hand. He removed his glove and shook it, and his rough hand dwarfed mine. "It's nice to officially meet you, Hudson."

"You, too. As I understand it, you're supposed to do some one-on-ones with all of us, right?"

"That's right."

"Never knew I'd be on a team that arranged dates for me, and I certainly don't mind the competition."

I laughed. "Not dates. Appointments."

"Sure, appointments." He sat next to me on the bench. "I usually find quiet Italian restaurants to be the best places for appointments. What do you say?"

"That will make it easier to hear your answers to my questions. I hate when background noise cuts into my recordings—it's terrible. I have to call you back and bother you again, and it slows the process down, which is awful for deadlines."

"And maybe afterward, we can hit a club or two. I can show you what else I'm known for."

"Clubs are notoriously loud, Hudson. Why would I want that?"

He smirked. "I'd like to see how you move on the dancefloor. How someone dances tells you everything about them."

"My job is to get to know you. Not the other way around."

His eyes danced down and up my body. "No reason it can't be both."

I was really hoping this was not where his line of inquiry was heading, and now, with all the guys around me, I decided to draw a line to make things clear in case anyone had any ideas like Hudson's.

First, I smiled to keep things light. "I'm sure you're a terrific dancer, but I am not."

"That's okay. We can—"

"We can't. My job is to interview you and nothing else. Professional interviews, with which I wield the power to make or break your reputation and, consequently, your career. I hope that's clear enough for you."

Hudson, the determined young man that he was, smiled, too. "Sounds like you could use some wine to help you relax. There's a great bar downstairs at my condo."

The kid would not let this go. I couldn't tell if that was because a half dozen players were watching us or because he was that kind of person, but I'd had it with his innuendo.

But before I could respond, a sharp voice sliced through the air. "Rice, that's enough."

I turned, startled to see Casey standing just off the bench, his arms were crossed and his jaw was tight. His expression was unreadable, but his tone carried a weight that silenced Hudson instantly. In fact, all the guys shut up and awaited further instructions.

"Keep it professional," Casey snapped.

Hudson raised his hands in surrender, his grin turning sheepish as he backed off. "Got it, Coach. Professional."

The rest of the players chuckled, the tension dissipating as they returned to their routine. But Casey's gaze lingered on me, his blue eyes steady and intense. It was the first time I'd seen him like this—protective, almost territorial—and it sent a shiver down my spine all the same.

Part of me knew I should bristle at the interference. I didn't need anyone to stand up for me, and I certainly didn't need anyone staking a claim. For that matter, it might egg some of the guys on if they thought flirting with me was forbidden.

But another part of me—a bigger part—couldn't help but like it. There was something deeply satisfying about the way Casey had stepped in, about the way his words carried a kind of unspoken message: she's mine.

After wrapping up my interview with Cole Maxwell, a hulking left winger, I made my way to Casey's office. I was riding the high from Casey's flirtation intervention and the buzz I got from prying secret information from a subject. Cole had a secret scented candle side hustle.

He sold them online using his female cousin's name, because he knew candles sold under a guy's name wouldn't sell as well. But now, she wanted a cut of the profits for the name usage, and he was having a hard time figuring out what to do. When I pointed out that they didn't need a person's name attached to them—he could have sold them under some generic name like Stone and Winter or something equally neutral—he blushed deeply, annoyed with himself that he hadn't thought of that. I suggested he pay her whatever she asked, but he really should talk to a lawyer to make things fair between them, and he agreed.

The players had already filed into the locker room, their

laughter and chatter echoing faintly through the hallways. The chill from the rink followed me as I pushed open the door, stepping into the warmth of Casey's office.

He was seated at his desk, a notebook open in front of him, but his pen wasn't moving. He looked up as I entered, his expression softening slightly.

"You didn't have to do that," I said, closing the door behind me.

"Do what?" he asked, though the faint smirk tugging at his lips told me he knew exactly what I was talking about.

"Barking at Hudson like that. He was just being playful."

"He was hitting on you," Casey said flatly. "And you're here to work, not deal with that."

I raised an eyebrow, leaning against the edge of his desk. "It's not the first time it's happened, and it won't be the last. I can handle a little flirting."

"You shouldn't have to handle it," he said, his tone softening but no less firm. "You're here to do your job, not fend off idiots who can't keep things professional."

The earnestness in his voice sent a flicker of warmth through me, and I felt my irritation melt away. It wasn't just jealousy driving him—it was something deeper, something protective and genuine. And the way he said it, I knew something more important about Casey. But I had to ask to confirm my theory.

"If we weren't...involved, you still would have intervened, wouldn't you?"

"Damn straight. I hate it when women get hit on while doing their job. It puts them in the awkward position of having to turn someone down while also not getting in trouble for being rude. It's unprofessional of men, and I won't stand for that kind of bullshit on my team."

I didn't know what to think. I had dated around, met some interesting men, and had a good time doing it. But this might have been the first time I had found a man with integrity, and for some reason, that turned me on more than anything else. He had shown me professional respect, not to impress me, but because he respected me outright.

Was it a turn-on because it was so rare? Maybe.

"I appreciate that."

He nodded once, but his eyes hardened. "Hudson's used to getting his way when it comes to women. He's a good-looking young man."

I half-shrugged. "I guess so."

His eyes dipped back to his screen, and he cleared his throat. "If, once the interviews are over, you're interested in him, I'm sure he'd be open to it."

Something twisted in my chest. "What?"

"It's okay, Gemma. We never said we were exclusive. I just ask that you don't mention anything to them about us. No point in stirring up drama."

I blinked at him. He was serious, and I didn't understand why. "Casey—"

"Don't feel you have to say anything to mollify me. Please. We're both adults—"

"You don't have to worry about the players," I said gently. I had to say something, or he would keep rambling. "I like you. A lot. And nothing they say or do is going to change that."

His lips went tight, but still, he didn't look at me. "Good to know where I stand among them."

I marched to the other side of his desk and spun his chair around so he faced me. "You're not standing among anyone! You're the only man I'm interested in. Period."

His blue eyes searched mine, and for a moment, the air between us felt charged. With what, I wasn't sure. Finally, he reached for my hand, his fingers warm and calloused as they closed around mine.

"Good," he said, his voice low. "Because I don't want to share you. I'm not interested in seeing other people. Are you?"

The simple honesty of his words sent a shiver down my spine, and before I could think twice, I leaned down and kissed him. It started slow, almost tentative, but the moment his hand slid to the back of my neck, pulling me closer, the kiss deepened into something hotter, more urgent.

"Gemma," he murmured against my lips, his voice rough with need.

The tension that had been simmering between us since the incident at the rink finally boiled over, spilling into every touch, every kiss, every whispered word. The papers on his desk tumbled to the floor as he lifted me onto the edge, his hands finding my waist as he pulled me closer.

"Are you sure about this?" he asked, his breath warm against my skin. "Here? Now?"

"Yes," I said, threading my fingers through his hair. "I've never been more sure."

The next moments were a blur of heat and sensation. His hands were strong and steady, his lips leaving a trail of fire wherever they touched over my clothes. The cold, professional atmosphere of the office melted away, replaced by the heady intimacy of being with him.

For the first time in what felt like forever, I let myself be completely vulnerable, completely open. And Casey met me there, his touch tender even as his kisses grew more desperate. Between those raw kisses, he locked the door, and when he came back, there was nothing to slow us down.

Except him.

He pressed his forehead to mine, and with excruciating slowness, he unbuttoned my shirt. I didn't care about that part of things—this was an office quickie, or so I thought. But Casey made me wait for his touch, and that spurred me on. By the time his hands brushed over my nipples, I was dying. I had to be. No one had ever left me on edge this long, and my patience had worn away completely.

"Casey, why are you moving so slowly?"

His lips quirked to the side. "Because I like seeing you want something."

"Someone."

He smiled fully at that. "Is that what you want, Gemma? Just one person?"

"You. I want you."

Without a word, he pulled me off the desk and stripped me in a rush of desire. He pulled a condom from his pocket, and his clothes melted away in a few moves. When it was in place, Casey picked me up, my legs around his waist, as he walked me back to the door. The cold wood drew a gasp from my throat as my spine hit the door. But he thrust home, and that was all I needed to warm up.

The door had less give than the tree we had fucked against in the park. Casey's thrusts were rougher this time, almost as if he understood I could take it now. But he kissed me tenderly, touched my face reverently. The dichotomy was dizzying–fast and hard down below, sweet and gentle up top. He overwhelmed my senses, and before I knew it, I came in a holler.

After, I straddled him on his desk chair. He nipped at my throat, groaning all the while. I loved the sounds he made. He was always so proper until he was naked, and I loved that, too. But this time, I wanted him unleashed, feral. So I rode him harder, throwing all my weight behind it. I bit his neck as I took control. His groans became growls, and when he swelled inside of me, my orgasm took hold. We almost howled together.

When it was over, we lay tangled together on the small couch in the corner of the office, the faint hum of the building filling the quiet space. My head rested on his chest, the steady rhythm of his heartbeat fascinating me for some reason. It was music to my ears.

"I meant what I said," I murmured, breaking the silence. "I like you, Casey. I don't want anyone else."

His arm tightened around me, his lips pressing a soft kiss to the top of my head. "I like you too, Gemma. More than I probably should."

The vulnerability in his voice made my chest ache, and I tilted my head to look up at him. "Why does it feel like you're holding something back?"

He hesitated, his gaze flickering away for a moment before he met mine again. "Because I want this to work. And I'm terrified of screwing it up."

"You won't," I said firmly, reaching up to brush a strand of hair from his face. "We won't."

But I might.

I put the thought out of my head as best I could. I knew

I had to tell him the truth about Winnie, but not now. His smile was small, and at that moment, I understood what worried him. He was afraid of messing up, and so was I. There was something real here. Whatever it was—whatever it could become—it was worth fighting for.

Chapter 15

Casey

The hook-up with Gemma in my office had been, without question, one of the most exhilarating moments of my life. Not just because it was physically intense—though it absolutely was—but because of what it represented. Her choosing me, reassuring me with words and actions that I didn't need to worry about the younger guys on the team. That connection felt real, solid, and I wanted to trust in it.

For a while, it worked. It silenced that part of me that doubted everything, that worried I wasn't enough for her. The age difference didn't feel so insurmountable when we were together. It wasn't even noticeable when it was just us. The way she had looked at me after, her lips slightly swollen from our kiss, was like a balm for every insecurity I'd ever had.

But Winnie kept creeping into my thoughts.

That kid was something else. She was sharp, quick on her feet, and bursting with a kind of restless energy that reminded me of someone I knew all too well. Myself. It wasn't just her personality that gnawed at the back of my mind. It was the birthmark. That oddly shaped café-au-lait spot on her shoulder had lodged itself into my thoughts like a splinter. It wasn't identical to mine, but it was close enough to make me pause every time I thought about it.

And then there was her face.

Winnie didn't look like me. She had Gemma's warm brown eyes and her hair, but there was something familiar about her expressions, her mannerisms. Little things that caught me off guard—like the way she furrowed her brow when she was concentrating or the determined set of her jaw when she didn't want to give up on something.

I knew that feeling too well. It was why her presence kept coming to mind.

And she ran hot like I did. Always taking off layers when convention said to leave them on. Hell, I never wore more than shorts and a fleece when I was on the ice. Sometimes less.

The timeline lined up. Winnie was four, almost five, which matched perfectly with the night I'd spent at the masquerade fundraiser. A night that had stuck in my mind ever since for reasons I hadn't been able to articulate back then.

Until now.

The whole thing was odd. A series of coincidences, some might say. Plenty of people had those same traits. There was nothing to work myself up over.

But I couldn't let it go.

I knew I needed answers, but I wasn't going to get them from Gemma—not yet, anyway. If she was hiding something, I had no idea how to broach the topic without risking the fragile connection we were building. I'd told her the honest truth about us—I was terrified of screwing this up. Nothing would screw it up more than prematurely claiming fatherhood of her daughter.

That left Nico.

He would know things about Gemma that she wouldn't necessarily think to tell me herself. If I could ask the right questions, I might be able to get the pieces I needed to put the puzzle together. But I had to be careful. The last thing I wanted was to make him suspicious.

The next morning, I called Nico into my office under the guise of discussing logistics for practice. He showed up in his usual relaxed way, still in his sweat-soaked practice gear, a water bottle in hand, and his easy grin firmly in place, dropping into the chair across from my desk like he didn't have a care in the world. "What's up, Coach?"

I leaned back in my chair, trying to project the same casual energy. "Nothing major. Just figured we should chat. With your sister hanging around the team so much, I thought I should get to know her better."

Nico raised an eyebrow, his grin turning slightly amused. "What, are you vetting her?"

"Something like that," I said, chuckling. "She's been doing a lot of interviews, spending time with the guys. Just thought it wouldn't hurt to get some context. I know she's doing a bang-up job for our PR, so Whit likes her. But you know me. If anyone's hanging around my team, I want to know them. Figured it makes sense to talk to you first."

"Fair enough," he said, shrugging. "What do you want to know?"

I hesitated, choosing my words carefully. "What's her story? I know she just moved back, but why now?"

"Because of Winnie," Nico said without missing a beat. "She was in LA for five years, doing her thing, but once my niece got old enough to start school, Gemma wanted her to grow up somewhere more stable. Atlanta made sense. I'm here, our dad's here—it's home."

I nodded slowly, filing the information away. Five years. The timeline fit perfectly into the widening hole in my heart. But I kept my casual smile in place. "How's she adjusting?"

"She's doing great," Nico said, leaning back in his chair. "She's tough. Always has been. But I think she's glad to be back. Even if she acts like she's too cool for Atlanta, I know she missed it. It's good for her to be around family again. I think the guys are warming up to her, too."

"And Winnie's dad? Is he here or LA or something?"

Nico's grin faltered, and he shook his head. "That's...a sore subject. Gemma's private about it—she won't even tell me who he is. I've learned not to push. All I know is he's not involved, and she seems fine with that."

"She's never mentioned him?" I pressed, keeping my voice neutral.

"Not once."

"You don't find that weird?"

"That's Gemma for you. She's always been independent. Doesn't like asking for help, doesn't like sharing her burdens. It's how she's always been. Not that Winnie is a burden—she's the greatest kid in the world. But it can't be easy, the whole single mom thing."

I nodded, though my mind was racing. If Gemma had

never mentioned Winnie's father, not even to her brother, it had to mean something. But what? "She looks familiar," I said, testing the waters. "Is there any reason I'd recognize her? Have we met before?"

Nico tilted his head, his brow furrowing slightly. "I mean, maybe? She's been around town for a while now. Oh, and she came to that big masquerade fundraiser we did right before she moved to LA."

My breath caught in my chest. "The masquerade?"

"Yeah," Nico said, laughing. "You know, the one we all hated but had to go to because it was for the pediatric hospital? Gemma came to that."

I swallowed, my brain blitzing from too many thoughts. "Why was she there?"

"She had just graduated, and I thought she needed a night of fun before she moved to LA." He shrugged. "She's not a party girl, but it's always good to try something new, right?"

"Right," I mumbled, still reeling as my stomach sank. "Did she tell you anything about that night? Did she meet anyone—"

"Like I said, she's a private person. I didn't ask. But come to think of it—she wore some kind of mask, so I doubt you'd actually recognize her from that night. Why do you ask?"

My pulse hammered in my ears, and I resisted the urge to use the blood pressure cuff I kept in my top drawer since Mom's heart attack. "Just curious. What kind of mask did she wear?" Don't say peacock.

Nico chuckled, shaking his head. "Man, I have no idea.

Do you think I was paying attention to stuff like that? It was five years ago."

I shrugged and smiled to hide the fact I was about to freak out. "It's like adult Halloween. Someone's mask tells you a lot about who they are or who they want to be. Thought it might offer some insight."

"Yeah, I always forget you go in for all that psychology shit."

"Thanks, Nico. You've been helpful."

He stood, stretching his arms over his head as he prepared to leave. "No problem. And, uh, go easy on her, all right? She's good people."

"I'll do my best." It was all I could do.

As soon as Nico left the office, I leaned back in my chair, my thoughts spinning in a hundred different directions. Gemma had been at the masquerade. The timing lined up perfectly—five years ago, right before she moved to LA. And she wouldn't talk about Winnie's father.

It couldn't be a coincidence. Could it?

I closed my eyes, letting my mind drift back to that night at the masquerade. As parties went, that one hadn't been too bad. I'd gone reluctantly, dragged there by the team for a good cause but fully expecting to be bored out of my mind. Whitney had been pushy like always, but it was for the good of the team, and her instincts were second to none. So when she told me to go talk to people, I did.

And then I saw her.

The woman in the blue dress and the peacock mask, the woman who had been unlike anyone I'd ever met. Confident, sharp, with a wit that had disarmed me within seconds. I'd been captivated by her in a way that had surprised me, drawn to her laughter and the way she carried herself. And her body. There was no denying that.

We'd spent the night talking, connecting in a way I hadn't thought possible in such a short period of time. And when the night ended when we'd shared that one unforgettable moment of passion, I knew I'd never forget her.

But I didn't know her name. She called me Red. I called her Blue. We had left our masks on the whole time.

Now, five years later, Gemma was in my life. Brilliant, beautiful Gemma, who had captivated me in the span of a brief conversation. Could it really be her? Could the woman who'd haunted my thoughts for years be the same woman who filled my days with light and warmth?

And if it was her, what did that mean for Winnie?

The rest of the day passed in a blur. I went through the motions of practice, giving instructions and feedback, but my mind was elsewhere. Scribbling in my playbook was pointless. I couldn't stop thinking about Gemma, about the possibility that she might be the woman I'd been searching for all this time.

That night, as I lay in bed alone, the questions swirled in my mind, refusing to let me rest. If Winnie was my daughter, if Gemma was the woman from that night...what then? What would that change?

Would she tell me the truth if I asked? Would she even want me to know? I was just an anonymous party hookup back then, but what we had now was real. Could I risk it for the possibility of the truth?

I didn't have the answers yet, but one thing was clear: I had to find them.

For her. For Winnie. For myself.

Chapter 16

Gemma

The small ice cream shop near the arena was one of those places that seemed frozen in time. The walls were painted a cheery pastel yellow, dotted with old-school posters advertising sundaes and milkshakes, and the faint scent of vanilla and freshly made waffle cones hung in the air. It wasn't busy—mid-afternoon on a weekday wasn't prime ice cream time—but a couple of teenagers hovered by the counter, giggling over their sundaes.

Casey was already there when I walked in, seated at one of the little booths by the window. He looked slightly out of place in his Fire jacket and baseball cap, his broad frame filling the small space. But even from across the room, he still managed to take my breath away. It was as if seeing him made the world disappear.

When did I become such a sap?

I didn't really care. I was so happy when it came to Casey that it made most of those judgy inner voices shut up. As it turned out, being deeply in like worked like a mute button for all that noise.

Deeply in like? Really? You can do better than that.

So, maybe it didn't shut all the judgy voices up, but it helped. And I did like Casey, but I knew it was bigger than that. I wasn't ready to touch that other l-word just yet. But it was coming.

I smiled as I approached, hoping to shake off the strange knot of nerves that had been following me all day. This was supposed to be a fun, casual date—just a quick break for him before he had to get back to work. That was why he picked this place. It was a few blocks from the arena. But as I slid into the seat across from him, I immediately sensed something was off.

"Hey," I said, setting my purse on the bench beside me. "How's your day going?"

"Busy," he said, his tone clipped. He didn't look at me right away, instead focusing on the menu in front of him like it was fascinating.

"Everything okay?"

"Yeah," he said, finally glancing up. His smile was small, but it didn't reach his eyes. "Just a lot on my mind."

I studied him for a moment, trying to read the tension in his posture, the way his shoulders were stiff, and he twisted his father's ring on his thumb. This wasn't like him—not with me, anyway. Casey was usually a rock in the whirlwind that was my life.

"Are you sure?" I asked, leaning forward slightly. "Because you're acting...weird."

He sighed, setting the menu down and rubbing the back of his neck. "I guess I am being weird."

"Want to tell me why?"

He hesitated, his jaw tightening like he was trying to hold something back. But then his eyes met mine, and I saw the conflict there, the storm of something dark he was trying to keep under control.

"Five years ago," he said slowly, "you were at the Fire's masquerade fundraiser, right?"

My stomach dropped.

For a split second, I thought about lying, about denying I'd been there and playing dumb. But I knew that wouldn't work. Casey wasn't stupid, and the look on his face told me he'd already connected the dots. Besides, all he had to do was ask Nico to check me. He had a source, so lying would be pointless. And I didn't want to lie to Casey any more than I already had.

"I was there," I said carefully, my voice steadier than I felt. "Why?"

"Your daughter is almost five," he said, his tone soft but pointed. "That means she would've been conceived right around then."

My heart started pounding in my chest, the blood rushing in my ears. I forced myself to keep my expression neutral, to pretend I didn't understand where this was going.

"And I've raised her on my own. I don't need you to recap my personal history to me, so what's your point?" I asked, my voice colder than I intended.

Casey's eyes didn't waver, his gaze locked on mine. "Did you hook up at the masquerade?"

I froze, my body going rigid as his words sank in. For a moment, all I could do was stare at him, my mind racing with a thousand different responses. I could lie, I could deflect, I could tell him the truth...but none of those options felt safe.

"That's none of your business," I said finally, my voice sharp. "And I'm offended that you'd even ask."

His eyes widened slightly, and he leaned back in his seat, clearly startled by my tone. "Gemma, I'm not trying to judge you. I just—"

"No," I interrupted. "What I did or did not do that night is not on the table. If you want to continue this date, fine. But I will not be interrogated or judged by you or anyone else."

He exhaled slowly, rubbing his hands over his face. "I'm sorry. I didn't mean for it to come out like that. I just..." He trailed off, his voice faltering.

"You just what?" I asked, my heart still racing.

"I hooked up with someone that night," he admitted, his voice barely above a whisper. "And I've been thinking about it ever since. Not because I regret it, but because until I met you, she had been my gold standard for sex."

Even now, with so much on the line, I couldn't help but be flattered by that. "Oh."

"That hook-up was amazing. My first and only one-night stand. Pretty much figured no one else could measure up to a memory, so why try to relive that high, you know?"

I swallowed. "I think I get it."

He blew out a breath, the lines near his eyes softening. "And I don't know...I got it in my head that if you were there...I thought Winnie might be mine."

It felt like the ground had shifted beneath me, like the entire world had tilted on its axis. My chest tightened, and it took everything I had to keep my face neutral, to keep my voice steady.

"I thought we were leaving our pasts in the past. The fact that you're older than me means you have a lot more experience than I do, and I don't judge you for that. I don't think you should judge me for my past, either."

"This isn't about judgment, Gem."

"Well, I don't think this is a conversation we should be having right now."

"Why not?" he asked, his eyes searching mine. "If there's even a chance—"

"There's not," I said quickly, cutting him off again. "I'm not doing this, Casey. Not here, not now." He opened his mouth to argue, but I held up a hand, silencing him. "I'm serious. If you want to keep seeing me, then drop it. Right now."

Frustration stiffened him right back up. He glanced out the large window, and if I had to hazard a guess, I would have said he was debating on a response. I hoped he chose wisely.

"Okay," he said quietly. "I'm sorry."

I nodded, swallowing hard as I tried to calm the storm raging inside me. "Apology accepted. Now, can we just... enjoy our ice cream?"

He managed a small smile, but I saw through it. I'd screwed up and hurt his feelings by shutting him out, and that stung us both. But he said, "Yeah. Ice cream sounds good."

The shop was a counter service kind of place, so we made our selections—his pistachio waffle cone and my dulce de leche milkshake—and sat back down. Awkward wasn't a heavy enough word for what happened until our food arrived.

We were silent. Not the comfortable silences we'd had before. This one was peppered with unasked questions and regret.

When the food came, we both dove in, thankful for something to do with our mouths that wasn't talking. I could tell Casey wanted to bring it up again, but he didn't, and for that, I was grateful.

But internally, I was falling apart.

He knew. Or at least, he suspected. And I couldn't hide it much longer. When we were parting ways outside the shop, he tipped his head to the side, his brow lined from deep thought. "You didn't ask why I thought it might have been you."

I swallowed. "You said you were at the same masquerade as me."

"Right, but why wouldn't I know the face of the woman I slept with?"

"I thought we were done talking about this, Casey."

"I'm not asking about that night. I'm asking why you didn't ask how it is. I wouldn't have known who I slept with."

I shrugged. "It was a masquerade. We were all wearing masks. I assumed people who hooked up that night kept their masks on for the sex."

"Hmm," he said stiffly. "I guess that's where you and I differ. That kind of thing wouldn't have occurred to me. If I'd been on the receiving end of those kinds of questions, the first thing I would have asked is how it is you don't know who you slept with. Strange that you knew we kept our masks on."

My heart leaped into my mouth. "Isn't that the point of hooking up at a masquerade? The spicy anonymity?"

"Yeah, but—"

"You obviously don't read enough romance novels, Casey. It's a thing. I'll send you some links to the ones I like."

Just like that, with one lie, his worry lines melted away. "That's really a thing in those books?"

I nodded, relieved he bought it. "You'll see." We said our goodbyes, and that was that, but nothing felt resolved because it wasn't.

Later that night, after Winnie was asleep and the house was quiet, I sat on the couch with my head in my hands, replaying the conversation over and over in my mind. I had done hours' worth of research for romance novels that had that plot in them and sent him the links. Thankfully, social media made it easier than reading the books myself.

That had been a welcome distraction from my guilt.

I'd always known this moment would come. From the second I figured it out, I knew it was only a matter of time before he put the pieces together. But I'd convinced myself I could handle it, that I could keep the truth buried until I was ready to deal with it.

I had lied to him and to myself.

Because the truth was, I didn't know if I could deal with it. I didn't know if I was ready to face what it would mean for Casey to find out he was Winnie's father.

Would he be angry? Hurt? Would he want to be

involved in her life? Would he want to be part of mine? And what if he didn't?

The thought made my chest ache, and I let out a shaky breath, trying to push it away. I couldn't afford to think like that. Not now.

But as much as I tried to push it aside, the truth loomed over me. I couldn't hide it much longer.

Chapter 17

Casey

When I walked into the arena after the ice cream shop debacle, something was off. I couldn't put my finger on it right away. The guys were bullshitting like always until they saw me. Then they averted their eyes or gave me a stiff, "'Sup, Coach?"

But it wasn't their usual greeting tone. More like they had something on their mind but couldn't say it.

The air felt weighty like unsaid words hung around like buzzing flies. It wasn't just the players, either. In the breakroom, Esai—one of our trainers—gave me a look that I'd only ever seen him give to players who half-assed things. Sharp disappointment.

"What's up, E?"

Esai was normally a go-getter, gregarious and friendly. So his formal, "Nothing at all. Anything you'd like to share with the rest of us?"

I had the sneaking suspicion I'd done something wrong and the absolute panic that they knew about me and Gemma.

My heart raced once I realized the problem. They knew. They all knew I'd been sleeping with a player's little sister. I was going to lose my job, and they were disappointed in me for breaking the rules.

For Gemma's sake, I covered. "No. Anything you want to tell me?"

"No. I have nothing to hide."

"Good. Then we're on the same page." I poured my coffee and left. By the time I reached my office, my gut was in knots. If I was fired for fraternization, I might not work in the league ever again. Pro hockey was my life, my calling. What would I do if not this?

When I opened my door, Whitney was already there, standing by the window with her arms crossed. She didn't turn when I came in, but the tension in her shoulders was obvious. The way she sighed when I shut the door behind me set me even more on edge.

"All right," I said, setting my bag on the chair. "What's going on?"

She turned, her expression grim. "You might want to sit down for this."

My stomach dropped. "Whit, just tell me."

She hesitated for a moment like she was trying to figure out how to soften the blow. But then she straightened, her tone sharp and to the point. "There's a rumor going around, Casey. A bad one. About you."

"What kind of rumor?" I asked, my voice low.

"People are saying you might have an illegitimate child," she said, her words landing like a slap. "That you bailed on the mother and left her to raise the kid alone."

For a moment, I couldn't speak. The room spun. This

was a worse rumor than just me sleeping with a player's sister. This was character assassination.

"What?" I finally managed, my voice barely above a whisper.

Whitney nodded, her jaw tight. "It started an hour ago, but you know how these things are. Nothing travels faster than your hero falling, and now it's all over the building. Staff, players, everyone. No one knows exactly where it came from, but it's spreading fast."

"Well, it's not true," I said, my voice rising. "I didn't—"

"I believe you," she said quickly, cutting me off. "I know you. You're not the kind of guy who would do this sort of thing. But you need to understand how this looks, Casey. People are upset. Some of the players are angry. They think you abandoned a kid and their mom, and that's not sitting well with anyone. A lot of those guys were raised by single moms, and they look up to you like a dad, so they're pissed. It's personal to them."

"Why the hell would anyone think that about me? They know me, too! How could they think that of me?"

Whitney held up her hands, her voice calm but firm. "I don't know who started it, but at this point, it doesn't matter. The speculation is already out there. If we don't get ahead of this, it's going to spiral out of control."

I paced the length of the room, trying to wrap my head around what she was saying. The thought of people believing that I'd abandoned a child—especially my team thinking that of me, the people who were supposed to trust me—made me want to rail at them for doubting me. Or, at the very least, set the record straight.

"I didn't abandon anyone," I said finally, my voice tight. "I swear to you, Whitney. That's not who I am."

"I know that, Casey," she repeated. "But if I'm going to help you fix this, I need to know everything. The truth. No holding back."

I hesitated. Telling Whitney was a big risk. But as much as she knew me, I knew her, too. I trusted her, and Whitney couldn't help me if I didn't give her the full picture.

"All right," I said, letting out a shaky breath. "Here's the truth..."

I told her everything.

I started with the masquerade fundraiser five years ago, the woman in the peacock mask, the one-night stand that had lingered in the back of my mind ever since.

Then I told her about Gemma. How we'd reconnected recently, how things had started to grow between us. That she had a daughter, Winnie, who was almost five—the exact timeline of that night at the masquerade.

"And the thing is," I said, my voice quieter now, "it took me a while to put it together, and when I did, I asked. Today, in fact, when we were at Sweet Nothings. I asked if Winnie might be mine, and...she didn't say no. She didn't say yes, either, but the way she reacted..."

"What do you mean?"

"She got angry," I admitted. "She shut me down, told me it wasn't my business. But she didn't deny it."

Whitney was quiet for a long moment, her eyes narrowing in thought. "So, you think Winnie might be yours."

"I don't know," I said honestly. "But I can't stop thinking

about it. The timing, the birthmark, the way she acts—it all lines up too perfectly to ignore. Or maybe I'm just an old fool who has always wanted children and a family, and I'm seeing things that aren't there. I don't know anything for certain."

Whitney exhaled slowly, running a hand through her long, dark hair. Somehow, it fell perfectly back into place, though I suspected that was because nothing of Whitney Dobson's would ever be out of place. She was always too poised, too perfect. A gorgeous woman, to be sure, but far too just-so for my liking. Probably because she was a former model. In all the years I'd known her, I'd never seen her look anything less than stellar.

It was easier to focus on Whitney than the vortex of possibilities I was being sucked into.

She sighed. "This is messy, Casey. Really messy. And the fact that it involves a player's sister..."

"I know. Believe me, I know."

She leaned against the desk, crossing her arms. "Okay. Here's what we're going to do. First, I'll try to figure out where this rumor started and find out what else they think they know. Second, I'll work on damage control—get ahead of it before it gets worse. But Casey, you need to be prepared for the fact that this might not just go away. Rumors like this don't die easy deaths."

"What do I do in the meantime?"

"Focus on the team," she said. "Keep your head down, stay professional. Don't give anyone a reason to think the rumors are true. Don't let them see you sweat. You're Coach. They need to remember who it is they're gossiping about."

I nodded, though the knot in my stomach didn't ease. "Thanks, Whitney. For everything."

She gave me a small smile, her tone softening. "You're a good guy, Casey. Don't let this mess convince you otherwise."

After she left, I sat at my desk, staring at the wall as her words echoed in my mind.

A good guy.

Was I? If Winnie was mine, what did that say about me? About the man I thought I was? I hadn't known she was out there, but how much did that matter to a child her age? All she knew was that she didn't have a daddy.

The more I thought about it, the more I realized that Gemma's reaction during our last conversation had left a lingering doubt I couldn't ignore. She hadn't denied it. She had only gotten angry that I was asking her about her past sex life. If Winnie wasn't mine, I could understand why she was upset.

If Winnie was mine, that reaction would also make sense.

So, it wasn't proof of anything either way. Which didn't help matters. And now, with the rumors swirling, I couldn't shake the sinking feeling that I was right about Winnie. There were too many coincidences that lined up.

That afternoon, I zipped up my Coach's jacket and stepped onto the ice for practice, hoping the jacket would remind my players who they were dealing with and that the routine would clear my head. But the tension in the arena was still there. The players were quieter than usual, their banter subdued as they skated drills.

A few of them shot me wary glances between drills. It

was clear the rumor had reached them, and the thought of my own team doubting me made me sick. Trust was a fragile thing, and they thought I had broken it.

After practice, I pulled a few of the veteran players aside.

"All right," I said, crossing my arms. "I know you've heard the rumors. Let me make one thing clear. They're not true."

The men exchanged glances, their expressions uncertain.

"Whatever you've heard, whatever you think you know —it's not true," I repeated firmly. "I didn't abandon anyone. If you've got a problem with me, say it to my face. Otherwise, keep your focus on the game. The other guys look up to you. They'll follow your lead. We're here for the game and for each other. Remind them of that."

There was a moment of silence before Nico nodded. "We hear you, Coach."

By the time I got home that evening, I was exhausted at every level. The day pressed down on me as I sank onto the couch, staring at the ceiling.

The anger in Gemma's voice when I'd brought up the possibility of Winnie being mine, it burned me. I thought about Winnie, about the way she'd smiled at me at the park, the way she'd called me Casey like it was the most natural thing in the world.

The way I wished she'd one day call me Dad instead.

I had thought of it in a stepdad capacity, and I knew I'd gotten ahead of myself by thinking like that all by itself. But now? Now, I was convinced I'd been left behind.

I hadn't done the abandoning in this equation. If Winnie was mine, that was.

Chapter 18

Gemma

My editor's email had been sitting in my inbox for hours, but I couldn't bring myself to respond.

"We need coverage on the Casey McConnell illegitimate child rumors. Given your access to the team, you're the best person to write this piece. Let me know if you need additional resources."

Each time I read it, my stomach turned. It wasn't just an assignment. It was a direct hit to everything I'd been carefully balancing. Not only that—this would be a hit piece on Casey, which went against everything in my heart.

How could I write this? How could I possibly report on rumors that were, in some twisted way, tied to me?

The professional answer was simple. I couldn't. No journalist could—or should—write about their own life disguised as someone else's story. But I couldn't exactly walk into my editor's office and tell him, "Hey, I might actually be the mother of the rumored illegitimate child in question. So, as you can see, this might be a little awkward."

No. I'd need to handle this myself before my boss ever found out. Before anyone found out. And that meant I had to talk to Casey.

The rest of the day felt surreal. I went through the motions of my job—reviewing notes, emailing sources, typing up drafts—but it all felt meaningless. The real task loomed ahead, and it made everything else seem small.

When I picked up Winnie from daycare, her joyful chatter barely registered. Normally, I'd hang on her every word, asking questions about her day and marveling at the way she saw the world. But this time, all I could manage was a few distracted nods.

"Mommy, are you okay?" she asked from the backseat, her voice small.

I forced a smile, glancing at her in the rearview mirror. "I'm fine, sweetheart. Just a little tired."

It wasn't a lie, exactly. I *was* tired—bone-tired, emotionally drained, and mentally running in circles. But how could I explain to a four-year-old that her entire world might be about to change?

When we got home, I focused on Winnie's bedtime routine, desperate for the comfort of structure. Dinner, bath, bedtime story. Each step helped calm the whirlwind in my mind, but only slightly.

By the time she was tucked in and snoring softly, I'd made my decision. I grabbed my phone, my hands trembling as I typed out the message.

Want to come over for dinner tomorrow? Just the two of us.

I hit send before I could second-guess myself. My heart

pounded as I stared at the screen, waiting for his reply. It came almost instantly.

Sure. What time?

I exhaled shakily, typing out a quick response and setting my phone down. Tomorrow. Tomorrow, I'd tell him everything.

But as I lay in bed that night, staring at the ceiling, doubt crept in. How could I say it? How could I sit across from Casey and admit that I'd been keeping the truth from him? I didn't know how he'd react, and the fear of losing him—of losing whatever fragile connection we'd built—was almost paralyzing.

The next day was a blur. I avoided my boss' email, ignored the gnawing sense of urgency at the back of my mind, and threw myself into preparing for dinner.

Cooking had never been my strong suit. I knew a few dishes well enough not to starve, but I was no culinary genius. My hands moved on autopilot, chopping vegetables and marinating chicken while my mind replayed every possible scenario for the night ahead.

If I told him and he laughed in my face, I'd send him packing.

If I told him and he broke down crying, I'd be there for him and choke on his anger at me while begging him not to take it out on Winnie.

If I told him and he stormed out...I had no idea what to do then.

When the time came, I set the table with a precision that bordered on obsession. Two plates, two glasses, and a carefully folded napkin at each place. Everything looked perfect. Weirdly perfect. I moved a fork askew so I didn't seem any more psychotic than I was feeling at this panicked moment.

I glanced at the clock. Any minute now.

When Casey knocked on the door, I thought I might vomit. I took a deep breath, smoothed my hands down the front of my sweater, and opened the door.

"Hey," he said, giving me a warm, easy smile. The smile that I couldn't get enough of.

"Hey," I replied, stepping aside to let him in.

He leaned down to kiss my cheek, and the gesture was so casual, so normal, that it made my whole body ache.

The scent of him—earthy like a forest—filled the room, unraveling me. I wished we could skip the next part of things. The arguments, the bickering, the truth. I wanted to go straight to the bed with my sins forgiven. Wasn't that what makeup sex was for?

But we couldn't get to the makeup sex without the other stuff first, so I'd take my lumps. I could do this. I had raised my baby girl on my own. I could do anything, right?

Right?

We sat down to eat, and Casey said, "Well, I have something to tell you."

He hates me. I know he does. "By all means."

"There's a rumor going around at work that I have an illegitimate child, and I abandoned her mother."

My fork clattered onto my plate. "What?"

"Obviously, it's just a rumor, but some of the players are convinced it's true. I've got your brother and the other veterans running defense for me, and Whitney. I'm doing what I can to handle it, keeping a tight leash on the guys while they figure out what's what." He sighed. "It's a headache, but nothing more."

I felt sick. "Glad to hear it's under control."

"Whitney's a miracle worker," he said with a chuckle, swirling the wine in his glass. "I don't know how she does it."

"Whitney's amazing," I parroted.

"What about you?" he asked, his blue eyes steady on mine. "How's work?"

"Busy."

"Anything interesting?"

I hesitated, my fingers tightening around my fork. "Just deadlines. You know how it is."

He nodded, but the way his gaze lingered told me he wasn't buying my deflection. "Glad you're making time for this tonight. Winnie around?"

I shook my head. "Megan's got her for the night."

"I'm glad you have that kind of support so close."

Numbly, I nodded. "One of the benefits of being in Atlanta." I rambled on about other things, but I knew better. Casey was too perceptive to miss the fact that something was wrong, and the longer I stayed silent, the harder it became to find the right moment to speak.

When dinner was over, he leaned back in his chair, studying me with a curious expression. "All right," he said, his tone calm but pointed. "What's actually going on?"

"What do you mean?"

"You invited me over," he said, gesturing around the room. "Just the two of us. No Winnie, no distractions. Feels like you've got something on your mind."

I considered lying with a, "Can't a girl ask her boyfriend

over for a romantic dinner?" kind of line, but that was disingenuous, and Casey was too smart to fall for it. I opened my mouth, then closed it again, my heart pounding.

"I just..." I hesitated, gripping the edge of the table. "I wanted to apologize. For the other day. For how I reacted when you brought up Winnie."

"You don't have to apologize, Gemma. I shouldn't have pushed you."

"No, you were right to ask. We're involved. You're bound to have questions," I said quickly, my throat tightening. "It's just...it's a hard topic for me. I've spent so many years being a single mom, and people judge. They judge everything. Not just me, but who the father is, why he's not around...I've gotten used to keeping it to myself."

He nodded slowly, his expression thoughtful. "I get that."

"Not to play the woe-is-me card, but I don't think you do. Society judges women on everything we do. Our hair, our bodies, our clothes, the way we sit—"

"The way you sit?"

A nervous laugh escaped me. "When I was twelve, a friend's mom told me to cross my legs, or I'd look like a whore with my legs open for men."

His eyes bulged. "Well, damn. That's messed up."

"Exactly. And when it comes to child-rearing, it gets worse. If we don't want kids, we're selfish. If we have a child out of wedlock, we're harlots. If we have a child, when are we having another one, and on and on and on."

"That's exhausting."

I nodded. "It really is. So, I'm sensitive when it comes to this topic, and I reacted poorly. I'm sorry for that."

"Understood." He drew a deep breath as he leaned forward, his elbows resting on the table. "But I need to ask you something. And I need you to be honest with me."

My heart felt like it was going to burst out of my chest. I knew what he was going to ask, and I still wasn't ready. "What?"

"Am I Winnie's father?" he asked, his voice calm but firm. "No deflecting, no dodging. Just tell me the truth. Whatever it is."

The walls closed in around me as his words lingered in my heart. For a moment, I couldn't breathe.

"Look," he said, his voice softening. "If I'm not, you don't have to tell me who her father is. But if I am—if there's even a slight chance—then I deserve to know, don't I?"

I stared at him, my hands trembling in my lap. My mind raced with a thousand thoughts, each one louder than the last.

"Gemma," he said again, his voice quieter this time. "Please."

Fight, flight, or freeze. Those are the common human reactions to fear. I'd always been a fighter, save for the two times in my past when I was in a bad situation. The first had been when a boy who was bigger than me cornered me in the school hallway and tried to forcibly feel me up. I slipped between the lockers and him and ran.

The other time was when the principal had caught Megan and me smoking behind the gym. It was the one time I had ever tried cigarettes, and of course, I got caught. I had apologized, said we would never do this again, that we never smoked, ever. Instead of three days of out-of-school suspension, we got one day of detention, helping clean the cafeteria.

The thought of Casey breaking up with me or not wanting anything to do with Winnie was too much for my brain to bear. I opened my mouth to speak, but the words were trapped, tangled in the sea of emotions swirling inside me. I couldn't force them out. For the first time in my life, I froze.

Chapter 19

Casey

The silence in the room was all I could hear. That and the blood pulsing in my temples. Worry sweat trickled down the back of my neck. That hadn't happened since the last playoffs. We'd won that night, but I didn't think my luck would hold out here.

And I wasn't sure what answer would qualify as winning this game.

Gemma sat across from me, her face pale, her hands trembling in her lap. I had asked her the one question I couldn't let go, and now I waited for the truth to drop like a bomb between us.

If I wasn't the father, why else would she not tell me? Did she not know who the father was? I'd never judge her for that, but after explaining the whole society-is-judgmental thing, I understood why she might not want to admit that. Maybe if I assured her I would never think less of her for that, she'd tell me.

But before I could get the words out, she nodded. "Yes."

The single word hit me like a sledgehammer, shattering my world apart.

I leaned back in my chair, the air rushing out of my lungs as I tried to process what she'd just said. She wasn't looking at me anymore, her eyes fixed on the table as if the weight of my gaze was too much to bear.

I should've expected it. Some part of me had, or I never would have asked. Somewhere deep down, I think I already knew. But hearing it confirmed was something else entirely.

Winnie was mine. I had a daughter. With a woman who had lied about her and kept her from me.

A thousand emotions surged through me at once—shock, anger, confusion, more, so much more—but cutting through all of it was a strange, unexpected sense of joy. Winnie. She wasn't just Gemma's little girl anymore. She was mine, too.

And she was amazing.

I thought back to the day at the park, the way she'd giggled when I pushed her on the swings, the way she'd run circles around Gemma with boundless energy. She was sharp and sweet and so full of life, and now I knew why I'd felt that strange connection to her.

But as quickly as the joy came, it was swallowed by the enormity of the situation.

Gemma hadn't told me.

For almost five years. That was how long she'd kept this secret. How long I'd missed out on being a father to my daughter. How long she'd chosen to handle this on her own, without giving me a choice.

Five years with my daughter, gone. The words rasped out of me, "Why didn't you tell me?"

Her head snapped up, her brown eyes wide with guilt. "Casey, I—"

"Five years," I said, cutting her off. "Five years, and you didn't say a word. Why?"

Her shoulders sagged, and she looked away again, her voice barely above a whisper. "Because I didn't know how. I didn't even know your name. And by the time I figured out I was pregnant, I'd already moved across the country. I'd started a life in California, and I wasn't ready to give that up. I needed that fresh start, Casey. After Dad...I didn't think..." She trailed off, shaking her head.

"You didn't think I deserved to know?" I asked, the anger simmering beneath my words.

"No, that's not it," she said quickly, her voice trembling. "I didn't think you'd want to know. Most guys, a hookup calls and says she's pregnant, he's ready to drive very fast into a brick wall, you know? Think about any guy you've ever known in that situation."

The truth was, there had been some surprise babies for my players, and each one handled it differently. Some were inclined the way she said it, others were overjoyed. "Men are not a monolith, Gem. You know me now. Do you think I would have been like that?"

She slowly shook her head. "No. But I didn't know you then, and I didn't want to burden you with a choice I'd already made. It wasn't your fault that I decided to keep her. That was my choice. Not yours. You shouldn't have to be saddled with a child and a stranger as your child's mother."

The words stung, even though I could hear the sincerity in her voice. She hadn't done it out of malice, but that didn't make it hurt any less.

"Do you know how much I've thought about that night?" I asked, my chest tightening. "How many times I wondered who you were if I'd ever see you again? And now, to find out like this—"

"I'm sorry," she said, her voice breaking. "I know I should've told you the minute I figured it out. I know I should've found a way. But I didn't, and now..."

She looked at me, her eyes shining with unshed tears.

"Now what?" I asked, my voice softening despite myself.

"Now I don't know what to do," she admitted.

Neither did I. So, I stood, pacing through her house as I tried to process everything. Pacing helped me think. The playoffs were right around the corner, the team was under immense pressure, and now this—this massive, life-changing revelation—was crashing down on me.

And then there was the other problem.

"Do you know what this means for us?" I asked, stopping to look at her.

"What do you mean?"

"It's against company policy for me to fraternize with a player's family," I said. "If anyone finds out—"

"And Whitney knows."

"She won't tell. Whitney's the only reason we've gotten this far without it blowing up in our faces. But if this gets out, I'm cooked."

"You're worried about your job," she said, her tone flat, as if she had any right to be disappointed in me.

"Of course, I'm worried about my job," I said, the frustration slipping into my voice. "This is my career, Gemma. My entire life. And now I've got a daughter I didn't even know about, and I don't know how...I don't know anything at all."

Neither of us spoke for what felt like an eternity. I resumed pacing and dragged my fingers through my hair, wishing that was her hand, her gentle touch. I loved when she did that.

Not today, though.

"I need to think," I said finally.

"Casey," she said, standing.

"I need to think," I repeated, my voice firmer this time. "And I can't think here. You're here. I'm too...you muddy things up in my head." I started toward the door, but before I could reach it, she was there, standing in front of me.

"Don't go," she said, her voice trembling.

"I have to," I said. The look on her face made it feel like my chest was caving in.

She grabbed my arm, her brown eyes locking on mine. "I love you."

The words stopped me in my tracks.

My body went numb. I was overloaded. I forced the words out, "How...how can you say that to me now?"

"I had to tell you."

"To make me stay?"

She shook her head. "I'm not trying to manipulate you, Casey. I needed to say it. I've wanted to say it for days—"

"After you drop this on me, you say that, and I'm supposed to...what, exactly? Say all's forgiven, let's be a happy family? Gemma, you're fucking with my heart, my livelihood, my life, and I have no idea how to handle any of this—"

"I know this is a lot," she said, her voice shaking. "And I

know I've handled it all wrong. For someone who writes for a living, I suck at saying things the right way out loud. But I love you, Casey. I love you so much, and I don't want to lose you."

My heart ached at her words, torn between the anger, the confusion, and the deep, undeniable love I felt for her. But it was too much—the playoffs, the team, the policy, and most importantly of all, Winnie.

If I said it back, if I told her I loved her, I couldn't be rational. I'd give into whatever she wanted, and I'd ruin my career over it. The career had given my life meaning when I was so lonely for so long that I thought love was a construct and the only real thing was my work. Whenever love had let me down, work was there for me. I couldn't just say screw it, could I?

Her house had become unbearably small and suffocating. I had to go somewhere I could breathe again. "I need time."

She nodded, stepping aside to let me pass, but the hurt in her eyes killed me. I opened the door and walked outside, the cool night air hitting me like a splash of cold water.

I didn't look back. If I did, I'd never get this figured out, and there was a very young child in need of me figuring it out. I had to leave for her sake.

Chapter 20

Gemma

I shouldn't have done it.

The words echoed in my head as I stood at the door Casey had just walked through, my hands trembling and my heart pounding in my chest. I shouldn't have said anything. I shouldn't have told him I loved him. And I definitely shouldn't have let him leave like that.

But I couldn't stop myself.

Telling him about Winnie was one thing. Telling him that I loved him was another. It crossed a different sort of line. I understood why he had asked me why I'd said it now of all times. From his end of things, it must have looked like I was trying to manipulate him. But on my end of it, the words had just come spilling out. It was not a plea to control him—it was my heart's declaration that I couldn't tamp down any longer.

I had to see him.

Even as the rational part of my mind screamed at me to give him the space he clearly needed, the rest of me—the part that couldn't imagine a life without him—was already moving, grabbing my coat, and slipping out the door.

The night air was crisp and cool, biting my cheeks as I hurried after him. I didn't know what I was going to say, but I couldn't let it end like this. If I had my druthers, we wouldn't end at all.

I caught up to him just sitting in his car on my driveway. His eyes widened when he saw me. When I came to his window, to my surprise, he rolled it down. Hopefully, that was a good sign.

"Hey—"

"I said I needed time."

"I couldn't let you leave like that," I said, my breath coming out in puffs of mist.

"You should've," he said, shaking his head.

"I can't just stand by and wait while you figure out how to deal with this. I need to be a part of the solution."

"This isn't just about us, Gemma," he said, his tone sharper now. "This is about a child. My child, who I didn't even know existed until tonight."

"I know," I said quickly. "And I know I screwed up by not telling you sooner. But you don't get to just walk away from this—from me—because it's hard."

"I'm not walking away," he said, his voice rising. "I'm trying to figure out how to handle this without losing everything I've worked for. Do you have any idea what this could cost me?"

"Of course I do," I snapped. "Do you think I haven't thought about that? About what it could cost me? My career, my reputation, everything I've built for Winnie—"

"Then why didn't you tell me?"

"Because I was scared!" I shouted, the words bursting out of me before I could stop them.

The silence that followed was deafening, broken only by the faint hum of a car passing in the distance.

He exhaled loudly. "If we're doing this, let's go back in your house. I'm not going to give your neighbors a show."

I hadn't even thought about that. But I nodded and stepped back, and he followed me inside. Once there, I repeated, "I was scared. I was scared you wouldn't want her. That you'd see her as a mistake, or a burden, or..."

"Gemma," he said, his tone softer now.

"I didn't want to burden you with a choice I'd made," I said, my throat tightening. "And I didn't want to risk you resenting me—or her—for it."

He sighed, running a hand through his hair. "You think I would've resented her? That I wouldn't have stepped up if I'd known?"

"I didn't know," I admitted, tears stinging my eyes. "But I couldn't take that chance. Not at the beginning."

"So you waited...for what, exactly? Was this all some kind of test?"

"No, not like that. I was scared you'd hate me for not telling you. That you'd be angry with me."

Casey stepped closer, his expression conflicted. "Angry that you cheated me out of five years with my daughter? I am. Deeply."

"I know you are," I said, my voice trembling. "And I don't blame you. But please, Casey, don't shut me out now. Not when we've finally found each other again. This thing between us is real, and we both know it."

His blue eyes simmered with struggle caught between

hating me and knowing I was right. He was at war with himself, and I was the enemy and the ally. His breaths, labored and ragged, sucked all the air out of the room.

When he finally moved, it was sudden, and I barely had time to react before his lips were on mine. The kiss was desperate, almost frantic, as if he was trying to erase the distance that had grown between us by sheer force of will.

I kissed him back just as fiercely, my hands clutching at his jacket as if letting go would send him spiraling away from me forever.

We stumbled back toward my bedroom, the argument forgotten in the heat of the moment.

He backed me against the hallway wall, ripping at my clothes, kissing and licking the latest bit of exposed skin.

The moment he stood, I shoved him across the hall, taking my own toll on him by pulling away the clothes that had the audacity to be in my way.

I dropped to my knees and took him in my mouth, and he cursed under his breath, slapping the wall behind him before digging his fingers through my hair to rock me back and forth down his length. But he growled and pulled me off of him, bringing me to my feet in a hurry.

By the time we reached the door, his hands were on my waist, pulling me closer, and my heart was pounding so hard I thought it might burst.

I didn't know who landed first, but suddenly, we were on my bed and tangled up in each other. His teeth grazed my nipples in turn, one after the other, as he made his way down my body. But I ran my fingers through his hair and pulled to signal what I really needed.

He climbed on top of me, and just before he thrust in,

he paused, catching himself. His voice was ragged with need. "Condom?"

I gently shook my head. "Birth control."

With that, he hooked a hand under my hip and lifted me as he plunged deep. My head dug into the pillows as I unleashed a cry, baring my throat to him. He licked me there as he pumped into me again and again. I took his face in my hands and brought him to my lips. Whatever this was, making love, fucking, something in between, I didn't know, but I needed it. Needed him.

Orgasms didn't seem to matter. I craved this connection with him more than any of that. When I came, mewling, he chased my orgasm harder, longer, faster, driving it through my entire body. I was lost in them, and he found me, kissing me to bring me back to life after every crashing wave.

When he pulled out and turned me over, it wasn't like the other times. He slid back in from behind, but this time, he caged me in his arms, pulling me up onto my knees. Like he couldn't be close enough to me. I understood the feeling.

I would have done anything for this. Would have begged for the honor.

Somehow, we ended up with me on top and his hands gripping my ass to drive us. He sat up against the pillows, and we shared breath. Our kisses had turned my lips raw, and I couldn't stop. Never wanted to stop. When he was close, his body went tense, and I murmured, "Just like this."

His sounds turned beastly before he kissed me as he came deep inside of me. He held me tightly, still kissing me as his body jerked and twitched in me. Eventually, our breaths slowed, and we separated—me to clean up and him to do the same right after. Once he was back in bed, I drifted off to sleep, too blissed out to recall much of anything beyond what we'd just done.

Sometime later, I woke to the sound of dishes clinking together. And I was alone in my bed.

I wrapped a robe on and found Casey by the sink washing the last of the dinner dishes. The tension that had been muted by passion came rushing back. He was quiet, his movements slow and deliberate.

"I should go," he said finally, drying his hands on a dish towel.

I nodded, wrapping my arms around myself as I leaned against the counter. "Okay."

He looked at me for a long moment, his blue eyes clouded. "We'll talk soon."

I nodded, incapable of speech at the moment.

He grabbed his jacket and headed for the door, but something about the way he lingered in the entryway made my chest ache. I wanted to call out to him, to ask him to stay, but the words caught in my throat.

He raced back to me, cupped the back of my head in his hand, and kissed my forehead as if kissing my lips was somehow too personal after what we'd done.

When the door finally clicked shut, the loudest silence followed.

I sank onto the floor, burying my face in my hands and sobbing. My heart was still racing, my skin still warm from his touch, but everything had gone cold and sick inside.

When I finally stopped the worst of the sobbing and stood up, my gaze landed on the sink—and the small object sitting on the edge.

It was a silver ring, thick and worn, with faint engravings on the inside. Casey always wore it on his thumb. He'd once told me it had belonged to his father, a constant reminder of the man who'd shaped him into the person he was today.

My heart clenched. He must've taken it off while washing the dishes and forgotten to put it back on in his rush to leave.

I reached for my phone to text him, only to find the battery completely dead. I groaned, plugging it into the charger before sinking back onto the couch.

The house felt unbearably empty without him. I traced my fingers over the edge of the ring, the cool metal grounding me even as my thoughts spiraled. Had I made everything worse by following him outside, by not giving him the space he needed? By taking him to my bed?

I thought about the way he'd kissed me, the way he'd held me like he was afraid to let go. But I also thought about the look in his eyes when he left—the pain, the uncertainty.

"I love you," I whispered to the empty room, the words feeling hollow without him there to hear them. I curled up on the couch, the ring still in my hand, and let the silence swallow me whole.

Chapter 21

Casey

The moment I stepped into the locker room the next morning, I knew it wasn't going to be a normal day.

The atmosphere was different—heavy, charged, the kind of tension that prickled at the back of your neck. I felt like prey. Conversations stopped mid-sentence as I walked in, and I caught the briefest flicker of glances exchanged before heads turned away. It was like high school all over again, only this time, the rumors were about me, as if I was finally one of the popular kids.

Is this how they always felt? No wonder they were dicks to everyone else.

Rumors always traveled fast in locker rooms, but this one had taken on a life of its own, spreading like wildfire through the arena. I'd always heard that saying about the bigger they are, the harder they fall, and I was Coach. It doesn't get much bigger than that. Whitney had done her best to contain it, but some fires couldn't be extinguished with words alone.

I stopped Luke, who dodged my gaze as he tried to walk by. But once I stepped in front of him, he couldn't avoid me. "Hey. What's going on?"

"Uh, nothing, Coach."

"Don't give me that. Why is everyone—"

"McConnell!"

I turned just in time to see Nico storming toward me, his jaw tight and his fists clenched. He knew everything. Somehow, he knew.

"Nico," I started, holding up a hand. "Let's—"

Before I could finish, he slammed me into the lockers with enough force to rattle the metal. My breath hitched, and for a second, I was too stunned to respond. The pain in my shoulder didn't register, but I knew it would soon. No one took a hit from Nico without feeling it for days after.

"What the hell is wrong with you?" he spat, his face inches from mine.

"Nico, calm down—"

"Don't tell me to calm down," he snapped. "You've been lying to me. Lying to all of us. We're supposed to be a team, Coach! How the fuck do you justify lying to us?"

"I haven't—"

"Don't lie to me," he said, his voice cold. "I know about Gemma."

The words hit like a punch to the gut, harder than the shove into the lockers. It wasn't even the words themselves. It was the disappointment in them. I knew how Nico felt about me—it was the same as a lot of the guys felt about me. I was a father figure to them, whether I wanted the role or not. That was why I held myself to a higher standard than other coaches did. I had to be someone they looked up to.

And now, Nico thought I failed him in the worst way.

"She's my sister!" Nico continued, his voice rising. "My baby sister! And you—what, you thought you could keep this a secret? That no one would figure it out?"

"Nico, it's not like that," I said quickly.

"Bullshit!" he shouted, shoving me again for good measure. The back of my head knocked against the cold metal. "You think I'm stupid? A redhead, a kid conceived the night of the masquerade, you asking me about the mask she wore—how long did you think it would take me to put it together?"

I didn't know what to say. I'd been so careful, so sure that we could keep this quiet, but in hindsight, it was obvious. Of course, Nico had figured it out. He wasn't just a teammate—he was family, and that connection made him sharper than I'd given him credit for. I deserved whatever he said or did to me. I just wished the rest of the team wasn't here to see this. They didn't need to see us fight.

Given he was Gemma's brother, I didn't want this fight to get any worse, either. Locker room fights were notoriously bad because every surface in a locker room is hard. Metal, wood, tile, none of that was good to the human body. That was why I always made the guys take their grievances out on the ice, if things got too heated in the locker room.

No chance of that happening now.

"You're supposed to be better than this," Nico said, his voice trembling with anger. "I looked up to you, Coach. We all do. But now you're just—what, another guy who couldn't keep it in his pants? Just another schmuck like every other asshole out there? Who are you anymore?"

I winced, the words cutting deeper than I wanted to

admit. I'd started to wonder about that myself. Worse, the players watched us, hanging on his every word. Whatever this was, it would not help the team. I had to get him out of here.

"You're too old for her," Nico snarled bitterly. "She's young, Coach. She's got her whole life ahead of her, and you—"

"Nico, stop."

"Why the hell should I?" he shot back. "Because you don't like hearing the truth?"

"Because this isn't the place for it," I said, stepping away from the lockers. "Come to my office. Now."

I was relieved when he followed instead of taking the chance to catch me with my guard down. But I trusted Nico—locker slams aside. He was a good man, and he wouldn't attack me from behind. I hoped.

The walk to my office was tense, Nico trailing behind me with barely restrained fury. I felt the weight of his glare on my back the entire way, and by the time we stepped inside, my own frustration simmered.

How dare he attack me in front of the team?

I couldn't just let that shit slide. If I did that, the team was lost. I shut the door and turned to face him, my hands on my hips. But what I saw on his face wasn't anger anymore. It was pain. I'd hurt Nico, and that took the steam out of me. "How did you figure it out?"

His jaw clenched. "Seamus."

I closed my eyes and sighed. Of course. I should have known. He'd been out most of the season with the flu and was just coming back. He had been trained for the clergy before joining the team, so ice cream was his only vice.

Perfect for helping him regain some of the weight he lost with the flu. I'd told him to eat as much of it as he could, which made this my fault.

How the hell had I missed him being there? Because I was too messed up about Gemma to pay attention to anyone else. So, it was doubly my fault.

I shook my head at myself. "Seamus was at Sprinkles, wasn't he? He saw us?"

Nico nodded once.

"All right. Let's get this out in the open."

"Yeah, let's," he said, crossing his arms.

I took a deep breath, steadying myself before I spoke. "Yes, I've been seeing Gemma. According to her, Winnie is my daughter. And I know it in my bones. She even has almost the same birthmark as me."

Nico's jaw tightened, his knuckles white where they gripped his arms.

"But it's not what you think," I continued. "I didn't know about Winnie, Nico. The night we met at the masquerade, I didn't know Gemma was your sister. When we met again here, I didn't know about Winnie—I didn't know about anything until recently."

"And you didn't recognize Gemma when you saw her again? Are you screwing that many girls that you can't keep up with them? You're just like the rest of them, aren't you?"

"The night at the masquerade...we didn't share names. We called each other by our mask colors. I was Red, she was Blue. We kept our masks on during the sex—"

He held his hand up to quiet me down. "That's enough. I don't need more details about that. She's my sister."

"Understood." I had to change the topic or he'd shut

down. I read it on his face. "If I'd known, Nico, I would've done things differently."

"Would you?"

"Yes," I said firmly. "I'm not proud of how this happened, but I care about her, Nico. I care about both of them."

"That's not the point," he said, his voice rising again. "You knew the rules, Coach. No fraternizing with family. You drilled it into all of us from day one, and now you're the one breaking the rules. You're a hypocrite."

I flinched, guilt twisting in my gut. "I know."

"You're supposed to be better than this, better than all of us," he said again, his voice cracking slightly. "You were like a father to me, Coach. To all the guys. And you're banging my baby sister? You were the guy we looked up to, the guy we trusted to set the example. And now—"

He broke off, shaking his head as he paced the room.

"I'm sorry," I said quietly.

He stopped, turning to face me with a look of pure disbelief. "Sorry? That's all you've got?"

"I don't know what else to say. What could I say that would make you feel better about any of this?"

"You could've told me about you and Gemma," he said, his voice trembling. "You could've trusted me. But instead, you snuck around behind my back, like a rat." He glared at me, part rage, part pain.

I had no defense, so I remained silent. He was right. The past aside, I had broken the rules. I had started seeing Gemma, knowing full well it was against the rules. I deserved whatever came next.

He shook his head in disgust. "You're not the man I thought you were."

And that hurt worse than any punishment my boss could dole out. Because Nico was right.

I'd been a different man since the moment I met Gemma all those years ago. Something had shifted in me after that night. I was more confident with women, more self-assured on the ice. Still played things safe, but I wasn't afraid to do a little free-falling every now and then. And now that she was back in the picture, I had broken all the rules for her.

Gemma had changed me completely. But I had fallen for her. There was no excuse for how I'd gotten there, but maybe if he knew that, then he'd understand. "Nico, I—"

Without another word, Nico turned and stormed out of the office, slamming the door behind him.

I sank into my chair. His words rang in my head. You're not the man I thought you were. It wasn't just Nico's anger that stung—it was the truth behind it. I'd let him down. I'd let the team down. And worst of all, I'd let myself down. I didn't regret anything with Gemma—I only regretted how I'd mishandled the situation.

A knock on the door pulled me from my thoughts, and Whitney stepped in, her expression worried. She leaned against the doorframe. "I tried."

"Tried what?"

"To stop the rumor," she said. "But it's out of control, Casey. Everyone's talking about it, and now that Nico ran off at the mouth and Gemma's name is in the mix..."

I held up a hand, cutting her off. "I get it. This is bad."

Whitney hesitated, then stepped closer. "Look, I know

this is a mess, but you've got to fix it. The guys are pissed. Nico isn't the only one who's disappointed in you. It's the team, and soon enough, it'll be Matthew. You know how he feels about this kind of thing. That's why it's in everyone's contracts. Family is off-limits."

I nodded slowly. This really was going all the way to the top, whether I liked it or not. "I'll fix it."

"How?"

"I don't know yet," I admitted. "But I will."

Whitney sighed, giving me a small, sympathetic smile. "You'd better. Because this team can't afford to fall apart—not with the playoffs coming up. We might be up for the Cup, and you know as well as I do, nothing can stand in the way of that where Matthew is concerned."

She left without another word, and I was alone again. I leaned back in my chair, staring at the ceiling as the guilt churned in my chest.

Nico was right. They all were. I'd broken the rules. I'd let my feelings for Gemma cloud my judgment, and now the entire team was paying the price. Team cohesion was everything, and I'd been the one to tear it apart. How could I live with that?

As much as I hated myself for hurting the team, I couldn't bring myself to regret what I'd done. Because the truth was, I loved her. I loved them both. Gemma was wonderful, and Winnie was amazing. How could anyone regret coming into their lives?

I didn't know how to reconcile that happiness with the responsibilities I had toward the team. But somehow, I had to figure it out. If I didn't, I was going to lose everything. I could survive losing my career. I had a good number of trophies under me and a clean track record. The professional coach-to-educational institution coach was alive and well. There were other opportunities, too. I just had to reach out and find them. Headhunters were always emailing me, calling me. Financially, I'd survive this.

But the team? Nico? I had to make things right with them. I just wasn't sure how.

Chapter 22

Gemma

"Oh."

That was my boss' reaction upon learning I couldn't do the article on Casey's illegitimate child.

Damn, I hated that phrase. As if my baby girl wasn't legitimate somehow.

Sitting in Gordon's office, I took a beat to collect myself. He was doing the same. I sipped my coffee to stall for time, but eventually, it was too awkward not to speak. "So, that's why I can't write the story about Casey McConnell. Professionally, it's an ethical conflict. Personally, it's too close to home. I'm sorry for the inconvenience—"

He huffed a laugh. "The inconvenience? Gemma, this goes beyond that."

I swallowed hard, bracing myself. "I'm sorry, Gordon. I know this is unprofessional—"

"Stop," he said, cutting me off. "You don't need to apologize."

I blinked, stunned into silence.

"I wish you'd told me sooner," he continued. "But I get it. We're just getting to know each other, so there's no reason you would have told me."

"Right, but I should have the moment I realized who he was. I'm too close to the team, too compromised to cover them. I'm sorry."

"Not another apology. Gemma, I was thrilled to use your connections to the team through your brother. Your child's father is just another link. Given the circumstances, yeah, you're compromised, so this isn't something you can cover objectively."

I almost apologized out of instinct, but he was right. I couldn't keep apologizing about this. I wasn't sorry about being connected to Casey or having Winnie. I was just sorry I had made things ethically impure. "Okay."

"More importantly, I wouldn't expect you to."

Relief washed over me, and I exhaled shakily. "Thank you."

"That said," he added, his tone shifting, "I think it's best if we give you some distance from the Fire. At least for a while. Until things settle down."

"What?"

"It's not a punishment," he said quickly. "It's just...you know you're too close to this, Gemma. We can't have a conflict of interest, especially on something this huge. We can't risk compromising your credibility—or the site's."

I opened my mouth to argue but stopped myself. Deep down, I knew he was right.

"What would you want me to cover instead?" I asked finally, my voice small.

"The college beats," he said. "It's a solid assignment.

Less pressure, less scrutiny. You can still write great stories for us."

I bit my lip, fighting back the frustration bubbling in my chest. "I appreciate the consideration, Gordon. I really do. But I can still cover the Fire. I can handle it."

"I'm sure you could," he said gently. "But this is for the site. We have to maintain our credibility, and if or when this gets out, your articles will be combed over, scrutinized, picked apart...it's going to be an issue. So, let's put you on the college beats for now. You're too good to lose, Gemma, and I need you to trust me on this."

There was no arguing with him. I nodded. "I get it. You're right."

"Please take care of yourself and your little girl. I'm worried this is going to get ugly before things calm down. You know how people are, especially hockey fans. They have a way of obsessing that puts other fans to shame."

I wanted to argue, but there was no point. I knew he was right.

The drive home felt endless. My thoughts swirled like a storm, replaying the conversation with Gordon over and over. I'd been taken off the Fire beat—the one thing that had made me feel grounded, connected, capable—and now, I felt untethered.

By the time I walked through the door, my chest was tight, and my eyes burned with the threat of tears. I was halfway to the couch when a knock at the door startled me.

I opened it to find Nico standing there, his jaw tight and his expression unreadable. "Can I come in?"

"Of course," I said, stepping aside.

He walked in, his movements stiff and deliberate, and I could feel the tension radiating off him. "We need to talk."

I nodded slowly, motioning for him to sit, but he remained standing, his arms crossed over his chest. "What's going on?"

"Is Winnie here?"

"Daycare."

"Good," he said, his tone morose. "How long has that been going on?"

"How long has what—"

"Don't. Don't do that. Don't lie to my fucking face, Gemma. You and Coach. How long has it been going on?"

I hesitated, my stomach twisting. I could have lied, but it would have been wrong. My new boss knew the truth, but I hadn't told my brother. That didn't sit right with me. "It's...recent."

"Recent," he repeated, his voice laced with disbelief. "And Winnie? How long have you known she's his?"

"Nico, it's not what you think."

"Then explain it to me," he said, his voice rising. "Because from where I'm standing, it looks like you've been keeping a hell of a secret from me."

"I didn't know, Nico. Not at first. I didn't even know his name that night, we kept our masks on—"

He winced. "I heard. Go on."

"I made the decision to keep Winnie, to raise her on my own. I didn't think—"

"You didn't think what?" he interrupted, his eyes flashing.

"I didn't think he needed to know, whoever he was," I

said, my voice trembling. "What man wants to hear they got their one-night stand pregnant, Nico?"

"Guess we'll never know."

"Don't do that. You tell me what you'd do if you got that call from a hookup. Tell me how happy you'd be to hear that out of some girl whose name and face you didn't even know."

He glanced away. "It'd be hard—"

I laughed sharply. "Hard?"

"But I'd deal."

"Right. You'd deal. Perfect Nico Grimaldi, always making the right choices. Always the good guy—"

"Stop, Gem," he said quietly. "This doesn't need to be a fight."

"Fine. I didn't think he'd want to know. And I was scared. I was scared of what he'd say, of what he'd do. Maybe he'd hate Winnie or me or worse. Maybe he'd want custody...so I kept it to myself."

He stared at me, his jaw tight and his fists clenched at his sides. "And now? What's your excuse for lying to me about this since you knew?"

"I needed to tell Casey first. She's his child, and Casey is your coach, so telling you first would have been wrong."

"I'm only your brother, so I don't count?"

"You know what I mean."

He exhaled loudly. "When did you tell him?"

"Last night."

Nico's shoulders sagged slightly, the anger in his eyes giving way to something more complicated—hurt, maybe, or disappointment. I hated this so much. Disappointing Nico made my stomach knot up. "I don't know what to think,

Gemma. I've always thought the world of Coach. He's been there for me. He's been like a father to me."

"I know."

"After Dad had his stroke, you remember what it was like. That weird lost feeling..."

I did. I remembered it well. We'd both been confused and lost after Dad's stroke, and Nico had had to step up to handle not just the household, but Dad's care, too. Initially, we tried to take care of him ourselves. It didn't go well.

I half smiled at the memory. "Do you remember that first time you tried to make oatmeal for him?"

He chuckled. "You mean when I almost burned the house down?"

I laughed, too. Mimicking his voice, I said, "It was only a small fire."

"I didn't know what else to tell the firefighters." He grinned. But that grin slowly died. "I know it's self-serving to say it, but after the fire, I knew we couldn't take care of him at home."

Initially, it had been a sore spot between us, but I was young and naïve, and I'd thought all we had to do was figure out how to cook. But the fire highlighted how wrong I'd been. It wasn't just oatmeal. It was physical therapy, speech therapy, bathing my father...I couldn't be at his beck and call twenty-four hours a day, seven days a week. I wasn't a nurse. I didn't know what I was doing. Neither did Nico. Thankfully, he'd been a hell of a college athlete and caught the eye of the talent scouts and ended up on the Atlanta Fire.

It was the only reason we had the money for the assisted living facility.

"I know we couldn't take care of him."

"You're not still mad at me for it?"

I shook my head. "I was an angry kid. I'm sorry for what I said back then."

He nodded. "It's all good. I'm not...we don't need to rehash that. Ancient history. Right now, I'm still not sure about Coach." Nico's anger tightened his face. "He's been sneaking around with my baby sister. He's the father of my niece—"

"He didn't know," I said quickly. "None of this is his fault, Nico. I didn't give him the chance to step up. I didn't give him the choice."

"That stuff isn't his fault, but breaking the team's rules is. There are rules about this kind of thing for the team, and that includes Coach. You can't fraternize with players or their families, it's just not done."

My knotted stomach flipped. "Will he lose his job?"

"I don't know." He let out a long breath, running a hand through his hair. "I just...I don't know how to feel. I'm angry. I'm disappointed. But more than anything, I'm surprised."

I bit my lip, fighting back the tears that threatened to spill over. "He's a good man, Nico. I know you don't believe that right now, but he is. He cares about me, and he cares about Winnie. He's just...overwhelmed."

Nico studied me for a long moment. "What are you going to do now?"

"I don't know," I admitted, my voice barely above a whisper. "I really don't know." I couldn't hold the tears back this time.

My big brother crossed the room and held me while I

cried. After I calmed down, he mumbled into my hair, "This is messy."

"Yeah."

"He took advantage—"

"Absolutely the fuck not. Don't do that. There was no imbalance of power between us, no deceit other than me keeping Winnie's paternity a secret. He did nothing wrong to me, Nico."

He drew a deep breath. "Gem, you're my baby sister. It's hard for me to wrap my head around all of this."

"Take all the time you need, but don't act like he's some asshole who hurt me. He's not."

He slowly nodded, his lips tightening in frustration. "Right. You good?"

"One day, I will be."

When Nico left, the house felt unbearably quiet. I sat on the couch, staring at the ring Casey had left behind. I didn't know what the future held. But for the first time, I was beginning to understand just how much I had to lose.

Chapter 23

Casey

The moment I noticed the empty spot on my thumb, my stomach sank.

I froze in the middle of tying my skate, staring down at my hand like it didn't belong to me. My father's wedding ring. The one I always wore. The one I never took off, except—

My breath hitched as the memory came flooding back. Gemma's kitchen. The sink. Washing the dishes before I left in a rush.

I had left it there.

Cursing under my breath, I yanked my skate off, the practice session now forgotten. My players milled around, focused on their own routines, but I felt their glances. The rumor hadn't gone away. It wouldn't for a while. Juicy gossip clung like smoke on your skin. After my run-in with Nico the day before, this—this ridiculous, personal slip-up—was just another log on the fire.

I was not the man I wanted to be. Not yet.

I needed that ring. It was a part of me as much as the

hand that was now unbearably naked. The ring was the last part of my father, a symbol that meant he wasn't truly gone. As long as I had that, I had him.

My father had been a truly stand-up guy. He was kind to strangers, went to church every Sunday, and loved my mother fiercely. For years, I held myself to that standard, and now...now who the hell was I?

A man in love. No, scratch that. An idiot in love.

Maybe love makes you stupid. Dad always said so.

I couldn't focus, not with the thought of that ring sitting on Gemma's counter. It wasn't just a piece of jewelry, and I needed it back. What if she knocked it into the sink? Or what if Winnie took it to play with and lost it?

I shot off a text to Gemma. No matter how awkward things were between us, I had to get my ring back. She wouldn't hold it hostage. She wasn't that type of woman. Even still, I didn't want to see her yet. I wasn't ready to face the mess we'd made, to have the conversations I knew we needed to have.

But this wasn't about that. It was just about the ring.

Her response came quickly. **Of course. I'll be home after 7.**

That was it. Simple. Neutral. Nothing about Winnie, nothing about the tension that had hung between us since the night I left. I wasn't sure if that was good or bad.

By the time I pulled up outside her house, my nerves were beyond frayed. I'd told myself this was just a quick visit, nothing more. I'd get the ring, thank her, and leave. Simple.

But as I walked up to the door, my heart pounded in my

chest. What if she wanted to talk? Was I ready for that? For any of this? What if—

She opened it before I could knock, and the sight of her made my brain fuzz out. A loose sweater and leggings, her pretty red hair pulled back into a messy bun. No makeup, no pretense—just Gemma, exactly as she was. Perfect.

"Hi," she said softly, her brown eyes searching mine.

"Hi," I replied, my voice rougher than I intended.

She stepped aside, letting me in, and the familiar warmth of her home wrapped around me like a blanket. The smell of something faintly floral lingered in the air, and I caught a glimpse of Winnie's toys scattered in the corner of the living room.

"Your ring's in the kitchen."

"Thanks. Is Winnie here?"

She shook her head. "Thought it would be easier if she weren't."

I nodded once as we hooked a turn into the kitchen. Dad's ring was exactly where I'd left it, sitting on the edge of the sink. I picked it up, turning it over in my fingers, and a wave of guilt crashed over me.

I'd left a piece of my father here. A piece of my past. A piece of myself. All because things had turned between me and the woman I loved. The woman who kept my daughter from me for five years.

That conflict warred in my head as I slipped the ring back onto my thumb. At least my hand felt whole again. "Thank you."

She nodded, leaning against the counter. Her arms were crossed over her chest, but there was something vulnerable in her expression, something that made my chest lock up. "Casey—"

"Gemma, don't. I didn't come here to talk."

"Then why did you come here?"

"For the ring," I said, though the words felt hollow.

"Is that really the only reason?"

I opened my mouth to respond, but before I could say anything, she closed the distance between us and slanted her mouth up to mine. The first touch of her lips was soft, tentative, but it was enough to unravel the fragile thread of control I'd been clinging to. No one had ever kissed me the way she did. Like she needed me.

I kissed her back, hard, my hands finding her waist and pulling her tight against me. The world burned away—Nico, the rumors, the playoffs—disappearing in the heat of the moment.

"Gemma," I murmured against her lips, my voice raw. Her name was a plea, but I didn't know what I begged for. Mercy? Absolution?

She didn't respond, her fingers threading through my hair as she deepened the kiss. When she moaned in my mouth, I was done. We stumbled toward the counter, my hands roaming over her back, her waist, the curve of her hips. She tugged at my jacket, pulling it off and tossing it aside before reaching for the hem of my shirt.

Something deep inside bellowed that this was a bad idea. No good could come from sleeping with Gemma now. There was too much left unsaid, too many logistics to figure out. The world tried to invade my thoughts, a cacophony of voices, each demanding attention. What about your career? What about Nico? The team?

But my body didn't give a shit about any of that. Neither did my heart. There was only one question left on my mind. "Are you sure about this?"

"Yes," she whispered, her voice barely audible. "I'm sure."

That was all I needed to hear. I growled, "Take off your clothes."

Her breaths made her breasts heave as she pulled the sweater over her head. They were perfect—a soft handful. She hadn't bothered to wear a bra. As she bent to peel her leggings off, I realized she hadn't worn underwear, either. Had she planned to seduce me?

It worked.

My heart stopped when she looked up at me under her lashes. "Now you."

I'd never undressed so fast in my life. I threw my clothes behind me without a care as to where they landed, and once I was naked, Gemma kissed me again. It felt so good to be pressed up against her. She offered that warmth I'd been missing.

I'd been missing it my whole life.

I breathed her in as we kissed, and when she palmed my cock, it was my turn to moan. She kissed down my pecs, fingers toying with my scant chest hair all the while until she kneeled before me. When she took me in her mouth, I hissed. She had done this once before and I liked it—of course I liked blow jobs—but I had other plans.

I laced my fingers into her hair and gently pulled her off of me. Her eyes had gone sex drunk. Half-lidded and penetrating. I nearly let her finish me off right then, but this wasn't what I wanted. "Your mouth is amazing, but I need you."

"How?"

I pulled her to her feet, then picked her up and set her on the countertop. She let out the sexiest little whoop when I did that, and as I spread her thighs, her full lips parted in a gasp. It was nothing compared to the sounds she made when I reached her wetness.

I peered into her eyes, watching her every tic, her every breathless word. This woman was perfect, from her hair to her toes. That messy bun on top of her head had fallen apart, and now, her hair was a red waterfall over her breasts, barely concealing her hard nipples. Her lips had pinked from our kisses, and ragged gasps rained from them. I fingered her, delighting in the feel of her clamping down on me. As my thumb grazed her clit, she squeezed tighter.

"Don't stop!"

I leaned on the cabinet next to her head. "Never." I kept at her until she finally cried out, her body spasming on my fingers again and again. She wrapped her hands around the back of my neck to kiss me as she came. It was heady, this thing between us. Somehow, getting her off was almost more satisfying than my own orgasm.

Almost.

I slipped her down from the countertop, then slung her across my arms to carry her the way a man carries his bride—

I couldn't let myself think about that sort of thing right now. This wasn't that. I didn't know what we were anymore, but that kind of thought would only get me in more trouble.

I refocused and took her to her bed, laying her down as gently as I could manage. But in the moment, all I wanted to do was slam myself to the hilt inside of her. To bury myself and my troubles away in the pleasure of her body.

She wanted it too, pulling me down on top of her, clinging to me. She wrapped her legs around my waist, so I took her, going deep at the start. There was no better feeling in the world than to sink into the woman I loved. We cried out together, with Gem scratching down my back as she arched her own. I clamped onto her throat, the need to bite overwhelming me.

I needed every bit of contact I could get.

I took her wrists and pinned her to the bed as I pounded her into the mattress. Close was not close enough. I needed this connection with her the way I needed oxygen. We kissed feverishly, ravenously. When she worked herself up to meet my thrusts, I could have died a happy man.

Her eyes widened in shock right before I felt her come on me. It was almost enough to make me join her, but instead, I rolled us over so she was on top. She still shuddered in the aftershocks as I grabbed her ass—that amazing ass—and pulled her back and forth on my cock. I jutted myself up as I pulled her down, and I had to fight the urge to come. She looked so damn hot like this. All orgasm weak and sexy drunk, her tits bouncing. The woman was a fantasy come to life.

She had a hard time speaking, but managed to say, "Gonna make me...again."

"Good girl," I grunted as I kept going.

This time, her head flung back as she gasped through the next one, and as she gasped, she came forward, nearly knocking into my head as she collapsed against my chest. I lifted my hips from the bed to fuck her from underneath at my speed. My balls tightened, and every sensation set me on edge.

"Can't take much more—"

"Yes, you can," I growled.

"Oh fuck," she whimpered.

I lost all control when I came, slamming deep and rough inside of her, losing myself in her. The world burst with color and light as I came, and I wrapped her in my arms to keep her there with me.

But the ecstatic frenzy wore away with unusual speed.

I did what I could to maintain that peaceful feeling. Afterward, we lay tangled together on the bed, the air between us ripe with unspoken words. I traced lazy patterns on her arm, my mind racing with everything I wanted to say but couldn't. This wasn't just passion. It wasn't just the heat of the moment.

It was about us. It wasn't some physical thing. There were vitally important things to talk about, but I wasn't sure how to start. Or if she wanted me to. She and Winnie were the life I hadn't even realized I wanted until it was staring me in the face.

But she kept my daughter from me for five years. That was a wound I didn't know how to heal. The thought of leaving her now made my chest ache, but I didn't know what else to do. I couldn't offer a solution to our situation, and staying would only make that worse. "I should go."

She nodded, her expression unreadable. "Okay."

I stood, grabbing my clothes from where they had fallen

on the floor. She followed me to the door, her hand brushing mine as I reached for the knob.

"Casey," she said, her voice stopping me in my tracks.

I turned, my heart pounding.

"Thank you."

"For what?" I asked, frowning.

"For tonight," she said, her eyes shining.

I didn't know how to respond, so I just nodded and stepped outside, the cool night air hitting me like a wake-up call. The drive home was quiet, but my mind was anything but.

Chapter 24

Gemma

The house was too quiet without him.

After Casey left, I sat on the couch, staring at the door like it might open again. Like he might come back, sweep me into his arms, and tell me everything would be okay.

But of course, he didn't.

He didn't have a key, so he couldn't just barge in here. We hadn't gotten that far along yet. It was stupid to sit there, waiting for it to happen when I knew it couldn't. And yet, I did.

My heart was an idiot.

The ring was gone, back on his thumb where it belonged, but it felt like he'd left something bigger behind—an ache that settled in my body and refused to budge. I could still smell his cologne lingering in the air, faint and earthy, and it made my stomach twist with longing.

I loved him.

I loved the way he looked at me, like I was the only

person in the room. I loved the way he talked to Winnie, the way he'd pushed her on the swings and played tag with her like it was the most natural thing in the world. I loved his silver hair, the lines around his eyes, the way his age gave him a depth and steadiness that no one else I'd ever met had.

And I missed him.

It was a physical ache, a hollowness in my body that made everything else seem dull and unimportant. I felt empty without him here. Could I be codependent on someone I'd known for so short a time? Was that a thing? I wasn't sure. But even now, I could picture the way he'd looked at me before he left, his blue eyes filled with emotions he hadn't put into words.

I wanted him back. But I didn't know how to fix what I'd broken.

I wound my way through the cottage, turning off lights and closing up for the night. I found my hairband on the floor in the kitchen. It had come undone when he reached into my hair to pull me off of him. For some reason, the sight of it on the tile made me weep. I wiped my eyes on the back of my hand, washed up, and went to bed, where I cried myself to sleep.

In the morning, I got a call I never wanted.

"We're running the story tomorrow morning," Gordon said, his tone brisk. "Don't worry, your name's not in it."

"Thanks," I said quietly, gripping the phone so tightly my knuckles turned white. "Who is covering the story?"

"Ian."

I groaned. "Ian? He'll shank the story, Gordon. He has no heart, no compassion. It'll be a hit piece!"

My boss sighed. "Well, I had my favorite journalist on it, but she has a conflict of interest."

Dammit. "You know what I mean."

"I do. And everyone else has other assignments. He's been wanting to cover the Fire for a long time. It was either let Ian do it, or we'd get scooped."

Which wasn't an option, either. "Shit."

"I meant what I said, Gemma. I made sure there's nothing in there that could link you to this. You're in the clear. Ian has no idea you're involved in any way."

I blew out a deep breath. "Thanks, Gordon. And thanks for the heads-up."

"You got it. Take care."

I ended the call and flopped onto the couch. I wanted to believe my boss, but the knot in my chest didn't ease. The truth always had a way of coming out, no matter how carefully it was buried. And it didn't matter if my name was in it or not, because this story could hurt Casey.

So, I texted him and asked if he could come over. **Can you stop by? I need to talk to you.**

He didn't reply right away, and the minutes stretched into hours. But just as I was about to give up, my phone buzzed. **I'll be there in 30**.

When he arrived, he looked as tired as I felt, his blue eyes shadowed and his shoulders tense. "What's wrong?"

I led him to the couch, sitting down beside him and folding my hands in my lap. "The story's coming out tomorrow."

He didn't react right away. The silence stretched out between us. I needed him to say something, anything. But the silent treatment? I hadn't thought him capable of something that cruel.

Eventually, though, he muttered, "I figured it'd come out sooner or later."

"My boss said he kept my name out of it," I continued, my voice trembling slightly. "But it's only a matter of time before other people put the pieces together."

Casey nodded slowly. "I'll deal with it."

"You don't have to—"

"Yes, I do," he said firmly, cutting me off. "This is my mess, Gemma. Not yours. I won't bring you or Winnie into it."

I stared at him, unable to breathe. We both knew the kind of media circus this could bring down on me and our daughter, and he was sparing us even though he didn't have to. In fact, spreading the media around would have lessened the burden on him. And he was protecting us anyway.

I whispered, "Thank you."

He nodded again, his gaze softening slightly. "You don't have to thank me for that."

When Casey left, the silence in the house was, once again, unbearable. I sank onto the couch, hugging a pillow to my chest, trying not to vomit. I'd told myself I could handle this, that I could keep moving forward without him, but the truth was, I felt untethered. Adrift. Lost in a sea of—

"Okay, Gemma, rein yourself back in." I took a deep breath and hoped talking to myself was not a sign of bad mental health. I missed Casey more than I thought it was possible to miss someone. But more than that, I missed the way I felt when I was with him—grounded, like I wasn't alone anymore.

I needed something to cling to, and I refused to be one of those single moms who depends far too hard on her child to do her emotional labor for her. Winnie didn't sign up to be my crutch.

The next day, I threw myself into work. The great thing about my job was that I was the one asking all the questions. I could bury myself under a mountain of editing and no one would be the wiser.

Since Gordon had reassigned me to the college beats, I'd already lined up an interview with some of GSU's star football players. The campus was bustling when I arrived, and for a moment, I let myself get caught up in it.

Part of me missed college. As complicated as some of my assignments were, as difficult as some of the professors were, I missed the days when my biggest worry was whether or not I got a paper in on time. Things were simpler back then, and simplicity sounded very appealing after everything I was dealing with.

I met the boys in a student lounge. My interviewees were Jacob Grainer, Ryan Weiss, Ennis MacIntosh, and Ty Dixon, each more muscular than the last, it seemed. Giant muscly babies, each of them. After spending so much time with Casey and hell, even the Atlanta Fire, these college boys all looked undercooked. Cute, but so very young.

I understood why they were the star players—more than once, some girl or girls came by to flirt with them. They were good-looking kids, perfect for putting their faces on every bit of team merch that they could. A googly-eyed girl asked Ty to sign her foam finger with his name on it, which he did with a sly grin before she took it and ran off to show her friends.

"So, guys," I said, trying to collect their attention once again. "According to our sources, your bios have been crashing the school's system. People keep trying to find out more about you. What would you like my readers to know?"

Ty chuckled, turning that sly smile to me. He flicked his dark eyes up and down over me. "What do you want to know? I'm an open book. For the right reader."

"Maybe something personal. Is that girl the right reader for you?"

He grinned. "Nah. I like my women grown. The girls around here are just that. Girls."

I softly laughed. "I can understand that. Jacob, how about—"

"Gemma," Ty said, stealing my attention for himself. "What I mean is, you're exactly my type."

"So you prefer older women?"

"I prefer you."

I laughed a bit louder that time. "Thanks, but I'm taken." Was that a lie? It felt like a lie. But getting into the specifics was not on the table.

He sucked air through his teeth and muttered, "Damn. Hey guys, did you see where that girl went?"

Jacob pointed down a hall, and Ty was off. The remaining players sheepishly smiled or shrugged. Jacob said, "That boy doesn't have the sense God gave a goat. I'm sorry about him running off like that."

"Most players I interview don't have it in them to sit still for long. No worries." After that, the players were polite, friendly, and eager to talk. Evidently, Ty had stifled their personalities, which made sense. His persona was almost too big for the room.

They were cute, sure—tall, athletic, and confident in that boyish way that college kids always seemed to have. But they all looked like kids to me, and even though they were young and full of potential, they didn't have the depth or the quiet confidence that Casey had.

Without meaning to, he had become my benchmark.

I found myself picturing him instead—the silver in his hair, the faint lines around his eyes, the way he carried himself like someone who'd lived and learned. He was the only man I wanted, and no amount of charming smiles or college boy bravado was going to change that.

By the time I got home, the ache in my bones was worse than ever. I dropped my bag by the door and sank onto the couch once again, staring at the ceiling as the events of the day replayed in my mind.

I wanted to call him. I wanted to hear his voice, to tell him how much I missed him and how badly I wanted to fix things. But I didn't. Instead, I sat there in the quiet, letting the guilt of it all wash over me.

I loved him. And I deserved to be alone after what I'd done.

Chapter 25

Casey

Buzzing. That was the only word to describe the hum of adrenaline in the locker room. It was electric in a way that only happened before a playoff game. The players were loud, hyped up, and restless, their voices bouncing off the walls in a chaotic din. Normally, this was where I thrived—channeling their energy, sharpening it into focus—but today, the noise felt different.

Today, they weren't listening to me.

It did more than bruise my ego. It worried me for the playoffs. They had to get their shit together so they could learn the new plays I'd come up with, but instead, they were screwing around while I talked. I stood by the whiteboard, marker in hand, trying to go over our game plan, but the guys weren't paying attention. "Reilly, put your phone down. You're at work, remember?"

He gave half a shrug and kept texting without even looking up.

Before I could reprimand him, Nico smacked the back of his head, which made Reilly's hand curl instinctively into a fist. Until he saw who had done it. Then, his brow furrowed in confusion. Nico gestured for him to put his phone down and pointed at me, so Reilly muttered, "Oh. Sorry, Coach."

Why had Nico gone from slamming me into the lockers to garnering some modicum of respect for me? I had no idea. But I'd take it where I could get it. The guys had been assholes for the past few days, and I'd had enough of that.

"Right. Reilly, you or the other centers will drive up the middle in this play, no risks on your part. When you get the puck this close to the goal, they're gonna try you. They wanna fight? You don't give it to them. Not this time. This is the playoffs. We're not here to jerk each other off. Your only goal is to get primed for your winger to slap it to you, got it?"

The centers nodded along. All but Sorkin, though I wasn't surprised.

Out of the lot of them, he had the worst habit of zoning out. His fingers were usually drumming on his knee when he spaced, and sure enough, right now he was playing some piece on his knee again, likely from his old days.

Before he'd joined the team, he was a drummer in a local band that had a loyal following until the lead singer got a record deal and left them all behind. Sorkin had turned to professional hockey as his backup plan. He had played through high school in Canada. He had almost been recruited back then, but music was his stronger calling. Too many talents.

It was a pity that paying attention wasn't also one of his talents.

"Sorkin—"

Nico nudged his knee and snapped his fingers in the big guys' face. "Sore, you in there today?"

"What? Huh?" He blinked himself back into the locker room, like he was coming out of a haze. I didn't know if he had smoked too much weed when hc played at dive bars or what, but the kid always appeared perma-baked until he was on the ice. Then muscle memory took over.

Nico firmly said, "Coach is talking to you."

"Oh," he said stiffly. A slight curl to his lip said enough of what he thought of me. "Yeah, well, sorry."

I ran through the play again, this time with more attention paid to me. But the moment I stopped talking, they were at it again. Some of them were cracking jokes, others were fiddling with their gear, and a few were having their own conversations like I wasn't even there. It was infuriating.

"Nico," I said, my voice sharper than I intended.

He looked up from where he was leaning against the bench, arms crossed. "Yeah, Coach?"

If I wasn't a professional, it would have grated my nerves to admit I needed his help. After the locker room attack, maybe I shouldn't have turned to him for help, but I didn't have much choice. He was the only person they were listening to today. "Get them in line."

Nico hesitated, and for a moment, I thought he might push back. But then he clapped and let out a sharp whistle, the sound cutting through the noise like a warm knife through butter. He barked, "Atlanta Fire! Shut the fuck up and listen!"

The guys quieted down, their attention shifting to Nico

instead of me. He had their respect and their trust, in a way that reminded me what I'd lost. It stung.

Right then, I realized just how much the team's loyalty had shifted. I took a step back, letting Nico have the floor. If they weren't going to listen to me, fine. I'd use every tool in the toolbox to get the job done. He was the senior-most center these days, so I knew he'd have pull with the others. But would the whole team hear him out?

He looked around the room, his eyes narrowing as he took in the group. "I get it," he said, his voice steady. "I know some of you are pissed. Some of you think Coach let us down. But let me tell you something—he didn't."

There were murmurs of surprise, a few skeptical looks, but Nico pressed on. Hell, even I was surprised. Not that he said that, but that he knew, and that he understood about me and Gemma. I didn't deserve that grace, but I sure as hell appreciated it.

"Yeah, the circumstances suck," he said, his tone blunt. "Yeah, it's weird. But you know what's not weird? Winning. We're good at winning. And the only reason we're here, the only reason we've got a shot at that trophy, is because of Coach."

The room fell silent.

"He's helped us win in the past. This year, he's gotten us this far again," Nico continued, his voice rising. "And if I can look past the situation, so can you. Respect the man who got us here. Respect the work he's put in, and give him everything you've got in here when he coaches and out there on the ice. We owe him that much and more."

The tension in the room shifted. To my surprise, I felt a little better after hearing Nico talk about the weirdness between us. It was a pretty good speech. One by one, the players nodded, their expressions serious as they turned their attention back to me.

I stepped forward, meeting their eyes as I spoke. "All right, let's get to it. Here's the plan."

This time, they listened.

I ran through our strategies, breaking down the opposing team's weaknesses and emphasizing our strengths. The players nodded along, asking questions, making suggestions, and falling back into the rhythm we'd built all season. Not a cell phone in sight. Even Sorkin paid attention.

By the time we hit the ice, the energy in the locker room had given way to what I always liked during these sessions. Hope.

Once the team was on the ice to run drills, I grabbed Nico by the arm, pulling him aside. "Got a minute?"

"Sure," he said. But he was stiff about it, enough to tell me there was still something about this that he didn't like. Maybe we weren't good yet. But I had hope that we would be.

I led him to a quieter corner of the arena, away from the noise and activity, and turned to face him. "I just want to say thanks for what you did in there."

"For what?"

"For getting the guys to listen to me," I said. "For sticking up for me, even though I know you didn't want to."

Nico shrugged. "I did it for the team."

"I know. But it still means a lot to me, and I believe in showing my appreciation, so thank you."

He nodded slowly, his eyes narrowing as he studied me. "Are you okay with all of this?"

The question caught me off guard. "Okay with all of what?"

"Being with my sister," he said, his voice careful. "Knowing what people are saying about you, knowing how it looks with you being so much older than her. Are you really okay with it? You've always been so careful about your reputation."

I hesitated. To be honest, I didn't know. If we somehow figured things out and tried to make this work, people would judge us. I was almost two decades older than Gemma. People were more likely to assume she was my daughter and not my girlfriend, and I'd have to find a way to live with that.

A small price to pay compared to what else it might cost me. "People will say what they're going to say, no matter what I do. I could be a Boy Scout, and someone would complain." I shrugged. "Some people won't like us being together. So what? They aren't the people I care about. But I care about Gemma. And I care about Winnie. They are what matters to me, Nico. Anyone else can fuck off."

He snorted a laugh. "Who taught you that kind of language, Coach?"

"Been hanging around you criminals for too long."

He smirked, but it faded fast into something else. Worry, maybe. "I'm not gonna lie, it's still weird for me. I don't love the idea of you and Gemma being together. Maybe I'm overprotective, but I'm her big brother, and that's my right." He took a beat, and as he did, his face relaxed. "But if this is what I think it is..."

He trailed off, letting out a long breath while I held my own.

"As it turns out," he continued, "my niece has a great dad she hasn't really met yet. And my sister seems happy with you. So I guess I'll get over it. At some point." The corners of his mouth twitched upward in a small, reluctant smile. "And maybe," he added, "our family will be all the better for the weirdness. I don't think anyone gets to have normal these days, and well, Gemma was never normal."

I hacked a laugh, trying to hold myself together. His words hit me harder than I expected. I hadn't thought he'd approve in any way, shape, or form. Not this soon, at least. My throat tightened, but I said, "Thanks, Nico."

"Don't thank me yet," he said, clapping me on the shoulder. "We've got a game to win."

As he skated out onto the ice, his confident stride and easy grin reminded me of why he was such a crucial part of this team. He wasn't just a great player—he was a leader, someone the others trusted implicitly.

And now, he was giving me the biggest trust I could imagine. He approved of me being with his sister. Tacitly, but the approval was implied. I felt honored, and I didn't know what to do with the emotions welling up inside of me.

Nico shouted from center ice. "You gonna run drills or what, Coach?"

I took a deep breath, stepping onto the ice to join the team. Hopefully, they'd come around like Nico had.

Chapter 26

Gemma

I sat in the stands, heart pounding as the final seconds of the game ticked away. The arena was electric, the crowd on their feet, chanting, cheering, and roaring with every pass and block. But I barely heard it.

My focus was on him.

Casey stood behind the bench, shouting commands, his face set in a mask of intensity as he directed the team. This was where he came alive, where his passion and skill met in perfect harmony. And watching him work, a surge of pride struck so fierce that it took my breath away.

He had done it.

The whistle blew, signaling the end of the game, and the arena erupted in celebration. The Fire had won. They were going to the Cup.

I clapped and cheered along with the rest of the crowd, a smile breaking across my face despite the ache that had settled in my soul ever since he'd left my place. He wasn't ready to let me back in—not fully, and maybe never again—but that didn't stop me from being proud of him.

The cheering crowd began to thin as fans filed out of the arena, but I stayed rooted to my seat, my eyes fixed on the ice where the team had celebrated their victory. It was empty now, like most of the stands. They'd left to clean up and go home.

I should've gone home, too. I could pour myself a glass of wine, and try to distract myself from the fact that Casey and I were still in this strange, painful limbo.

But I didn't. I wanted to be there for him—in the good times and the bad.

Before I could think it through, I was on my feet, weaving my way through the crowd and out to my car. Thankfully, this wasn't the Cup, or I'd have to deal with tailgaters and drunken fights that inevitably followed those wins. I didn't even remember starting the engine, my mind already racing ahead to his place.

When I knocked on his door, my heart was pounding so hard I could feel it in my throat. For a moment, I thought he might not answer. Hell, he might not be home yet. Had I sped all the way here for nothing?

But then the door swung open, and there he was. He looked tired, the adrenaline of the game fading, but his blue eyes still held that sharp intensity I'd seen on the ice.

"Gemma," he said, his surprise obvious.

"Hi," I said softly, my hands twisting together.

He stepped aside, motioning for me to come in, and I slipped past him into the warmth of his home.

"I wasn't expecting you," he said, closing the door behind me.

"I know," I said, turning to face him. "I just...I wanted to see you. To talk."

"Talk about what?"

But before I could answer, his hands were on my waist, pulling me closer until he kissed me. He knew I wasn't here to talk. And even if I were, I would have shoved it aside for this. All the emotions I'd been holding back—the pride, the longing, the frustration, the love—spilled out as I kissed him, my fingers tangling in his hair as he pulled me flush against him. He gripped my ass, picking me up just a little, just enough to put me on edge.

We didn't make it far before clothes started coming off, leaving a trail from the living room to the bedroom. Our kisses weren't slow or gentle—they were heated, desperate, like we were both trying to erase the pain of the last few days with sheer physical intensity.

And for a little while, it worked.

"I've missed you," he whispered between kisses.

Those words. Those damn words. They threatened to slice right through me. "No talking." I groped him over his boxers.

He grunted and nodded once, before he pushed me backward onto the bed. I hadn't kept up with how naked I wasn't, until he ripped my underwear apart before diving between my legs for a snack. That man's tongue was a gift. My heels dug into his shoulders when I crested, and I gripped his hair to keep him on target. Not that he needed the help. Maybe I just needed something of his to hold onto when he made me come on the tip of his tongue.

When I finished, he flipped me over onto my stomach and split my legs apart right before penetrating me. The weight of him on me pinned me to the spot, and I craved the feel of him like that. Solid. Grounding.

But then he pulled me onto my knees with my head still down on the pillows, and he fucked me hard that way. Our bodies smacked together, harder and faster with every thrust. I pushed back to meet him, taking as much as he could give. Only then did he find my clit with his free hand—the other hooked around the opposite hip. When he touched me there, I rocketed into the next orgasm, too tight with tension to breathe through it. A scream pealed out of me as I came, that delicious tremor riding me like a wave.

He turned me over yet again, his wet hand hooking under my jaw as he slid back into me. Not a choking hold, but a claiming one. His wordless way of telling me that I was his.

Maybe not forever. But for now, at least.

His body went stiff, and his cock swelled inside of me. It almost triggered another one for me, and just as he gasped from his own, that look on his face tipped me into it. As primal as this had been, his face was nothing but loving as he came inside of me. It shattered me, and I came so hard I thought I might pass out.

I may have.

The next thing I knew, he was spooning me. We lay snuggled in the sheets, the room quiet except for the sound of our rapid breathing. My head rested on his arm as my mind raced.

"Why did you come here, Gemma?"

I hesitated, turning around to look at him. His expression was calm, but there was something in his eyes—something guarded, almost wary—that made my chest tighten. The guilt I'd carried promised to suffocate me. But he deserved answers. "I wanted to talk. But we...skipped to the part we're good at."

He huffed a quiet laugh, though it didn't reach his eyes. "Yeah, we're good at that." He sighed. "If you wanted to talk, you could have said no to this."

In theory, sure. But how do you say no to this kind of sex? The kind that tears you apart and puts you back together, the kind people go to war for. This connection was too important. It overrode my good sense.

Eventually, I said, "I know I could. Probably. One day, when I have some self-restraint around you. But I didn't want to say no to this."

He silently nodded.

I sat up, pulling the sheet around me as I searched for the right words. "I came here because I wanted to tell you how proud I am of you. Of what you've done with the team, what you've done for them. It's amazing, Casey. They're that good because of you."

He sat up too, leaning back against the headboard with a weighty sigh. "Thanks."

"But that's not all."

He glanced at me, his expression unreadable. "What else, Gemma? What is there to say?"

I bit my lip, my chest tightening. "So much."

"Like what?" he asked, his voice hardening. "Like how you didn't think I was worth being a father back then? How you decided for me that I didn't deserve to know my daughter? What has changed since then?" His words stung, but I couldn't blame him. He was right to be angry.

"Everything has changed since then, and you know it."

He shrugged. "Do I?"

"I was wrong about you," I said quietly, my voice trembling. "I was scared, Casey. I didn't know how to tell you. I didn't even know your name! And by the time I figured it out, I thought it was too late. But everything's changed now. You have changed everything."

He stared at me for a long moment, his jaw tight. "You think that makes it better?"

"No. It makes it worse," I admitted, tears stinging my eyes. "But I'm trying, Casey. I'm trying to make it right."

He shook his head, running a hand through his silver hair. "Gemma, I can't...I can't do this right now."

I froze. "What do you mean?"

"I mean I need time," he said, his voice tired. "Time to figure out what the hell I'm doing with my life, with my career, with you."

"I understand." I did and I didn't. He was hurting, and I wanted to do anything I could to fix it. But when someone asked for time, that meant they were figuring a way out, not a way in. My heart stuttered to a stop from grief. But I refused to make it his problem. I swallowed my tears down and vowed not to make him feel badly about this.

"It's not just my career on the line. I know you used your position as Nico's sister to secure your new job, so this puts your career at risk, too. I can't have that. You're a hell of a journalist, Gemma. You deserve more than what I—"

I pressed a finger to his lips. If he had, I would have lost it right then and there. "Don't finish that sentence. Please."

He reached out, his hand brushing mine. "It's not about not wanting you. It's about not knowing how to have you without losing everything else. I can't think around you. All I want to do is more of...well, this. Because we're good at this, and the other stuff...I haven't figured it out yet. I have to ask you to leave."

Tears blurred my vision as I stood, clutching the sheet around me like a shield. "Okay." I grabbed my clothes and some of his on my way out. Dressing while casually fleeing was not a skill I had, so I pulled on his T-shirt and my heavy sweater over it, and I did not care whatsoever if I looked undignified. My jeans went on next, followed by his socks and my shoes. By the time I was dressed, I must have looked exactly like a woman who had the hell fucked out of her and back into her.

He walked me to the door, his hand lingering on the knob as he opened it. "Take care of yourself, Gemma."

"You too," I said, my voice breaking.

And then I was gone, stepping out into the cool night air with my heart burning to ashes in my chest.

Chapter 27

Casey

Asking Gemma to leave was the hardest thing I'd ever done.

The sound of the door clicking shut behind her echoed in my head long after she was gone. Everything echoed, now that she was gone. My thoughts. The ticking clock on the wall. I sat on the edge of the bed, elbows on my knees, staring at the floor. The weight of empty silence was unbearable.

I'd buried both of my parents in relatively quick succession. I'd stood at their graves and said my goodbyes, feeling like the foundation of my world had been pulled out from under me. Somehow, this felt just as bad. How was that even possible?

I loved her, right down to my marrow.

That thought circled in my mind, a vulture soaring over the corpse of my ability to think about anything else. I loved Gemma. I loved everything about her. I loved her fierce independence. That was what kept her going in LA as a single mom, doing everything on her own for five years.

As much as I hated that she had kept me from my daughter that whole time, I knew it was no cakewalk for her, either. She was alone for all the milestones. Had to do everything herself. Be everything by herself. She was all Winnie had. I couldn't imagine that kind of pressure or how hard that must have been on her.

And yet, the pressure didn't show itself in bitterness or resentment. She was still warm. Still easy-going. The little things didn't bother her the way they did most people. Instead of becoming aggrieved, she turned that energy into warmth for everyone around her. She was friendly and outgoing in a way I admired. And she had a way of making people feel like they were worth knowing, a gift in her line of work.

And Winnie—God, Winnie. She was bright and funny and sweet, and the thought of all the years I'd missed with her was enough to bring me to my knees. I didn't know how to get past that loss, or if it was even possible to get past something like that.

And that was my flaw.

Love wasn't enough right now to push me past that pain, which meant I wasn't enough for them right now. Holding onto that anger made me weak, and they didn't deserve that. I didn't know how to be what they needed me to be, and the uncertainty was eating me alive.

I needed to get out of my own head, even if just for a little while. If I stared at the same four walls all night long again, I'd go crazy. The relentless quiet of my house was more than I could take. So I grabbed my jacket and headed to Smokey's, the kind of bar where the lights were dim, the drinks were strong, and everyone loved hockey.

Gabriel Moreau was a right winger out of Alberta, and when he came to Atlanta, he had opened Smokey's. His son, Xavi, was a great defender for the Fire, so between the two of them, they had plenty of real memorabilia on the walls of the bar. The place was otherwise wooden—the floor, the walls, the bar itself. All highly polished and well-maintained. The perfect place for a drink after a long day.

Maybe it was the post-sex haze, but I'd forgotten the guys would be here to celebrate going for the Cup.

Smokey's was overtaken by a raucous party. Beers and cheers in every direction. Sliding onto a stool at the bar, I nodded at Gabe and ordered a whiskey. The first sip burned going down, but I welcomed the sting.

Out of the corner of my eye, I noticed a few of the guys from the team sitting at a table in the back, laughing and talking. Some flirted with the puck bunnies that hung around the bar, just waiting for my players to show up. None of them had seen me yet, and I wasn't in the mood to join them. They were celebrating, while I was...well, I just needed a quiet drink, and a little time to let the noise in my head die down.

I was halfway through my second whiskey when a woman slid onto the stool next to me. She was tall and slim, with dark hair and a confident smile that didn't quite reach her eyes. Before Gemma came along, I might have been interested. Now, she was just a pretty woman, and the world was full of those.

"Rough night?" she asked, her voice smooth and casual, as if she hadn't just arched her back a little to thrust her breasts into the conversation.

"I've had rougher."

"You don't seem like the Smokey's type."

I glanced at her then, raising an eyebrow. She was a little older than most of the crowd. Like me. As far as I could see, neither of us belonged at Smokey's. "And what's Smokey's type?"

"No one drinks alone in a place like this," she said, smiling as she motioned to the bar around us.

I huffed a quiet laugh, shaking my head. "Maybe I'm just bad at blending in. Never really mastered the skill."

Her smile lingered, and I turned back to my drink, hoping she'd take the hint. Sadly, she didn't. "So, what brings you here?"

"Just needed a drink."

"Alone?" she pressed, her tone shifting to something more suggestive. She rested her hand on my forearm.

Before I could respond, an enormous man appeared behind her, his expression hard and his size imposing between us. "You hitting on my girl?"

I turned slowly, meeting his glare with a calmness I didn't feel. Must have been the whiskey doing its job. If he slugged me, I'd probably fall right off the stool. Right now, I didn't care that much. The truth was, the moment I realized I wasn't good enough for Gemma and Winnie, I had given up.

I wanted to figure something out, but the questions kept coming, and I had no answers. So, letting this guy beat the tar out of me sounded like as good a plan as any other.

But he was huge, and I liked my teeth. "Not hitting on her, no. We were just talking."

"Didn't look like just talking to me. Looked to me like you were touching her."

"I wasn't touching her. She was touching me," I said, holding up a hand. "I don't want any trouble."

"Too late for that," he said, raising his fist.

Before the guy could take a swing, someone caught his wrist. "Hey!"

I turned to see Nico and a few of the guys from the team standing nearby, their expressions just as hard as the gorilla threatening me.

"That's our coach," Nico said, releasing his wrist. "You got a problem with him, you got a problem with all of us. I don't think you want a problem with all of us, do ya, pal?"

"Coach? What are you, some kinda cheerleading squad?"

Luke stepped up to him, big guy to big guy. "We're the fucking Atlanta Fire, asshole. You wanna fight a hockey team? And their fans?"

It was then I realized the whole bar had watched this play out. The music had died. Gabe stood behind the bar, baseball bat in hand, ready to jump in. Xavi had popped behind the bar to grab a stick off the display over the cash register. Every person in this bar was ready to jump in.

The man's jaw clenched as he assessed his odds. Glancing at the group of large, imposing hockey players, as well as an entire bar staring him down must have shaken him out of his fighting stupor. He muttered something under his breath, grabbed the woman's arm, and stormed out of the bar.

The music came back on, and Gabe shouted, "Free round on the house!" which lightened everybody's mood, turning things back to the party atmosphere his place was famous for.

I let out a breath I hadn't realized I was holding, turning to face the guys. "Thanks."

Nico shrugged and clapped my shoulder. "We've got your back, Coach."

At their table, the guys settled into their chairs, waving for me to join them. I hesitated for a moment before grabbing my drink and heading over. They'd just saved my ass, so my inclination was to go to them. But things had been weird for a while now, and I wasn't sure what was best for the team.

For the sake of good manners, I joined them.

Luke grinned. "Didn't think we'd see you here tonight."

"Didn't think I'd be here," I admitted, sinking into a chair.

Nico leaned forward, resting his forearms on the table. "You okay?"

"Yeah." How was I supposed to tell him that his sister had the unfortunate habit of shredding my heart? Or that I wasn't worthy of her and Winnie? There were some things you couldn't say to a group of guys. One-on-one, maybe. But not to a group and definitely not to my players. I had to keep some level of decorum.

"You know," Luke said, "we're still behind you, Coach. Even with...everything."

I looked around the table, the sincerity in their faces and nods hitting me harder than I expected. It was odd, but I believed them. "I appreciate that."

"Yeah," Nico added. "We're a family. You can get mad at family, but at the end of the day, you're still there for each other."

The word family stuck in my head, looping over and

over like a broken record. Especially after hearing it from him. After losing my folks, the team had been my family, my anchor, the thing that kept me grounded. But now, the word meant something entirely different.

Because when I heard that word, Gemma and Winnie's faces came to mind. Family meant the life I'd been too afraid to embrace. Not just afraid, but stubborn, too. I'd dug my heels in about missing those years with Winnie, and what had that gotten me?

I was alone in a bar, nursing my feelings, when I could have been spending time with my girls. If Gemma didn't hate me for turning her out.

I sat there with the team, their laughter and banter drowning out the music, but my thoughts kept drifting back to the empty house I'd left earlier that night. To the woman I couldn't stop loving, and the daughter I couldn't stop aching for.

And for the first time, I wondered if I'd ever figure out how to bridge the gap between the life I had and the one I wanted.

Chapter 28

Gemma

The faint hum of my laptop and the occasional tapping of my fingers on the keyboard were the music of my day. Winnie was at school, the morning rush had long since passed, and I was finally able to dive into my work.

The college beats were starting to grow on me. The players were lively and enthusiastic, hungry for the win. More than any of that, though, they loved talking about themselves. Maybe it was the hubris of youth, but the first chance they got to spill their guts, they took it. There was something pure about it—kids chasing their dreams, playing with everything they had, their futures still ahead of them. They were doing it for the love of the game, the fans, the campus clout.

But this beat didn't hold the same thrill as the Atlanta Fire coverage. No matter how many stories I threw myself into, my thoughts always found their way back to Casey.

I hated how much I missed him.

I hated that no amount of logical reasoning or self-preservation could stop my heart from aching for him. And I hated that every time my phone buzzed, my chest tightened with hope, only to deflate when it wasn't him.

It wasn't healthy, this constant longing, but I couldn't help it.

Maybe the college kids were getting to me. I remembered what it was like back then, chasing after new love and the possibilities therein. I'd never been lucky in love, not even in my college days. But I had tried to make it work a few times. Never went anywhere, but I tried.

Maybe that was my curse. Maybe I was destined to fall in love and never have it returned.

"That's a depressing thought," I said to no one but me.

The more I thought about it, the more I replayed every encounter I'd had in my youth. It was always the same. I threw myself at love, and it never caught me. I'd had a high school boyfriend I thought I'd have babies with, and another in college who made me want to be a better person.

Neither ever said the l-word to me. And after I had Winnie, guys tried to date me, but most weren't interested once they found out I had a kid. Those who were still interested after learning I was a mom proved themselves to be either untrustworthy or, worse, boring.

Maybe I really was destined to be alone in one-sided relationships.

I sighed at myself and rolled my eyes. I didn't believe in destiny or a higher power. All of that was just a fairytale we told ourselves to feel better about our bad choices, and I wasn't a child, so I didn't believe in fairytales.

Was love a fairytale, too?

I was so caught up in my thoughts that I almost didn't

hear the knock at the door. Frowning, I set my laptop aside and padded to the entryway, glancing through the peep-hole. My breath caught when I saw him.

Casey stood on the porch, looking more nervous than I'd ever seen him. He held a bouquet of roses in one hand, a box of chocolates in the other, and had a bottle of wine tucked under his arm.

What the hell is going on?

I opened the door slowly, my heart pounding.

"Hi," he said, his voice soft.

I slowly said, "Hey."

His eyes flicked over me, taking in my oversized sweat-shirt that hung just above my knees, the messy bun I'd given up on straightening out, and my bare feet. For a moment, he just stared, his blue eyes softening, and whatever he'd planned to say seemed to vanish. "Can I come in?"

I hesitated, then stepped aside, watching as he shuffled in awkwardly, his hands full of gifts. I closed the door behind him. "What's going on?"

"I, uh..." He cleared his throat, setting everything on the table before turning to face me. "I had this whole speech prepared."

I raised an eyebrow, leaning against the doorframe. "A speech?"

"Yeah," he said, running a hand through his silver hair. "Something about how I'm sorry for being an ass, and how I don't deserve you, and how I'm probably going to screw this up again, but I'm willing to do whatever it takes to try, but there was more..."

I held my breath, afraid if I took another, I'd wake up.

"But then I saw you," he continued, his voice dropping.

"And my brain went blank." He stepped closer, his gaze locking on mine. "You're so beautiful, Gemma."

I let out a shaky laugh, trying not to cry as I motioned to my huge sweatshirt. "Like this?"

"Especially like this," he said, his voice rough.

Before I could respond, he cupped my face in his hands and kissed me, soft and slow at first, then deeper, more urgently. I let myself get lost in it for a moment, my hands curling into his shirt.

No. Not again.

I pulled back, placing a hand on his chest to stop him. My voice still shook as I told him, "Casey, we can't keep doing this."

He frowned, his hands dropping to his sides. "Doing what?"

"This," I said, motioning between us. "Coming to get a ring or visiting to celebrate a win or showing up with flowers and wine, and expecting sex to fix everything, and then hurting each other all over again. I'm not strong enough for that."

His face fell, and for a moment, I thought he might leave. But then he straightened, his jaw tightening with determination. "You're right," he said. "Presents don't fix this, and sex doesn't either. I just got caught up. But that's not why I'm here."

"Then why are you here?" I asked, crossing my arms.

"Because I want to give this a real shot. If you still want to."

I stared at him, my heart pounding. Did he even know what that meant? Did I? I cleared my throat to stop from crying or laughing or some other hysterical reaction from coming out of me. "A real shot? And what does that look like to you, exactly?"

"It looks like me trying."

"I don't...know what that means. And what about the team?" I asked, narrowing my eyes. "What about the rules? What about your career?"

"I'll talk to the owner. I'll explain everything. If that means stepping down, I'll do it."

He'd give up his job? But he loves his job. Does that mean he loves me?

I couldn't let myself get carried away. "What about my job?"

"I know your connection to the team has helped your career," he said, his voice softening. "But you're amazing, Gemma. You don't need me or the Fire to prove that. I'm sure your boss knows that, too, and if he doesn't, then he's an idiot and you should quit."

I shook my head, tears welling up in my eyes. I laughed behind my hand. It was all so easy when he put it that way, and nothing was easy in life. "It isn't that simple, Casey. It's not just about us. It's about Winnie, and our families, and—"

"And I want to figure it out, but I want to figure it out with you," he said, stepping closer. "I think that's where I kept screwing this up. I thought I had to figure out a plan without you. That's what I do."

"I don't understand."

"At work, I make the plays, I make the calls. All the planning is on me. I make plans without my players, alone. So, I think when it came to us, I tried to make the plan alone, because that's what I do."

I shook my head. "That doesn't work in a relationship, Casey."

"Exactly the problem. I don't have all the answers, but I'm willing to find them with you."

I took a quick breath, trying not to get my hopes up. "Do you know how to let me in like that?"

"Not yet. But I want to learn. Just like, I didn't know if you were a flowers, chocolates, or wine-as-an-apology type of woman, so I brought all three. I want to learn everything about you, Gemma. I want to know what you love, what you hate, what makes you laugh, what makes you cry. I want us to work this out. And if you're willing to give me a chance, I'll spend the rest of my life proving that I'm worth it."

I stared at him, my heart breaking and healing all at once, again and again. The words came out in a whisper. "You're serious about this?"

"Without a doubt."

"What's changed?" I asked, my voice trembling. "You said I didn't think you were worth being a father back then, and you were so angry about that. So what's changed?"

"Everything," he said simply. "You. Winnie. Me. I've changed, Gemma. And I don't want to miss out on another moment with either of you. I know I was angry, and part of me still is, but I refuse to let that anger stand in the way of me and my family being together."

I bit my lip, the tears spilling over despite my best efforts. "I love you," I whispered.

His face softened, and he stepped closer, pulling me into his arms. "I love you, too."

The words hung between us, weighty and light all at once, and when he kissed me again, it felt like the beginning of something new. We moved together slowly, deliberately, as if we were trying to rebuild what had been broken with every touch, every kiss, every whispered word.

There was no hesitation this time, no doubt. As our clothes fell away and our lips met, I had the strangest sinking and floating sensations come over me. I didn't recognize it at first, but for once in my life, love had come for me, too.

I backed toward my bedroom with Casey following me, his eyes never leaving mine. What did it mean to give things a real shot with him? Where would we move? My place or his? Or would we get a new place together? We'd have to get Winnie to a new daycare, and that would be a hard—

"Where did you go?" he asked with a smile.

"Hmm?"

We stood in my bedroom near the foot of my bed, naked and smiley, like two lunatics in love. But he was right. I had gone somewhere else. I didn't want to admit it.

But if we were doing this, I had to be honest with him. "I think...this is big for me, Casey. I've never had a guy say the l-word back and mean it, and I think my brain panicked and made me focus on the logistics of being with you instead of the emotional stuff, because that is much bigger and scarier than logistics. I can't wrap my head around this, and now I'm rambling, please say something to stop me."

His smile had fallen the longer I rambled. "No one has ever said it back?"

"No. If they ever said—and most didn't—they weren't serious about it. They just said it to get what they wanted from me. It was never real."

His fingers brushed along my cheek. "I love you, Gemma Grimaldi. With everything I am, I love you."

I couldn't stop the tear that fell. But he kissed it away, and I turned to take his lips for the next kiss. There was something about the way he held me, so tender and so supportive that I fell in love with him all over again every time his grip changed. How had I survived without this?

I backed onto my bed, and he followed. I had thought he meant to jump me, but instead, he took his time. We laid on our sides, kissing and touching and exploring this new love like we had all the time in the world.

His rough palms on my breasts shot sensation through me, urging me to hook my leg over his narrow hip. From that angle, I pressed myself against his cock, slicking him with my wetness as I ground on him, but not close enough to take him inside of me. We moaned together, two voices in sync with one another. Two souls, the same.

Casey grabbed my ass and rolled onto his back, pulling me on top of him. He laced his fingers with mine as I slowly sank onto his cock while he watched from the flat of his back. But he couldn't take it for long. He sat up and closed his arms around me as we kissed with him fully seated inside.

This was so different from every other time, and the absolute love in his eyes made me want to cry. How could I be worthy of it after all I'd done? But he had decided that I was worthy of his love, and I silently vowed to do my best to make him never regret that choice.

Normally, I knew when I was going to come. Not this time. This time, it caught me completely off guard. It was as if, once my body knew we were truly going to be with

Casey, that question was answered. I was no longer alone, and I could finally relax. And it led to the biggest orgasm of my life. I lost myself in it, in him. And when the pleasure died down, I was in his arms, his mouth on mine as he came, too.

Maybe it was because, in that moment, he understood he was no longer alone, either.

Chapter 29

Casey

The morning sunlight filtered through the baby blue curtains, bathing Gemma's bedroom in a pale glow. I lay there for a long time, watching her sleep. Her hair was a mess, falling in loose tangles around her face, and her lips were slightly parted as she breathed in a steady rhythm. She had even drooled in her sleep.

She was beautiful. And she was finally mine.

The weight in my chest had lifted since yesterday. We'd finally said the things that needed saying, peeled back the layers of pain and fear that had been keeping us apart. There was a lot yet to be done, but not much left to be said. Getting things out on the table had been cathartic.

I hadn't known about her past relationships, that she'd been with guys who lied and used her. It made sense. No wonder she was so torn up about whether or not to tell me about Winnie. She had no reason to think I was any different from the others. She didn't know me back when we had conceived Winnie.

And I was a different person back then, too. Was I ready to be a dad five years ago? It would have been a change, that was for sure. I would have taken on the role, but I hadn't been ready for it back then.

Not that it mattered now. Things had worked out the way they were meant to. I had Gemma, and I'd set things right.

Lying next to her, I felt a kind of peace I had never known. It felt as if my long, winding road had led me to this moment in time. All the follies, all the successes, everything had lined up for this. For the first time since we had begun things, I felt like we had a real chance. But there was still so much to figure out.

The team. Her career. Mine. Winnie.

That last thing was why I had had the world's most awkward night. I'd dozed off after we had made love, and when I woke up hours later, it was because Gemma was bringing my clothes in from the living room. She begged me to stay in her room for the night, because she didn't want to have to explain anything to Winnie about me being there. Thank God her bedroom had an attached bathroom, or I would have never made it.

I promised to leave in the morning before Winnie left for daycare, but right now, all I wanted to do was lay here and watch Gem sleep. This was where I belonged. By her side. Always.

It was certainly easier than figuring everything else out.

The logistics, as she put it, swirled in the back of my mind as I slipped out of bed, careful not to wake her. I wasn't going to screw up the first time I stayed over by letting Winnie catch me. So, I grabbed my clothes from the chair in the corner, dressing quickly and quietly. In the process, I stubbed my toe on Gemma's bed. I smacked my hand over my mouth to stifle the instant curses that came out. The last thing we needed was for Winnie to hear me swearing like that.

Things were complicated enough without having to explain to a child why she woke up to a man cursing in her mom's bedroom, and we had a sleepover and didn't tell her about it.

Once I got myself together, I leaned over Gemma, pressing a soft kiss to her forehead. She stirred slightly but didn't wake. I whispered, "I'll see you later." Then I slipped out of her bedroom. Now came the tricky part.

I closed the door as quietly as possible, but I knew little ears were good at picking up faint sounds, so I took my time letting the door slowly latch. It barely made a sound.

Gemma had given me a spare key last night so I could lock up behind myself. No way was I leaving my girls asleep in an unlocked house. The front door key sat in my pocket as I tiptoed down the hall.

That might have been overkill. Her floor was carpeted. But I was paranoid.

We had to handle everything exactly right for Winnie, and nothing good would come from rushing that process. We didn't want to scar her for life about sex or relationships or the rest of it. Nothing she'd spend years on a couch telling her therapist about, we agreed on that last night. So, once Gemma came to bed, we kept things PG. Just some kissing that led to nothing else until we figured out what we were doing and how thin Winnie's bedroom wall was.

I made it to the front door when a heavy truck rumbled

down the street, rattling the windows. I froze up, holding perfectly still and praying they wouldn't wake Winnie. The tell-tale beeping of a big truck backing up followed, and I cursed my luck. But eventually, the truck made its way down the street. Once I was sure she hadn't woken, I made my escape and locked up behind me.

I'd done it. A clean getaway.

The crisp morning air hit me as I stood there, the now-quiet suburban street a sharp contrast to the storm brewing in my mind. Every step toward my car, another factor sprang to mind. What would I tell Matthew? How fired would I be? I'd breached my contract, so that was that. I'd deal. Somehow.

"Coach McConnell!"

I froze, my head snapping up to see a man walking up to my car, a camera slung around his neck and some kind of device in his hand. A recorder, like Gemma's. My stomach dropped. A reporter. Worse, a reporter who knew too much.

I didn't know if he had tailed me to Gemma's house, or if he just happened to find my car, but the press and the Atlanta Fire were barely on speaking terms, so I assumed the worst. I'd brought the press to my girls' otherwise quiet life. I had to handle this just right.

"Got a minute?"

"No," I said, my voice clipped.

"Just a couple of questions," he pressed, stepping closer. "Rumors are swirling about you having an illegitimate child. Care to comment?"

"No comment," I said firmly, unlocking my car.

"Come on, Coach," he said, his tone turning sharp. "The public has a right to know. You've always come off as this uptight stiff, and now this? How long have you been hiding your kid in this neighborhood so far away from your posh condo? And how does it feel knowing you abandoned your child? That you're living the high life, while your child lives here?"

I turned to face him, my blood boiling. I wanted to smack the taste out of his mouth. But I knew better. "I said no comment."

Before I could say anything more, the front door opened, and Gemma stepped out in her robe and slippers, marching toward us with fury in her eyes. I'd never seen her so angry. "What the hell do you think you're doing, Ian?"

The journalist smirked and flicked his device on. "My job. Care to comment?"

"Your job?" she shot back, her voice rising. "Your job is to harass people on their front lawn? To spread lies about things you know nothing about?"

"Lies?" he asked, raising an eyebrow. "Are you saying that Coach McConnell isn't the father of your child? Because rumor has it, he's Dear Old Dad."

Gemma's jaw tightened, her hands curling into fists at her sides. "Leave. Now. While I still let you walk out of here."

I stepped over to him, crossing my arms. I had no doubt she could take this guy on, but now that we were together, taking out the trash was my job. "You heard the lady. You leave on your feet or on your ass. It's up to you. Ten seconds."

"This is a public interest story," he said, a little shaken. "And it's going to make one hell of a headline." With that, he jogged to his car parked on the street, climbing in and speeding off before either of us knew what else to do.

I let out a long breath, running a hand through my hair. I was almost disappointed that I didn't get to feed him his teeth. But then I saw the look on her face. She was bereft. I put an arm around her shoulders and quietly uttered, "This is bad."

"It's more than bad," Gemma said, her voice trembling slightly.

"Let me handle it."

"What are you going to do?"

"Call the best we've got." I pulled my phone from my pocket, dialing Whitney's number.

She picked up on the second ring. "Casey? It's early. What's wrong?"

"We've got a problem," I said, my voice grim. "A journalist showed up outside Gemma's house this morning. He was asking questions about Winnie. It's going to get out sooner rather than later, and—"

"See you in twenty." The line went dead.

I relayed the message and followed Gemma back inside. Winnie was up, and somehow, all the energy she had before was gone. My daughter was not a morning person.

My daughter. Those words filled me with inexplicable joy, even now, while everything else was falling to shit.

I helped get her ready for daycare—though I felt like I was in the way more than anything else. I didn't know the routine yet. But I'd learn.

After that, Gemma poured us a pair of coffees just as Whitney arrived, stepping into the house with her usual brisk efficiency. She took one look at Gemma and me, then shook her head. "This is a mess."

"We know," I said. "Trust me, we know."

She set her bag down and crossed her arms. "Okay, let's talk options. Are you two sure about this relationship? Because if you're not, now's the time to say so."

I didn't even have to think about it. "I'm sure."

Gemma glanced at me, her eyes softening. "So am I."

Whitney nodded, her expression serious. "Then here's what I think you should do. Go public. Take control of the narrative before that journalist can spin it into something salacious."

Gemma frowned, crossing her arms. "Go public how?"

"You're a journalist, Gemma. You know how this is done," Whitney said. "Call your editor. Write the story yourself. Make it personal, make it honest. Tell the truth—about how Casey didn't know, about how you've both been navigating this together. In this situation, the truth is the best defense."

"That's a lot to ask," Gemma said hesitantly.

Whitney looked at me. "Casey, are you willing to put yourself out there for this?"

I looked at Gemma, at the way she was watching me with equal parts hope and fear, and I knew there was only one answer. "Whatever it takes."

Gemma nodded slowly, her resolve hardening. "Okay. I'll do it."

Whitney smiled faintly, giving Gemma's shoulder a reassuring squeeze. "You've got this. And you're not alone in this, either of you."

After Whitney left, the house was quiet again. Gemma

and I sat on the couch, her laptop open on the coffee table between us. "Are you scared?"

"Terrified that I'll lose my job," I admitted. "But it's worth it. You're worth it. Winnie's worth it. Come what may, you're stuck with me."

Her eyes shimmered with unshed tears, and she reached for my hand, squeezing it tightly. "We'll figure this out. Together."

"That's all I've ever wanted."

Chapter 30

Gemma

The weight of what I was about to do pressed on my chest like a stone. Writing the truth felt right in theory, but it also meant exposing everything I'd spent years trying to protect—not just for myself, but for Winnie and Casey. I wasn't willing to let go of the fragile connection we'd only just started to rebuild.

Things were too new to survive this kind of scrutiny, and if I didn't have absolute faith in him, I would have thought we were doomed. But everything he did showed me who he was, as a partner to me and as a father to Winnie.

He was so good with her this morning. He had no clue what he was doing, but he made sure she took her coat, even if she wasn't going to wear it. He cut the crusts off her sandwich, looking like it was the most fun he'd ever had while she sleepily told him about her friends at daycare. The man was born to be a dad. And now, he'd get to be.

Was I getting ahead of myself? Maybe. Did I care? No.

Thinking about his impending fatherhood was more pleasant than thinking about the article. Publishing this story, of putting my dirty laundry out there for the world to see, made my stomach churn. But I couldn't run from it anymore.

This was coming out, whether I wanted it to or not.

When Gordon had agreed to let me write the piece, I'd felt a brief surge of relief. Finally, I could get my story out there—our story—and tell it from the most genuine perspective possible. Firsthand accounts were always a good draw for readers, and there were plenty of people who had wild stories about how they got pregnant. Maybe not exactly like mine, but near enough. People would understand. I could stop covering things up. I could finally be honest with the world.

But now, staring at the blank document on my laptop, that relief was gone, replaced by what it meant to tell the truth. This was going online, which meant that one day, Winnie would learn how she came into the world. The best kind of surprise eventually but still, not necessarily ideal from a kid's perspective.

Gordon's voice had been matter-of-fact when I'd pitched him the idea. "You think your version will outshine the one Ian's already working on?"

"I don't think it will," I'd replied firmly. "I know it will. At least, it will with some of the readers. Some will glom onto the salacious bullshit Ian will publish, there's no doubt about that. If it bleeds it leads." I always hated that journalistic mantra, but it was as true now as when it was coined.

"Exactly. So why will your story make an impact?"

"For anyone who has ever chosen the wrong path or made a mistake, my story will suck the air out of Ian's. That's most people, Gordon, and most people are going to see right through Ian's sensationalistic hit piece. Casey has been an upstanding citizen in Atlanta for a long time, and we always love to see someone like that fall—"

"People smell blood in the water, Gemma. The Fire has been a hot commodity for us for years, scandal after scandal. That team is cursed."

"Believe me, I am aware of that charming rumor, too. But if we tell the real story—honest, emotional, and grounded—it'll resonate with readers in a way the gossip can't. We can do more than get their attention. We can make them care about the team in a way they haven't in a long time. This isn't just good for me or Casey or the Fire. This is good for Atlanta. Let's give them something they can be proud of—"

"All right, before you start singing the national anthem, give me a sec." I could almost hear him mulling it over, debating the merits of both stories, the optics, all of it. I didn't envy Gordon's job. He had to make hard calls all the time and hope they paid off. Journalism was a dying artform, and he was one of the few editors who gave a damn about integrity. "Okay, fine. You've got until five. With the Cup match looming, there's only so much time. Get me something good I can run with."

"I'm on it."

Except that I wasn't on it.

The call had ended, and I'd felt the full weight of the task settle on me. I didn't have much time. As I sat at the kitchen table, staring at the blinking cursor on my screen, the words didn't come. Or maybe that was just me.

For years, I'd told myself that keeping Casey out of the picture was the right thing to do, even when I didn't know he was Winnie's dad—for him, for me, and for Winnie. I'd convinced myself that I was protecting her from disappointment, from a father who might not want to be involved. Apathy was the worst thing imaginable at the time.

I knew what that was like, thanks to my father's stroke. He had lost so much of himself in it, so much of me and Nico. His memories of us were cloudy or missing completely. The first time I visited Dad in the nursing home, there was no recognition. No hint that he knew who I was. To him, I could have been just another nurse, coming for his bedpan. It was that apathy that drove home what I was dealing with. It was why I had to leave Atlanta, if I was honest with myself. I couldn't stand seeing that apathy in his eyes.

So, I refused to expose Winnie to that. I had to protect her from even the possibility of it.

But was that really the truth? Had I kept her from him to protect her, or had I been protecting myself?

The wind had been knocked from my lungs by that thought. I didn't want to dig deeper, but I had to. So, I forced myself to think about it. No more avoiding the messy shit. I owed them this much.

I'd made the decision for Casey, deciding he didn't need to know about Winnie, didn't deserve to know. After all, he was just a man, and they were all disappointments. And in doing so, I'd taken away his chance to be a father, to be there for Winnie in the way she deserved.

Winnie.

I glanced toward the living room, where her toys were scattered across the floor. Last night, as poor Casey waited in my room, we had played Princess Knight, a story she had made up last year. She loved making up stories for her toys, as much as I loved helping her do it. Princess Knight had been her favorite for a long time.

The princess was a secret knight, and her kingdom was under attack from a dragon. But the queen had forbidden the princess from slaying the dragon because it was too dangerous, so she had to hide in a metal suit—Winnie's term for a suit of armor—and sneak out of the castle to hunt the dragon. I played the dragon, and I changed up my part of the story each time.

Last night, I'd made the dragon a vegetarian who wasn't really attacking people—he just needed someone to get a splinter out of his foot. Winnie had giggled and helped him, even though she didn't like touching someone else's foot. Peace in the kingdom at last.

She deserved better than her own father hiding out in my bedroom. She deserved to have him in her life all the time. And Casey deserved to play Princess Knight.

The thought of how happy she'd been since we moved back to Atlanta only made the guilt worse. She'd taken to Casey immediately, their connection effortless and genuine. And I'd kept that from them for years.

Tears pricked at my eyes, and I wiped them away quickly. This wasn't the time for self-pity. I couldn't rewrite the past, but I could take responsibility for my mistakes and make things right now.

I was so lost in my thoughts that I didn't hear Winnie approach until she was standing beside me, her little hand tugging on my sleeve. She had come home from daycare early—a lice outbreak. She was clean, but I'd have her during the day for the rest of the week.

"Mommy, what's wrong?" she asked.

I forced a smile, pulling her onto my lap. "Nothing, sweetheart. I'm just thinking."

"You look sad."

I hugged her tightly. She had always been too observant. I always tried to pretend everything was fine. Sometimes, I got away with it. More often than not, I didn't. But I had to try. "I'm okay."

"Is it about Casey?" she asked, tilting her head.

I blinked, unsure why she had figured things out so easily. "Why do you ask that?"

"Because you look upset, but you always smile when he's around." Her childlike logic was both sweet and piercing. "Is it because he's not around?"

"You're too smart for your own good, you know that?"

She grinned, but her smile quickly faded. "If he made you upset, I don't like him anymore. If you don't like him, then I don't like him either." She folded her arms and tried to look tough. "He's a bad man."

Her words sent a fresh wave of guilt crashing over me, and I hugged her tightly again. "Oh, honey. That's very sweet of you, but Casey didn't make me upset. He's a good man. That's not why I'm asking."

"Then why?" she pressed, her small brow furrowing. Right then, she looked so much like him that my thoughts dried up.

How had I not seen it before? Didn't matter now. I had to put my thoughts back together. "What do you think about Casey?"

"I told you. I like him if you like him."

"I need your opinion, Winnie. Me aside, what do you think of him?"

She took a deep breath, brow still furrowed, still looking like her father. But then she looked guilty, like the time she spilled her orange juice on the couch and tried to hide it by covering it with her blankie. "I like daycare. But he's my favorite part about Lanta."

Lanta. Her word for Atlanta.

It was a relief to hear that she liked him that much. I took a deep breath, as I prepared myself for what I was about to say. "Winnie, there's something very important I need to tell you."

Her expression turned even more serious, and she nodded for me to continue.

"You know how you've always asked about your dad, and how I told you he lived very far away when we were in Los Angeles?"

Her eyes widened slightly, and she nodded again, her small hands clutching at my sweater.

"Well," I said, my voice trembling, "the truth is...Casey is your dad."

She blinked, her mouth falling open as she processed my words. "He's my dad?"

"Yes. He didn't know before we came here, but now he does. And he cares about you very much."

She was quiet for a long moment, her little face scrunched in thought. "Is he going to live with us? Martina's dad lives with her."

"She's the friend you've been telling me about?"

"Uh huh," she said, nodding. "She lives with a mom and a dad and a buela."

"I think you mean she lives with an abuela."

"That's what I said. So, will Mr. Casey live with us?"

"Maybe one day," I said, my throat tightening. "If we're lucky. And you can still call him Casey, if you want. But I think he'd like you to call him Dad."

Her expression brightened, and a small smile spread across her face. "I like that idea."

Tears blurred my vision as I pulled her into another hug, relief and guilt warring in my chest. Seeing her so happy at the thought of having her dad around made my heart ache in a whole new way.

As Winnie scampered off to play, her excitement clear in the bounce of her step, I sat back down at the table as a searing guilt crowded my heart. There had been so many moments Casey had missed. The birthdays, the scraped knees, the bedtime stories, the bath times. Princess Knight. He hadn't been there for any of it, and that was my fault.

I'd convinced myself that I was protecting Winnie, but the truth was, I'd been protecting myself from the fear of rejection, from the possibility that Casey might not want to be a father. But he did. It was obvious in the way he looked at her, the way he lit up when she laughed, the way he melted whenever she called him Casey.

I couldn't change the years they'd lost, but I could do everything in my power to make sure they didn't lose any more. I turned back to my laptop, my fingers hovering over the keyboard. It was time to tell the truth. All of it, good, bad, or ugly.

And I was the ugly part of the equation.

Chapter 31

Casey

The phone felt heavier than usual as I stared at Gemma's name on the screen. My thumb hovered over the call button, but I hesitated. Her text had been straightforward.

"Story's going live this afternoon. Just wanted to let you know."

Simple words. Dramatic possibilities.

This was it. The truth would finally be out there. No more rumors, no more half-truths or gossip. I should've been relieved, but all I could feel was dread. What would it mean for her? For Winnie? For me? For us?

Too late now. The truth would be out there, whether I wanted it to be or not. Part of me was terrified, but the other part wanted this. No more secrets. I finally hit the call button.

She answered on the first ring, her voice soft but tense. "Hey."

"Hey there," I replied, trying to keep my tone steady. "You okay?"

There was a pause, the silence growing between us. Finally, she let out a shaky laugh. "I guess we'll find out. Gordon's publishing the story before the game tonight. It'll be posted in a couple of hours."

In a couple of hours, I might be unemployed.

I closed my eyes, exhaling slowly. "I'm glad it's coming out. Maybe once people know the truth, this whole thing will die down. No one pays attention to old news, and after the playoff game, hopefully no one will care anymore."

"Maybe," she said, but something in her voice—an edge of uncertainty, maybe fear—made my chest tighten.

"Matthew's going to read it," I said, saying my fear out loud. I had hoped voicing it might take away its power, but I was wrong. My stomach knotted down. My boss wasn't the kind of man to take things at face value. "I just hope he reads the whole thing before making any decisions."

"You think he'll fire you?" she asked, her worry palpable through the phone.

"I don't know," I admitted, running a hand through my hair. "I broke the rules, Gemma. I didn't know the other stuff, but I knew you were Nico's sister when you returned, and I pursued you anyway. That's on me. But maybe he'll make an exception under these circumstances. There's a child in the picture now. That changes things, doesn't it?"

Her hesitation on the other end told me she didn't have an answer, either. "I don't know. I don't know him or how he thinks about these things," she said, her voice barely above a whisper. "But I guess we'll find out soon enough."

I wanted to reassure her, to tell her it would all work out. But the truth was, I didn't know that it would.

I ended the call and tried to focus on my pregame ritual.

Everyone had their sports superstitions for their own reasons. Mine was something I'd done for years, a routine designed to clear my mind and get me in the right headspace to lead the team.

The ritual was simple. Meaningless to anyone else but me. I switched my socks from one foot to the other, thanks to an old girlfriend. She was Irish and said doing that brought good luck. I'd started doing it ever since, but when I looked it up, I couldn't find any lore on the practice, so I was pretty sure she was bullshitting me, trying to sound mysterious. Or maybe it was to get me to look like a gullible idiot. But the team had better luck when I did it, so I continued the practice.

After the socks came touching everything navy or gold in my line of sight. The team's colors reminded me of everything we'd worked for, and touching them grounded me.

The last part of the ritual was balancing a puck on my head and walking south to north until I no longer could. In my small office, the trip was a few steps. It was something my uncle had told me the great Toe Blake had done before games. I couldn't find anything to back up his claim, but like the sock thing, we had better luck when I did it, so I kept it up.

But today, it wasn't working. None of it.

My socks felt like they were on the wrong feet, even though they were the same sock, just on a different foot. I got a static electricity shock when I touched the gold corner on my bookshelf. And the puck kept falling off my head, no matter how straight I stood as I walked.

I flopped onto my desk chair, staring at the open playbook on my desk. It didn't take long before the words and diagrams blurred together, my thoughts too loud to let anything else in.

Matthew's reaction loomed large in my mind. He wasn't forgiving, and he valued the rules above all else. My relationship with Gemma had been a gamble from the start, and now, with everything out in the open, I wasn't sure how much longer I'd have this job.

And then there was Gemma.

I couldn't stop picturing her sitting at her laptop, pouring her heart into that article. I hadn't asked to read the article ahead of time. I thought she'd be too self-conscious or uncomfortable if I read through it before publishing. Whatever she wrote, she did it all to set the record straight on my behalf.

Guilt ground down my spine. What would she say to salvage my reputation? Was she ready for the backlash? For the judgment? I doubted it, and the thought of her facing it alone made my stomach twist.

A knock at the door pulled me from my thoughts, and I looked up to see Whitney stepping in.

"You decent?" she asked, holding up her tablet.

"That's a matter of opinion." I tried for levity, straightening in my chair. When she didn't budge, I asked, "What's up?"

"Gemma sent me a copy of her story to approve before it goes live," she said, scrolling through the screen. "Wanted to make sure it's fair to the team."

I swallowed hard. Gemma was nothing if not thorough, but knowing she'd looped Whitney in made me worry. "And?"

"It's good, Casey. Really good. For you, for the team. But you're not going to like it."

"Why?"

She hesitated, then sighed. "Because you come out of it looking like a good man done wrong by a bad woman."

The bottom dropped out from inside of me. "What?"

"That woman clearly loves you. She puts everything on herself. She takes full responsibility for not telling you about Winnie, for keeping you in the dark, for all of it. She makes herself the villain so you can come out clean."

I stared at her, my mind reeling. Gemma was throwing herself under the bus—for me.

"I can't let her do that," I said, standing abruptly.

Whitney raised an eyebrow. "Casey, the story is set to go live in less than an hour. What are you going to do?"

"I need to talk to her," I said, grabbing my phone. "Privately, if you don't mind."

"Of course." When she was in the doorway, she added, "Don't let her retract it if you want to keep your job."

Like I needed another thing heaped onto the pile.

When the door was shut, I dialed Gemma immediately. The phone rang only once before she answered, her voice shaky. "Casey?"

"Explain the article," I said, trying to keep my tone calm but firm.

"It's the truth. This is all my fault. I should have reached out. I should have told you about Winnie. I should have—"

Her voice broke, and I could hear her sobbing on the other end of the line. It shattered me.

"I should have done everything differently," she cried. "You didn't deserve this. You didn't deserve to have your life turned upside down because of me. I deserve this. I deserve all of it."

"Gemma, stop," I said, my voice softening.

"It's true," she sobbed. "I kept your daughter from you. I kept her from knowing you. How do I justify that? How do I make up for that?"

My heart broke at the sound of her crying. There was nothing for her to make up for. Maybe I felt that way when I first learned about the situation, but I was angry and lashing out back then. It wasn't how I actually felt. "Gemma," I said gently. "It's not like that."

"Yes, it is. I'm sorry," she whispered. "I'm so, so sorry. I know how wonderful Winnie is. She's the best little girl in the world...and I kept her from you. The world needs to know that none of this is your fault."

I stood, pacing the length of my office as my mind raced. I needed to see her, to hold her, to tell her that we'd figure this out together. "I'm coming over—"

"No, you're not," she said quickly, her voice trembling. "You have a game tonight. *The* game. The team needs you. The Seattle Razors have been at the top of the Western Conference for a long time. You have to focus. Just forget about this for now. Please. Show Matthew why he shouldn't fire you."

"I can't—"

"The Razors have put two centers and three wingers into the hospital this season, Casey. My brother is going to be on the ice. I need you to have his back, and you can't do that if you're worried about me. Please do this for me."

I already hated myself for the lie I was about to tell her. "All right, baby. I'll do this. For you."

She sniffled. "Thank you."

But there was no way I wasn't going to be by her side right now. She needed me. I heard it in her voice. I was halfway to the door when Nico appeared, his expression tense.

"What are you doing?" he asked.

"Nothing," I said quickly, brushing past him.

"You're supposed to be getting the guys ready," he said, his voice sharp. "It's almost game time, Coach. They need you."

I stopped, turning to face him. "Gemma—"

"Gemma will be fine," he said firmly.

"You don't know what you're talking about, Nico."

He shook his head. "I know my sister. She's handled bigger shit than some article."

"She told you about it?"

"She mentioned that you'd hate it. Didn't take a genius to figure out you might bail tonight." He stood there, solidly blocking me from going down the hall. "Don't do it, Coach."

"You didn't hear her crying, Nico. I have to go."

"That's where you're wrong. An article won't break Gemma. But you fucking up tonight, might. She needs you to be all-in on the game. We all do."

"She needs me."

He huffed. "Tonight isn't about you or Gemma or Winnie right now, Coach. This is about the team. You've gotten us this far, and we need you to get us to the goal tonight. The Razors aren't here to play—they're here to dominate. So whatever's going on, squash it."

His words stirred up more guilt inside. He was right. The team did need me. But so did Gemma. I was torn between the job that had defined my life and the woman who had redefined my future.

I swallowed. "This isn't fair. I need to be with her."

His heavy hand clapped on my shoulder, and he stared me down. "What you need is to be the man she fell in love with. That man is strong. He supports the people who depend on him. He coaches the Atlanta Fire. Show her who you are."

"You're actually advising against me comforting her when she's upset?"

"I'm advising you to trust that my sister can handle herself. Upset or not. If you think you need to run to her every time she's unhappy, you're not giving her enough credit."

Chapter 32

Gemma

The smell of buttered popcorn filled the kitchen, a scent so familiar it almost calmed me. Almost. The microwave timer ticked down, and I listened to the unpredictable arrhythmia of popping kernels, trying to focus on the mundane sound instead of the nerves twisting in my stomach.

The game was starting soon, and even though I wasn't at the arena, I felt like I was waiting for my own face-off. Casey was leading the team into the season's biggest game, and I was here, stuck in my head about everything else—the story, the fallout, the fans. He was up against the meanest team in the league. They weren't beyond pulling some bullshit to win this. I hated the thought of my brother facing off with those guys, but if the Fire won tonight, they'd be legends. More importantly, a win would make it harder to fire Casey.

Will the article be enough to save his job? Only time will tell.

I glanced toward the living room, where Winnie sat

cross-legged on the floor, crayons spread out like a rainbow explosion. Her little brow furrowed in concentration as she colored a picture of what looked like a hockey player, complete with a stick and a jersey that vaguely resembled the Fire's colors.

Megan perched on the couch, pouring wine into two glasses. She caught my eye and grinned. "You're going to need this more than I do tonight," she said, holding up a glass.

I forced a smile, wiping my hands on a towel as the microwave beeped. "You might be right about that."

"What's done is done," she teased lightly. "But don't worry, we'll get through this game together. And hey, if it's terrible, we have wine. If it's amazing, we'll still have wine. Win-win."

Her voice was light, but I knew she sensed my tension. Megan had been my rock through any mess, always babysitting at a moment's notice, or making me laugh. Tonight was no different, and I was grateful for her.

"You ready to cheer for your hockey hunk?"

"I'm here to watch the game," I said, delivering popcorn bowls all around.

"Sure you are," she said, smirking as she handed me a glass.

The knock at the door was so sudden that it startled both of us. I nearly dropped my wine, which would have been a crime. It was delicious. I froze, the popcorn bowl in one hand and my wine glass in the other.

"Expecting someone?"

"No," I said, frowning. "Casey's at the arena. He wouldn't..."

Winnie looked up from her drawing, her face lighting up. "Maybe it's Uncle Nico!"

I shook my head, dismissing the idea as I set the popcorn down. "No, baby. He's got a game to play."

But when I opened the door, there he was—my brother, standing on the porch with his usual easy grin.

"Nico?" I asked, baffled. "What are you doing here?"

He held up his phone like it was obvious. "You should really check your texts more often."

"My phone's dead."

"Again? Do you ever charge that thing?" he asked with a dramatic sigh.

"What is going on?"

"Go get dressed. Wear something warm. The arena's cold."

I stared at him, my confusion deepening. "What are you talking about?"

Ignoring my question, Nico stepped inside, his gaze immediately landing on Winnie. His face lit up, and he scooped her into his arms like she was the center of his world. "Hey, kiddo! Want to come to the game tonight?"

Her squeal of delight was answer enough.

"We don't have tickets," I said, crossing my arms and giving him my best "mom" look. It always worked on Winnie, but I wasn't sure it would work on my big brother.

He scoffed, waving me off. "You don't need tickets. You have me."

Megan raised an eyebrow, looking from him to me. "Aren't you supposed to be, you know, playing tonight?"

"I will be," Nico said casually like it was no big deal.

"But first, all of you are coming to the game. Megan included."

Her jaw dropped. "Me? Really?"

"Really," Nico said, flashing one of his charming smiles. "Now hurry up. The limo's waiting."

"Limo?" I repeated, my voice incredulous.

"Yeah. I went a little overboard. But it's for Winnie, so it's worth it."

Winnie clapped her hands in excitement, her eyes wide with delight. "A limo, Mommy! Can we go? Wait—what's a limo?"

Nico laughed. "It's a great big, fancy car with treats. You'll love it."

"Mommy, can we?"

The three of them gave me expectant eyes, the kind that said I'd be an asshole to turn them down. I sighed, glancing at Megan, who was already halfway to grabbing her coat. But I didn't want to go anywhere tonight.

The article had been posted, and the comments got so bad that Megan had forced me to step away from my laptop. People called me everything from a selfish bitch to the Wicked Witch of the West. Casey had come out shining in the comments. Everyone poured pity and affection on him, some even saying they wanted his number. So, the article did what I wanted it to, but I certainly didn't want to be anywhere near the arena. It was full of people who hated me.

But the longer I hesitated, the more upset Winnie looked.

"Fine," I said, shaking my head. "Let me get dressed."

Winnie cheered, Nico bounced her up in the air, and

Megan ogled his abs when his shirt hem lifted from tossing my daughter. He caught Winnie, and Megan looked away so he wouldn't see her checking him out. Which gave him a chance to spy down her sweater.

I didn't know why, but it unsettled me and made me happy.

Megan had had a crush on Nico when we were kids, and until now, I didn't know if it was mutual. But it wasn't just a subtle cleavage glance that clued me in. I overheard the small talk he tried with Megan when I was changing in my room.

"So, Megan. How's...things?"

"Um, good. Mostly. I guess."

The following pause could not have been more awkward.

But then he asked, "Are you a hockey fan?"

"Well, I don't know much about it," she said. "But I'm always willing to learn."

"Maybe tonight will help with that. If you want to learn, I mean."

Never in my life had I heard Nico fumble around a woman like that. He was suave, cool, effortlessly casual about these things. But in my hallway, he sounded like a nervous teenager.

Which meant he liked her. It was weird for me, though. The thought of my brother and a woman who was like a sister to me...being intimate. I squirmed, thanks to the heebie-jeebies of that thought. But the truth was, it wasn't such a bad thing.

As long as they were happy, I'd manage.

The limo waiting outside was sleek and extravagant, its

polished black surface gleaming under the streetlights. Winnie practically bounced into the backseat, her hands running over the plush leather seats with giddy enthusiasm. The passenger area was light blue and purple, giving every shiny surface a glow.

"This is so cool!" she squealed, her little feet swinging as she settled in.

Megan immediately zeroed in on the champagne stash, pouring herself a glass and holding up the bottle. "Want some?" she asked, already halfway through her first sip.

"Not yet," I said, settling into my seat.

Nico sat across from us, looking far too pleased with himself. "What?" he said when I gave him a pointed look. "You deserve it. Let yourself have some fun. You're not driving tonight."

I couldn't argue with that. Seeing Winnie this happy made it all worth it, even if the extravagance felt a little over the top.

"Thanks, Nico," I said quietly, my chest tightening with gratitude as I took a champagne flute from Megan.

"Anything for my baby sister."

"Are you nervous about going against the Razors?" Megan asked.

I'd expected him to flash a grin, vowing that he was never nervous. But instead Nico said, "They're a good team full of bad apples. This season, they pulled out some wins I never saw coming. They've been so unpredictable that the bookies in Vegas have been talking about it. The odds are against us for tonight, and the bookies are almost always right."

I nearly dropped my champagne out of shock. "Nico

Grimaldi, are you being humble for the first time in your life?"

He smirked. "Realistic. I expect the Razors to come after me tonight, so it'll be good to have you three in the stands in case I get carted out on a stretcher. You can ride in the ambulance."

Winnie clapped. "An ambulance ride, too?"

"Only if I get hurt, Win," he said.

Her little face fell. "Don't get hurt."

"I'll do my best." He ruffled her hair and smiled, but I saw the pinch at the corners of his eyes. He had never been good at hiding his worry from me.

The drive was short, thankfully. Once inside the arena, it was hard to hear each other at first. Crowd noise drowned our voices. Winnie's excitement was infectious as we made our way to our seats—prime spots behind the glass with an unobstructed view of the action. I couldn't believe Nico scored us these seats. When I said as much, he said I shouldn't doubt him.

"This is amazing!" Winnie said, her face pressed against the glass as she took it all in.

"It's definitely something," Megan agreed, sinking into her seat with a second glass of champagne. I had no idea how she had snuck it to our seats.

Nico handed me a tray of concessions before kneeling to give Winnie a quick hug. "All right, kiddo, I've got to get out there. You three have fun, okay?"

"Good luck!" Winnie called, waving as he jogged off toward the locker room.

I turned back to Megan, catching her watching Nico

with an expression I'd almost never seen before on her face. But there was no mistaking that look. "You like him."

"What? No," she said quickly, her cheeks flushing.

"You totally like him," I teased.

She huffed, crossing her arms. "Even if I did, it'd be weird. He's your brother."

"It'd be weird for *me*, but that doesn't mean it'd be weird for you, and I'd get over it. And, for the record, I wouldn't interfere. You two are grown adults, and you make your own choices."

Megan didn't respond, but the darkening blush on her cheeks said it all.

"Besides, you've liked Nico since the seventh grade."

She laughed. "I was a kid when I told you that."

"And some things never change."

The game started strong, the Fire dominating the ice with an intensity that had the crowd on their feet. Winnie was glued to the action, cheering and clapping with every play. She didn't understand much of it other than the cheering. She followed the crowd's cues, getting into the game more than I had expected, and the people nearby encouraged her enthusiasm. She was having the best night ever.

But as the cameras panned across the audience, my stomach sank. I hadn't noticed it when we walked in. People always held up signs for their favorite players, and I had brushed past them without a second thought when we found our seats. The cameras told a different story.

Scattered throughout the crowd were signs—"Justice for Coach!" "Gemma Pucked Up!" and similar phrases scrawled in bold letters.

Megan's mouth dropped almost immediately, her brows furrowing. "What the hell?"

"It's fine," I said quickly, trying to keep my voice steady. "As long as no one says anything to us, we'll stay."

"But—"

"It's fine," I said firmly, cutting her off.

The signs were a harsh reminder of the scrutiny I was under. There was judgment that came with putting our lives out there. But I wasn't going to let it ruin the night for Winnie. I could overlook it as long as they didn't bother us directly.

This was Winnie's moment, her chance to see her uncle in action and enjoy the game's magic. I could take the heat. I deserved it, after all.

Chapter 33

Casey

The arena pulsed with noise, hitting deep in your chest and vibrating in your bones. This kind of thing gave me strength, knowing my city was behind me. I loved it. I lived for it. Fans cheered and shouted, their voices merging into a single, deafening roar that filled every inch of the space. This was where I thrived. The energy, the passion, the stakes, the purpose—it was the air I breathed. Pure sustenance.

But tonight, things were different.

This wasn't about me or the team or even Atlanta. The story Gemma had published, and the scrutiny hanging over us all pressed down on me. Even if we won the game, Matthew was not guaranteed to keep me on. In fact, several clauses in my contract stated the exact opposite. He was within his rights to fire me. He could show up and with a wave of his finger, I was gone.

So, I had to make tonight count. If this was the end of my professional career, I'd damn well make my mark. That thought pushed me forward.

At least I tried to get caught up in the wave of it. But it was a struggle. Before we took the ice, I had texted and called Gemma, but to no avail. She knew what I wanted—for her to retract the article. It was the only way to save her from the public scrutiny.

So, she didn't respond.

I understood her side of it, but I hated this. It ate at me every second I wasn't with her. She shouldn't have had to be the bad guy in this. There were no bad guys in this, only people doing their best at the time.

She made her call when it came to Winnie, and she wasn't wrong to doubt me. She didn't know me. How could she trust that I would have been a good father to our daughter? It would have been crazy to trust a stranger with your child, and I supported that decision once I had cleared my head about it.

I could have gotten caught up in the what-ifs of it, but that wasn't going to move things forward. Neither was Gemma ignoring me. Or maybe she was. With her lack of response, I had no choice but to focus on the game. And even still, it was hard.

Nico was right. I had to trust Gemma. She had been a single mom on her own across the country for five years. She had no family, no friends in LA whom she spoke of. Pregnancy, labor, delivery, having an infant, and raising her into the quirky, sweet girl I knew, Gemma had done all of that on her own while making a name for herself in her industry.

That woman was stronger than I gave her credit for, which was my mistake. Nico was right about that. She could handle an article that she wrote about herself. She made that choice clear-eyed and level-headed. I had to stop underestimating her, and I vowed to do exactly that in the future.

The game itself was brutal. The Seattle Razor's defense was air-tight, their reads sharp, and they'd studied us well. Every move we made, every play we tried to set up, they were a step ahead or countered us. Matthew had been right about me. I'd grown too predictable if the Razors could read my plays on the ice like this. It wasn't just skill that we faced. It was strategy, discipline, grit, and the willingness to get their hands dirty.

The first period had been relentless, and I had to shift gears by the time the buzzer sounded.

The intermission came quickly, and I didn't waste a second. During the game, my eyes had stayed locked on the ice, watching their defense's patterns. I saw the openings, the moments they overcommitted to speed, but we weren't exploiting them yet. Speed and brute force were their strengths. We had to play to their weaknesses.

I grabbed the whiteboard and called my centers over.

"Nico," I said, my voice cutting through the locker room noise, "when you're back out there, fake left. Make it big—sell it hard. Their winger's overcommitting every time. He spends too much time building speed. He doesn't have enough power behind it, zero agility, and that's your advantage. When he bites, drive the puck straight through the center. Lopez will be open. He always is because he's new, and they think I don't trust him yet. Let's make them regret that."

Nico's grin stretched wide, the kind of confident smirk that only came from years of knowing how good he was. "Got it, Coach."

"Don't overthink it," I added. "Just trust the play. They won't see it coming."

He nodded, and I watched as he carried that confidence back to the ice. Moments like these were why I loved this game—seeing the pieces fall into place, the adrenaline of knowing we were about to turn the tide.

When the team hit the ice together, it was like poetry in motion. Nico executed the play perfectly, faking left so convincingly that their winger nearly tripped over himself trying to follow. All his momentum had him going the other way, but Nico could pivot with the best of them. Lopez was in position in the blink of an eye, and his stick met the puck with a resounding *clack* before it sailed into the net.

The crowd erupted, and I couldn't help the grin that spread across my face. Tied game.

Despite the brief rush of that victory, my nerves were shot.

I glanced at my phone, and still there was no response. I'd tried everything. I hated feeling disconnected from her. It felt like missing a limb. Whether it was her dead phone or intentional silence, I didn't know, and it didn't matter now. The truth was out there, and the fans were already reacting. They were quick to jump on any information about the team, and they certainly pounced on this one.

A secret child kept from her father? A sneaky mom who wanted to have her cake and eat it, too? It was scandalous enough to make the fans forget they were at the Stanley Cup. The signs in the stands were proof enough that they had bought her story hook, line, and sinker. Instead of anything about the importance of the game, the signs read things like, "Gemma Pucking Sucks!" "Coach is King!"

They were rallying behind me and had directed their anger squarely at her, just as she had planned.

It was sweet in a way. Fans were diehard loyalists in hockey, and most of the time, that was great. We needed that kind of loyalty. Hockey played a lot of games each season, and without loyalty, there were no ticket sales. Hockey was like any other pro sport—a business first.

But this wasn't one of those times when people would see the signs and think they were sweet or supportive. I was glad we had rules about what they could write on their signs, but several pushed the boundaries of what we allowed. Sometimes, the P in Puck didn't connect how it should have, leaving them to read, "Fuck Gemma!" Those signs would likely not get broadcast, I hoped.

But Gemma had gotten what she set out to achieve. She had flipped the narrative, just like she said she would.

It didn't sit right with me. I didn't want her painted as the villain while I came out looking like a hero. And Winnie...God, what about Winnie? Could she read those signs? Would she understand them?

The thought of my daughter seeing those signs and hearing the whispers about her mom made my stomach churn. I'd spent my career teaching my players to take hits, to get back up, but this was different. I couldn't take these hits from them. I couldn't cheer them on to get back up if this hit landed.

Life was not hockey. It was unpredictable and spun out in ways you never saw coming. As much as I tried to treat everything like hockey, there was no playbook for life.

This wasn't about me anymore. I didn't want this bullshit for my family. The more I thought about it, the more pissed off I got. I had to do something.

Whitney found me during the second intermission, her ever-present tablet in hand. She looked calm, but I knew her well enough to see the sharpness in her eyes. "You look like hell."

"Feel like it, too, thanks," I muttered, rubbing the back of my neck.

She stepped closer, lowering her voice so only I could hear. "The fans are with you, Casey. The story's trending, and it's working. People are rallying behind you. Matthew won't touch you with this kind of support. You're golden, so enjoy it."

I shook my head, the tension in my chest tightening. At my age, I should have been worried about my chest tightening so much lately, but I had Gemma and Winnie to think about. "They're rallying against Gemma. Nothing gets people riled up like a common enemy."

"She knew what she was doing. This was her choice."

"I didn't want her to do this," I said, my frustration bubbling to the surface. "She never asked me what I wanted. Not with Winnie and not with the article." It was high time I made it clear what I wanted. I'd already planned to, but this solidified things.

Whitney studied me for a moment, her expression tensing. "Why do I see the gears turning in your head, Casey?"

It was funny how calm I felt after the decision was made. It felt like a puzzle piece falling into place in my mind. I smiled, finally feeling at peace for the first time in a long time. Maybe for the first time ever. "Sorry, Whit. Get ready for a long night."

"What does that mean?"

"You'll see," I said, already moving past her toward the locker room.

Nico waited near the locker room, already suited up. His helmet was tucked under one arm, and there was a fire in his eyes that reminded me of why he was one of the best.

"You good?" I asked, stepping up beside him.

"Yeah. You?"

"Ask me after the game," I said, trying to keep my voice light.

Nico smirked, but his eyes stayed locked on mine. "Plan B, then?"

I nodded. "I'm not even sure if there was a plan A, to be honest. This is the only thing that makes sense. It feels right."

"You're absolutely sure about this?"

"Are you trying to talk me out of it?"

He shook his head. "You saw the signs. If you do this, the fans could turn on you. They could make things very hard for you and Matthew."

"Out of everything that's happened today," I said firmly, "this is the easy part."

He tilted his head, studying me for a moment before his smirk softened into something closer to a smile. "All right, Coach. Let's do it."

I clapped him on the shoulder. "Let's." Whatever came after this—Matthew, the media, the fallout—we'd handle it.

The final period loomed, the crowd chanted, and I stood behind the bench, watching the team gather. This was it. Whatever chaos awaited me off the ice, it didn't matter now. This moment was everything.

And I was ready.

Chapter 34

Gemma

The second intermission always felt like the longest part of the night, but tonight, it was excruciating. Megan had been distracted by her phone, giggling, and suddenly offered to take Winnie to the bathroom. I figured she wanted an excuse to hunt Nico down and flirt with him. Maybe they'd been texting back and forth. I wasn't sure why she was so giggly before she left, but she was happy about something, and I was glad to see it.

Megan wasn't like most people. It took a lot to make her happy. Nico was a lot. So, the two of them seemed to fit. Not to mention the fact that she'd been crushing on him since she first came over to my house when we were kids. I could still see her in my mind, eyes wide, mouth open as he breezed past her to dig through the refrigerator. She nearly dropped the orange juice. At the time, I didn't understand what was wrong and had asked her, "Are you feeling okay? You look like you're about to throw up."

I learned that was not the thing to say to your new best friend when she was staring at her very first crush.

I shook my head at the memory. Felt like a lifetime ago, around the same time Megan and Winnie had left. I was alone in the sea of excited fans, so it wasn't too bad. Everybody was in a good mood, enjoying the game. The arena buzzed with anticipation for the final period, the energy thick enough to feel it in the air. It was almost enough for me to forget about the signs sprinkled through the stands. But then I read some of them.

"Puck Gemma!" a sign read. That was a particularly popular phrase. Some posters were more colorful. None were flattering. Only then did I realize people were glancing my way.

I sank lower in my seat, pulling my jacket tighter around me as if it could shield me from the stares in my direction. The article had a photo of me at the bottom, so only the dedicated readers knew what I looked like, but by the number of signs, it was easy to assume there were plenty of them here. Given the finger-pointing and glares, I was sure I'd been spotted.

I had to suck it up, though. I'd earned this.

I deserved the scrutiny. I'd invited it the moment I decided to write that article. It was a calculated risk worth taking to save Casey's job. I knew this was coming. It wasn't the first time the public had collectively decided to hate someone. But it was one thing to know it would happen and another to sit here in the arena, vulnerable and alone, feeling the sharp edges of the crowd's judgment.

The Zamboni made its slow laps around the ice. I stared at it, trying to zone out and dissociate. Anything was better than watching people gossip about me. I hadn't felt this dissected since I told my brother I was pregnant with Winnie. Granted, I was already in LA by then, so at least I didn't have to face him right away.

It took half a day, thanks to flight delays. But he had shown up at my apartment in LA, looking for the asshole who had "knocked me up." When I told him I wasn't going to tell him who the father was, and we had a few more ugly exchanges, he took off, having spent less than an hour in LA total. He was so angry, and he had no outlet for that anger, so he threw himself into practice after practice until he cooled down. Now, he attributed his increased skill to that time period, but we both knew that wasn't where he got his talent from. He worked hard for it, period.

It took a long time for him to forgive me for not telling him who the father was. I wondered how long it would take an arena full of strangers to get over the article.

I glanced around, looking for my best friend and my daughter, only to be met with more scowls. A woman pointed at me, and her friend mouthed, "Disgusting." At least, I thought that was what she said. Thankfully, at this distance, I couldn't hear them. I didn't want to know anything else, except for one thing.

Where are Megan and Winnie?

Not that I wanted them to face this with me. But I was fairly certain no one would mess with me if my adorable daughter were with me. Plus, Megan threw a mean right hook from taking boxing at computer summer camp. These days, she liked to play on the boxing machines in bars to earn free drinks from guys who thought they could beat her. It was one of the few outings she actually enjoyed.

I was surprised she had jumped on the trip to the arena. It was filled with everything she didn't like: people, loud noises, and the cold. But when it came to Nico and Winnie, she was a trouper.

The seconds ticked on, and they were still gone, making the minutes stretch unbearably. I glanced around, darting toward the aisle where I hoped they'd appear. That was when I saw her. A woman a few rows up was staring at me.

Not just staring, either. She'd been holding one of the signs earlier, and now her eyes locked on me with a level of intensity that made me want to hide. Her face was stern, her jaw set, and her anger radiated through me.

Please, no.

She stood abruptly, clutching her sign as she marched toward me. Her movements were purposeful, her expression unwavering. There was no avoiding this. Did she plan to wield the, "Coach can get it!" fan sign as a weapon? Or would she go personal and use her fists?

My heart pounded as I gripped the edge of my seat, my breath coming shallow and quick. I didn't know what she would say, but I braced myself for the worst. I was not much of a fighter. I preferred avoiding confrontation if I could, and I'd never fought a woman before. Handsy guys, sure, but a woman? She knew how to hurt me because she had all the same parts.

I didn't even know if security was around to stop her. Fights in hockey stands were nothing new, though they usually happened during the game, not the intermission. I looked for any of the men in a security jacket, but they were nowhere to be seen.

Once other fans figured out who I was, they might join

in. My phone had died long ago. I was on my own now. I had to handle the mess I'd made.

You deserve this, Gemma, I thought. *You did worse to Casey. An ass-kicking is nothing compared to that.*

The woman stopped a few feet away, her eyes narrowing as she looked me over. "You're her, aren't you? The bitch who hurt our coach?"

I opened my mouth, but no words came out. How could I explain myself to a stranger? Who would understand the choices I made back then? There was nothing I could say to her to make her not hate me before she took a swing. Stale beer scent wafted off of her, so I also had that to contend with. How do you calm a drunk woman fueled by righteous anger?

The answer was, you don't. You just do what you can to mitigate the damage. I braced for whatever came next.

She growled, "You're the one who—"

Before she could finish, the announcer's cheesy voice boomed through the speakers. "Ladies and gentlemen, it's time for the Kiss Cam!"

The woman froze as everyone's attention shifted toward the screens. The crowd cheered, their excitement palpable as the camera began its sweep of the audience.

I had always hated the Kiss Cam schtick, but not tonight. Tonight, it had saved me. Or it had postponed my beating. I exhaled shakily, grateful for the unexpected distraction. My nerves were still raw, though. Tonight had been harder than I had thought it'd be.

I considered using the distraction to get the hell out of there, but my would-be attacker blocked my aisle on one end and the other side had too many people to crawl over.

My choices were to face her or try and grapple with a dozen people, half of whom were standing. In these tight quarters, I didn't like my odds.

The Kiss Cam usually focused on couples in the stands, drawing laughter and applause as the camera coaxed them into a kiss. It was the perfect distraction for her to use to attack me. But tonight, something was different. The camera didn't stop on any of the usual suspects.

Instead, it focused on me.

What the hell?

I wasn't there with anyone except for the woman who wanted to wring my neck and the knot of people at the other end of my row. Before I could shake my head or signal them to get the camera off me, I thought better of it. *Keep the camera on me, so she'll leave me alone.* But then the lights lowered. The next shot was of the ice, where the Fire players were skating onto the rink in an unusual spreading formation.

I frowned, stretching up straighter as I tried to understand what I saw. My attacker did, too, preoccupied by the spectacle instead of me. The players moved deliberately, their movements coordinated and precise, until they formed a giant heart at center ice. The crowd gasped, murmurs and light clapping rippling through the arena as the spotlight zeroed in on the center of the heart.

There, standing proudly, was Winnie. She held a bouquet of flowers so large it seemed to dwarf her tiny frame, and she was waving at me with a grin that could light up the entire arena.

"Hi, Mommy!" her voice echoed through the speakers,

clear and full of excitement. Someone had put a microphone on my baby girl.

My heart leaped into my throat. *What is happening?*

Before I could fully process what I was seeing, movement caught the corner of my eye.

I turned, and there he was.

Casey.

The camera put us on screen for everyone to see.

He kneeled beside my seat, looking up at me with a nervous smile that made time stop. Even with the whole arena staring at us, the world shrank until it was just him and me, and the crowd's roar faded into a dull hum.

"Casey," I whispered, my voice barely audible over my heart pounding. I thought I knew what this was, but it couldn't be that. People like me didn't get things like this.

He slipped the ring from his thumb and held it out to me in his open palm. The one I'd seen him wear every day. The one he had come back for, despite what I'd admitted to, despite his pain and suffering. It was that important to him. His father's wedding ring.

And now, he offered it to me.

Before he said a word, I laughed, trying to stop tears from pricking my eyes. "We always do things the weird way, don't we?"

My voice echoed through the arena. He must have worn a microphone. "Yeah, I think we do," he said with a chuckle. "I love you. I love Winnie. Let's make weird things our family tradition."

I gulped, and the tears welled in my eyes. "You mean that?"

"Gemma Grimaldi, will you marry me?"

The arena went silent, the question spreading like a ripple through the crowd. Thousands of eyes stared at us, but I saw only Casey. I wanted to throw my arms around him and never let go. A smile broke across my face, or maybe it had been there since I realized he was by my side. That was Casey in a nutshell. If I said yes, he'd always be by my side. What else could I possibly ask for?

I nodded, tears spilling down my cheeks as I whispered, "Yes."

The crowd erupted, their cheers crashing through the arena like a tidal wave. Casey slipped the ring onto my finger, his hands steady even as mine trembled. It didn't fit at all, so I clenched my fist to keep it safe.

He stood, pulling me to my feet, and cupped my face in his hands. He kissed me so hard that I went limp in his arms.

When we pulled back, I grinned mischievously, the teasing words slipping out before I could stop them. "Under one condition." My voice echoed—I'd forgotten about his microphone.

His brow furrowed, his expression shifting to one of concern. "What's that?"

I gestured toward the ice, where the team was still in formation. "You have to win tonight."

The crowd ate it up, their cheers even louder than before. Even the angry sign lady cheered along with them.

His grin returned. "Consider it done."

Chapter 35

Casey

The crowd bellowed as the team skated back onto the ice for the third period, and the energy in the arena reached a fever pitch. After the proposal, people had gone nuts, cheering and shouting for us. Gemma hate signs had miraculously vanished, which I was particularly grateful for. The game was tied, and everything was on the line—not just for the team, but for me.

This wasn't just about hockey anymore. The proposal intermission had thrown everything into overdrive. The moment her shaky voice had said yes had filled me with a fire I hadn't felt in years. And seeing Winnie out there on the ice, her grin lighting up the arena, reminded me exactly why I needed to win tonight—this was not for me. It was for them.

It was so odd. I'd never considered myself to be a selfish person before I got together with Gemma, but now, I wondered. Before them, I didn't know what doing things in someone else's name was like. I was always worried about my reputation and my good standing. I worked hard in *my* name, and it was hard work to do so.

But doing things for them made the hard work easy. It strangely lightened the load, knowing failure was no longer an option.

There was no room for distractions now. The team needed me to focus. The city needed a win. It was no longer about me or what I wanted. In one way or another, the final period was for everybody else.

I glanced down the bench at Nico, his helmet on and his expression sharp with determination. He caught my eye and gave me a slight nod. He was ready.

So was I.

By the end of this, he'd be my brother-in-law. If I had the time to think about it, I might have laughed. When we met all those years ago, he was a smirking punk who was good on the ice. Now, he was still those things, but he was even better on the ice. One of the best I'd ever seen. The man was built for power, but he had a good head on his shoulders, too.

He had grown up a lot, too. When we first met, there was no way he would have come to understand me and Gemma. He was a black-and-white thinker, only seeing enemies or friends, good or bad, nothing in between. But over time, he had matured into the man I thought of as a friend.

And soon, I'd call him family.

The puck dropped, and the game's intensity immediately ratcheted up to eleven. The Seattle Razors came out swinging, their defense as tight as ever. Once they'd figured out Lopez was a secret weapon, we had to adjust. I swapped him out for Luke, hoping they wouldn't notice, but they did.

Of course, they did.

Those bastards had been on our shit all game long. A player swap wouldn't change that. I had to do something bigger. It was time to call in the Russian squad.

"Ivanov, Petrov, Sokolov—"

Lopez said, "Coach, Sokolov is Defense."

I smiled. "Exactly." I sent them on their way, pulling my other guys out. "Socks, I know you and the other Russians have been working on some stuff. Ready to show the Razors?"

He grinned. "We got you, Coach." Then he said something in Russian to his compatriots, who nodded once, firmly.

"All right, you guys, listen up. Petrov and Ivanov, I want you to hit a V-formation as soon as you're on the ice. Cut in toward the goalie. Your only focus is reaching the goal until Socks gets you the puck. Socks, this is a lot riding on you. Screw around out there—"

"Wait, what?"

Each of them looked at me like I had a screw loose.

But I continued, "Act like you have no business being out there on the ice. You're an offensive defenseman—it's not hard for them to underestimate you. Look like you've never seen a play before, and you're just there to pester them. Get them to drop their guard, swoop in around their left winger—they've been protecting him the whole game—and I'd bet the Cup that they're about to send the puck his way. Get me that puck. Bring it to your boys, either one, don't care who. Surprise me."

"But that puts me in Nico's zone. He'll be pissed."

I shook my head. "Nico knows I put you out there for a reason. I trust him. He trusts me. Go."

They hauled ass onto the ice, each to their respective posts. Socks played the fool, *accidentally* cutting into Nico's path, being a menace to everyone—the Razors and the Fire alike—at that end of the ice.

It would have been great. They wouldn't have seen it coming. It was something new which would make Matthew happy. Everything was going according to my plan.

If only they hadn't put in the Bulldozer.

The Bulldozer, AKA Max Martin, had quickly built himself a reputation for fighting. He'd worked his way up from the minors with bruised knuckles and missing a tooth. He had been responsible for two of their opponents ending up in hospitals in the past season alone. He took hits like they were nothing but doled them out like it was his personal mission. The man was huge. Commentators joked that they didn't know how his skates didn't bend under his massive form.

Socks had speed and agility on his side, but the Razors' coach, Derek Pendleton, had paid too much attention and sent the Bulldozer after him. He knew Socks would not be able to take a beating, and he did it anyway. In his own way, Derek was worse than the Bulldozer.

Socks veered left, the Bulldozer went right. Socks spun around Nico to dodge, but the Bulldozer caught up to him with shocking speed, sending him straight into the boards. Nico slapped the puck to Ivanov, who shot it straight past their goalie, bringing us one step closer.

But I felt the crunch of the hit on Socks from across the

arena. Sokolov tried to get up and couldn't. My stomach lurched as I bolted for the ice to check on him, but the medics got there first. His nose was bloodied, but he gave me a thumbs-up. "Bet I bled on his jersey. Messed it all up. That'll teach him."

I chuckled. "You're a lucky son-of-a-bitch, Socks."

They rolled him onto a stretcher. "Tell that to my arm."

"I'll tell it to Pendleton's ass when I hand it to him."

They lifted him to cart him out. "Don't bother. But win this thing for me and for that cute kid of yours."

"I promise."

As he held his less injured thumb up to the arena, the crowd cheered while he was taken away. They loved to see a fallen man defiant against the odds, especially when it was one of their own. But their cheers wouldn't make Ivanov and Petrov any happier about what had happened to their boy. They were too Russian for that, their emotions easy to read on their faces.

We were all pissed off.

That was how the last play of the season began, with anger and to honor our fallen comrade. Our players had given it everything, and I saw the exhaustion setting in. The long season, the pressure of the Cup—it was all catching up to them. And now, there was no more Sokolov to cheer up the two other naturally grumpy Russians.

I leaned forward, gripping the boards as I shouted instructions. "Stay tight! Watch the left wing! Cover the slot!" The guys were listening, their movements sharp and focused, but the Razors still matched us blow for blow. I was grateful the Bulldozer had been penalized and now rotted in the box. We didn't need more of him out there.

Two minutes after that bullshit he had pulled, they scored.

The arena went quiet for a split second before the Razors' fans erupted in cheers. I clenched my jaw, forcing myself to stay calm as the scoreboard updated. 2-3.

There was still time.

I called for another line change, and the players skated to the bench with sweat dripping from their faces. "Listen up!" I barked, my voice cutting through the noise. "They're overcommitting on every rush. We can exploit that. Nico, I want you to hold back a beat before you break for the puck. Make them think you're out of position. Maxwell, you're going to hang closer to the net. When Nico takes the shot, you clean up the rebound."

The guys nodded, their eyes locked on me.

"You've got this," I said firmly, meeting each of their gazes. "We've fought too hard to let it slip away now. Let's finish this. For Socks."

The next shift was pure chaos. The Razors pushed hard, their forwards swarming the zone like sharks. But we held strong, blocking shots and clearing the puck with precision.

And then it happened.

Nico intercepted a pass in the neutral zone, his stick moving like lightning as he broke away. They scrambled to catch him, but he was too fast, too smart.

He held back for a split second, just like I'd told him, and then unleashed a blistering slapshot from the blue line.

The goalie made the save, but the puck rebounded straight to Maxwell, who was exactly where he needed to be.

He buried it.

The arena exploded, the noise so loud it felt like the building was shaking. I pumped my fist in the air, my heart racing as the scoreboard updated. 3-3.

We were back in it.

With only a minute and a half left on the clock, the tension in the arena was palpable. Every second felt like an eternity as the puck moved back and forth across the ice, each team fighting desperately for the winning goal.

I barked instructions from the bench, my voice hoarse. "Keep it tight! Don't let them set up! Stay on them!"

Nico was everywhere—blocking shots, winning faceoffs, and setting up plays with the kind of skill that made him one of the best. Despite having the most time on the ice, he was in the zone, and the rest of the team fed off his energy. I didn't know how he did it until I saw Winnie. Jumping up and down, cheering her uncle on, arms flailing like the best little cheerleader anyone could ask for.

That was everything.

The puck was deep in the opposing zone, and Nico battled for it in the corner. He dug it out, spinning away from a defender with a smooth move that left the guy flailing. Nico skated toward the net, his eyes locked on the goalie.

Time stopped as I held my breath. He pulled back his stick and fired a shot so perfect it felt like fate. The puck sailed past the goalie's glove and into the top corner of the net.

The horn blared, and the arena erupted in a deafening roar.

We did it. We actually did it.

The team swarmed Nico, their cheers and shouts echoing through the arena as the fans went wild. I stood behind the bench, my chest heaving as the adrenaline coursed through me.

As the players celebrated on the ice, my gaze drifted to the stands, where I spotted Gemma and Winnie. Winnie was still jumping up and down, her little hands clapping with glee, and Gemma was smiling through tears, her eyes locked on mine.

I felt a lump rise in my throat as I raised a hand to her, and she grinned, waving back. This wasn't just a win for the team. This was a win for us—for our family, for the future we were building.

We have the Cup. I have my girls.

Nico skated over, his grin as wide as I'd ever seen it. "Told you we'd pull it off, Coach."

"You did good."

"So did you," he replied, his tone sincere. He threw an arm around my shoulders for a back-pat of a hug. "Glad to know you're joining the family."

The knot in my throat threatened to choke me. "Same here."

Chapter 36

Gemma

Arena noise had bored its way into my brain like a prion, and it didn't let up as we made our way through the place. The excitement of the game, the energy of the fans—it all felt like a blur now. Between that behemoth crashing into Sokolov, the proposal, the woman I thought would kick my ass, too much concession food, I was cooked. It was a hell of a game, one for the books. I was so proud of Nico and Casey. But the only thing I could focus on was how wildly my heart raced whenever I thought about my fiancé.

Just thinking that word made me giddy.

"You're thinking about him again, aren't you?" Megan asked.

"Maybe."

She giggled. "You should have gotten engaged years ago. It makes you silly."

"Mommy's silly!" Winnie teased.

Maybe I was. That was okay. Nico and Casey had secured the Fire's place in history, and the victory had been nothing short of electric. But now, as we gathered outside the locker room, my thoughts shifted from the win to what came next. I was allowed to be silly about it. I was engaged after dating a man for less than a year, something I'd sworn I would never do.

Maybe that had always been silly. Rules like that were ridiculous. Love came when it came. You couldn't put a timetable on it. I never understood that until now.

Megan held Winnie's hand, the two of them still buzzing from the game. Other than to tease me, Winnie hadn't stopped talking about how amazing her uncle was, and I couldn't help but smile at her. She'd be a lifelong hockey fan. I was sure of it. Between her uncle, her father, and me, she was destined to love the sport as much as we did. Maybe more.

Starting tonight, hockey was going to be a huge part of our lives, even more than before. My brother playing center for a pro team was a good reason to pay attention to the sport. My boss in LA had put me down for the hockey beat because of Nico. I was one of the few women on staff who understood the sport as intimately as the players. But now, with Casey joining the family, Winnie didn't stand a chance of falling in love with any other sport.

Unless she did it just to annoy us when she became a rebellious teenager.

Then the question struck me—would she have younger siblings? Did Casey want more kids? Did I? I hadn't thought about it much. When life was just me and Winnie, I definitely did not want another one. I adored my daughter, but she was a handful. Being on my own, I figured I could handle her and only her. But everything had changed when I said yes.

I toyed with the ring on my finger, trying to make sure it didn't fall off as we waded through the crowd. Did I want another kid? The thought of having a second Winnie instantly filled my heart with joy. I had to talk to Casey. Right now.

"Megan," I said, catching her attention. "Would you mind taking Winnie home tonight?"

Her eyebrows shot up, and a sly grin spread across her face. "A *private* celebration for the victors?"

"It's not like that," I said quickly, though my cheeks flushed. "I just...I need to see Casey. Alone. To talk. Possibly all night long."

She waved me off, her grin widening. "Say no more. I've got it covered."

"Thank you."

Nico appeared at that moment, his hair still damp from his postgame shower. He looked between us, his brow furrowing. "What's going on?"

"I'm taking Winnie home," Megan said breezily.

"Not without me, you're not," Nico said, crossing his arms. He assured me, "I'll make sure she gets home safe."

Megan rolled her eyes but didn't argue. "Fine. But you're paying for the rideshare."

"Are you kidding? We're going home in that limo," Nico said with a smirk, ruffling Winnie's hair.

"Yay!" Winnie shouted.

Once we said our goodbyes, I wasted no time tracking down Whitney. If anyone could make this happen for me, it was her. She was by the press area, managing the chaos of postgame interviews. When she saw me, her expression softened. "Gemma. Congratulations on your engagement. Did you get lost? Need a tour guide down here? I know the tunnels can get confusing."

"Thanks, but no. I need a different kind of favor."

"What kind of favor is that?"

"Can you get me into Casey's office? And get him there in ten minutes?"

Whitney stared at me for a moment before a slow smile spread across her face. "Nothing nefarious, I hope. Don't want you to have to write another article."

I hesitated, then decided to go for honesty. "I just need to see him. After everything that's happened tonight...I need to speak with him. Privately."

"You're lucky I like you. Fine. I'll stall him with postgame interviews for a few minutes and send him your way."

"Thank you."

Everything inside Casey's office was quiet, starkly contrasting the noise outside. It was a relief after everything. My ears still rang, though. I plugged my phone into the charger on his desk, finally giving it some much-needed juice.

It wasn't long before the screen lit up with a flood of notifications—texts, missed calls, emails. All from Casey, except for those from Nico. I opened the first one, my heart sinking as I read it.

Don't do this. Don't tank your reputation to save me.

Another text followed.

I'll take the heat. Please, just let me be the bad guy.

Email after email carried the same message, his pleas

growing more desperate. I'd missed them because Megan demanded I close my laptop. I'd missed the calls and texts because my phone was dead. They spelled out his plan. He didn't want me to bear the weight of public scrutiny, not when it could be turned on him instead. Doing that would have cost him everything important to him, and he knew it, and still, that was what he wanted me to do.

Tears pricked my eyes as I stared at the screen. He would ruin himself to save me.

My heart stuttered in my chest. I set my phone down and inhaled deeply, trying to steady myself. My hands moved almost without thought as I slipped out of my clothes, leaving me in just my undergarments. I draped my jacket over the back of his chair and perched on the desk, waiting. I was both aroused and overwhelmed. Knowing he'd leave everything behind for me...it was his ultimate sacrifice. I was glad he didn't have to do it, but the fact he was willing to do so was enough.

The sound of two voices outside the door pulled me from my thoughts. The door was almost soundproof, which meant they were close. I froze. Casey was coming. But he wasn't alone.

Hide!

Panicking, I darted to the storage closet, easing the door shut as the office door opened. The closet was stuffed, so I had to hold perfectly still, or I'd knock into something and expose my nearly naked presence.

I watched through the slats of the closet door as Casey entered, followed by an older man I didn't quite recognize. He carried himself with authority, and the way Casey straightened when he spoke made it clear this man was in charge. He looked familiar, but I couldn't place him.

"You know why I'm here," the man said, calm but firm.

Casey nodded, his jaw tightening. "I figured you'd come by."

The older man crossed his arms. "You've always put the team first. So what's changed?"

Casey's expression softened, a small smile tugging at the corners of his lips. "Everything."

"Go on," the man said, his tone leaving no room for argument.

"You read the article that came out today, didn't you, Matthew?"

Matthew... Matthew Edwards. The owner. Oh hell. I'm about to watch Casey get fired.

It was all but impossible to remain in the closet. I wanted to run out there and demand he keep his job. But a half-naked woman is not exactly the best negotiator. Or maybe she could be. But I wouldn't do that until I knew it was coming.

The old man stood taller, haughtier. "I read it. There were some interesting details, including that the woman who bore your child is a player's sister. You know the rules, Casey. I am well within my rights to fire you, as I'm sure you're aware."

Casey took a deep breath. "I am. So go ahead and fire me if you want, but either way, I'm marrying that woman."

I loved hearing that out of him.

"Is it really so easy for you to throw away everything you've built with my team? Your ethics, the rules—"

"I've always lived by those rules. Until I couldn't."

The old man sighed. "I always thought of you as the most ethical person I knew, the dullest, the most oatmeal-and-bran kind of man in the world. You actually got my players eating healthy. Healthier than any other team in the league, even in the offseason. You've always been a stand-up guy. Dependable. Loyal. Boring. And a woman was enough to get you to break the rules?"

"She's more than just some woman. She's everything to me. Gemma is clever, strong, determined, everything I could ever ask for," he said as he smiled. "And I've got a daughter with her. Winnie. She's amazing—smart, funny, full of energy. And she's got her mother's kindness."

The older man's eyebrows lifted in surprise. "I see."

Casey paused, his gaze distant momentarily before turning back to the older man. "As much as I love this team and this career, they don't compare to my real family. Nothing could."

Tears streamed down my face as I listened, his words hitting me like a tidal wave. My chest ached, and every part of me needed to go to him. I clamped a hand over my mouth, fighting the urge to sniffle as his declaration sank in. It was one thing for a man to say nice things to your face. But to say them under these circumstances meant more.

Matthew studied Casey for a long moment before nodding slowly. "That's what I needed to hear."

"What's that supposed to mean?"

"I'm happy for you, Casey. Your priorities are finally in order."

I held my breath.

Casey blinked, clearly caught off guard. "You're...okay with this?"

"I'm more than okay with it," the man said with a faint smile. "You've got a family now. This means you will need this job, since families are expensive. And since I don't foresee you carousing with anyone else's sister—"

"Ha! No!"

"Your job is safe, Casey. I'm going back to Texas for the offseason. For what it's worth, congratulations. Make sure I get a wedding invitation." He gave a short nod and smiled, before leaving the office, closing the door behind him.

Chapter 37

Casey

The sound of my office door clicking shut behind Matthew was like the first breath of air after being underwater for too long. How long had I been holding my breath over this? It felt like forever. I leaned back against my desk, running a hand through my hair, my chest heaving with relief.

I hadn't been sure how that conversation was going to go. Matthew had a way of keeping me on edge. That quirky bastard never revealed his thoughts until the very last moment. I figured he liked to make people nervous—it was some kind of powerplay that amused him. Truly wealthy people had odd hobbies. I'd known only a few, and each was a unique snowflake who made life challenging in their way. For most of the conversation with Matthew, I'd braced myself for the worst—for the possibility that tonight would be my last game as the Fire's head coach.

But what a way to go out.

The game had been an all-timer. I looked forward to the highlight reel because every second of that game could be featured. Even the Bulldozer wasn't enough to secure the Seattle Razor's win. It had been the game of a lifetime, and, because Matthew had an odd sense of morality, I still had more games to go.

I couldn't believe he'd let me off the hook. More than that, he had congratulated me and wanted an invitation to our wedding. The same man, who'd once told me hockey should come before everything else, had smiled and said he was glad my priorities were finally in order. I had to stop thinking I could predict him, because he proved me wrong time and time again.

For the first time all night, I felt like I could breathe again.

Gemma was safe from the fans. My job was safe from Matthew. We were getting married. Somehow, the stars had aligned, and things worked out.

I pulled my phone out of my pocket, already scrolling to Gemma's name. I needed to tell her everything—about Matthew, how much I loved her, that we could finally move forward without this cloud hanging over us, and how I wanted to wake up beside her every day for the rest of my life.

But then the storage closet door creaked open. I nearly jumped out of my skin, my heart racing as the door swung wide, my fingers scrambling not to drop my phone.

"What the hell?" I started, my voice catching in my throat. But I lost that train of thought when Gemma stepped out, wearing nothing but her bra and panties and an expression that left no room for misinterpretation.

For a moment, I couldn't speak. I couldn't even think. The sight of her pooled all the blood low in my body, and my mouth went dry. "Gemma...what are you—why are you—"

Before I could finish my question, she crossed the room in three determined steps and grabbed my face, her lips crashing against mine.

Any thoughts I'd had—confusion, coherent words—disappeared the instant she kissed me. Every kiss we shared was that way. Each kiss coalesced priorities into the meeting of our mouths. Her soft hands slid to the back of my neck, her fingers tangling in my hair as she kissed me with a desperation that stole my breath. I wrapped my arms around her, pulling her closer, the feel of her satiny skin against my hands setting off sparks in every nerve of my body.

"Gemma," I murmured against her lips, trying to catch my breath, but she didn't give me a chance to say more.

"No talking."

I wasn't about to argue.

She pushed me back against the desk, her hands sliding under my shirt as she kissed me like she couldn't get enough. Her warmth against my cold chest lit me from the inside. My jacket hit the floor first, followed by my shirt, and when her lips trailed down my neck, my brain officially short-circuited.

I lifted her onto the desk, her legs wrapping around my waist as I kissed her deeply, pouring every ounce of love and passion I felt into the moment.

The office faded away, the arena noise a distant hum. It was just us, lost in each other. She shoved my pants down, grabbing me in her hot little hand and stroking me as I pumped against her palm. She rubbed the head of my cock against herself, wet and ready for me. When I entered her, nothing else existed. Not the team, not the arena, not time, not space. I sank deep into her there, wishing for a bed to do this right.

But I did have a door.

I lifted her from the desk and carried her so her back was against the door. Every thrust, a new sensation threatened to make me spill right then. But when she stared into my eyes with her every gasp, *that* was the thing that sent me near the point of no return. I felt her love for me in some cosmic way, and it was everything I ever needed.

Her kisses were something animalistic. She fed off my lips the way I fed off hers. Nothing else mattered but her. She was my end and our beginning. My blood thrummed in my ears, my balls, my heart, all at once. I needed her more than I needed anything in my life. When she squeezed around me, rapturous sounds trickled from her mouth, and I devoured each one as she came on me, shuddering until she slowed.

She gasped, "Set me down."

I did, and she dropped to her knees. "Are you okay—"

I thought she had fallen. But she swallowed me into her mouth, working me into her throat as she stared at me through her lashes the whole time.

Fuck.

Gemma took everything I had to give her and wanted more. So I gave it all to her, weaving my fingers into her long red hair to keep her on my pace. Her tongue flicked against the head, and that extra sensation got me there even faster. I pumped into her lips, ecstatic and verging on delirium. It was too much, too fast, and exactly what I needed.

Something unholy erupted from my throat as I came in hers.

After we pulled ourselves together, I needed the support of my desk chair. This crazy woman had made me weak in the knees. I leaned back against my chair, my chest heaving as I tried to gulp air in. Quickies weren't our normal thing, but fuck, that was amazing. Gemma curled onto my lap, her fingers tracing lazy patterns on my shoulder as we basked in the afterglow. She was tracing my birthmark.

It felt like that mark had brought us full circle. Without it, I might never have known Winnie was mine. I still couldn't believe Gemma was here. Or that she had agreed to marry me.

I didn't believe in fate or luck. I believed you made your own path through hard work and dedication. But ever since getting to know Gemma, I had begun to wonder if some force in the universe had gotten us together. Whatever the case, this felt as though it was meant to be. Everything with her felt right.

Except the fact that she had been in my storage closet. "You were in the closet that whole time."

She grinned, propping herself up on one elbow. "Guilty."

"And you heard everything," I continued, watching her carefully.

Her smile softened, and she nodded. "I did. And if I had any lingering doubts about you—which, for the record, I didn't—but if I had, they would've disappeared the second you told Matthew you'd give up your job for us."

I cupped her cheek, brushing my newly naked thumb

over her skin. "You don't know how close I came to losing it all tonight. If Matthew hadn't—"

She silenced me with a kiss. "But he didn't. You're still here, and so am I. And I'm glad it didn't come to that."

"Same here."

Gemma's grin turned mischievous as she sat up, her eyes sparkling. "Let me guess—Whitney was behind getting you back here?"

"She's behind everything good around this place."

"More than you know," Gemma said, laughing. "I asked for her help with this—"

"That's how you got into my office? I thought it might have been some journalism school thing."

Her eyes widened. "How so?"

"The intrepid reporter, breaking into buildings...it's practically a staple trope in film noir."

She pressed her forehead to mine. "You're adorable. And for the record, no, we don't learn how to break into buildings in journalism school."

"Probably safer that way."

"I learned how to do that from my mother, not college."

I chuckled, but her expression didn't break. "Wait—you're serious?"

"Nico used to lock himself out of the house a lot when we were little kids, so Mom showed us how to break in safely by picking the lock."

"Oh. I guess that's a good skill to have if you're bad at remembering your keys. Maybe you should teach Winnie."

She smiled and shook her head. "I forget to charge my phone, Nico still forgets his keys. We'll wait to see what she forgets and go from there."

"So, it's a family trait?"

"Yeah. Mom used to forget which bills came at the start of the month, and Dad always left the stove on."

"Damn." I made a mental note to watch for the stove thing with her and Winnie. After a beat, fleeting concerns came to mind. I sighed, running a hand through my hair. "I thought Matthew was going to fire me. Honestly, I'd made peace with it. If losing this job meant being with you and Winnie, it was a no-brainer. I'd even looked into other jobs—"

"But you love it here."

I shrugged. "It's like I told him. You and Winnie are all that matters."

Her expression softened, "Casey..."

I kissed her again, slow and deep, trying to convey everything I couldn't put into words. Out of the two of us, she was the one who was good with words, so I had to show her how I felt. Unfortunately, this time, it couldn't lead to anything more than a cuddle. Tiredness was starting to sink in as the night's adrenaline wore away.

Eventually, we straightened up and began to dress. I couldn't help but feel a sense of lightness I hadn't felt in months. Matthew was headed to his ranch in Texas, my job was safe, and most importantly, the woman I loved was by my side. Truly, she was the woman of my dreams. I hoped I could be the man who made her dreams come true.

I asked, "Can we go to my place for the night?"

"Yes, please." On our way out the door, she asked, "Do you want more kids?"

I laughed. The abruptness of her question had caught

me in the middle of a fantasy of what I wanted to do to her at my place. Shifting gears, I asked, "Do you?"

"I asked you first."

"Fine." I hoped this went well. "I do. If you're up for it. If you're not, that's okay, too. Winnie's plenty for us. But I don't want you to feel pressured—"

She spun on her heel, facing me. "I want more, too. Maybe not right away—I want to spend time with it being just the three of us for a little while. But, on the off chance, we could make another Winnie, I want to try."

My heart swelled. I stroked her cheek, and she leaned into it, smiling. She was perfect. I knew that before, but now, I had all the confirmation I needed on that point. "Then let's do that. One day."

Chapter 38

Gemma

The morning sunlight hadn't begun to peek in yet as I stretched lazily under the sheets. My man had good taste in linens, from his flannel sheets to his super soft towels, and I luxuriated in them, while just thinking in the early morning hours. I never slept well after a crazy night or even a night out. It was a curse that had led to many long mornings replaying the events of the night before.

It had been the best night of my life after one of the worst days. Replaying every detail, I should have seen each surprise coming a mile away. But hindsight was twenty-twenty. How could I have known Nico's sudden appearance was part of Casey's proposal plan? Or that when Megan had been texting before she vanished with Winnie, it was with Casey, not Nico? Or, for that matter, that a proposal could save his career?

Strange how much could change on a dime and how unrelated things could add up to something wonderful.

I had thought my article would be the best approach

possible, but I was wrong. Casey's incredibly public proposal had flipped the entire arena's energy. I went from a pariah, targeted for her actions, to the arena's sweetheart in a matter of minutes. Even the woman who had come down to attack me had flashed me a smile after his proposal. Others sent us food and beer, and a particularly nice old woman bought Winnie a jersey.

People loved to have a villain to hate, but, as it turned out, they loved love even more.

I stretched again, trying to wake up. I knew Nico and Megan would take care of Winnie, but I also knew she could be a handful. She wasn't a morning person, but I could picture her powering through, thanks to their presence. Still, I didn't want to move. I was so cozy, and Casey's arm was draped between us, his hand splayed possessively on my hip.

He was so handsome that it made my chest ache. That chiseled jaw, those perfect lips. Staring at him in the faint darkness of his room, listening to his shallow breaths...I would get to wake up to this face every day now. I could hardly believe my luck.

"Morning," he murmured, his voice husky with sleep.

My heart did that fluttery thing it always did when he smiled at me like I was the only thing that mattered. I'd never take that privilege for granted. "Morning."

He leaned in, brushing his lips over mine in a kiss that started sweet but quickly deepened, his hand sliding up my hip to my back to pull me closer. He was already hard, his cock pinned between our bodies as we kissed.

I sighed against his mouth, threading my fingers through his hair. Whatever plans I'd had for the morning were forgotten the moment he rolled us over, his weight pressing me into the mattress in the most delicious way.

He reached between my thighs, rubbing, coaxing, playing. Nothing too fast, nothing hurried. I loved that about him. He played my body like he'd known me for years, but he had been able to do that since our first night together. The man knew all my spots, all the ways to light me up. His thumb circled my clit, fingertips toying at my entrance and setting me alight. They didn't enter me—he was still taking his time. When I opened my eyes, pale purple light had snuck in through the curtains. I bit my lip as everything in me went tight.

He whispered in my ear, "I love when you make that face."

I could hardly speak. Instead, I cocked my hips so his fingers slipped inside of me.

"Greedy girl."

I nodded coquettishly, and he fingered me until I trembled.

"That's it, isn't it? Right there? You're so wet for me now. Do you want more?"

"Yes," I whimpered.

Another finger joined the party, stretching me further as I dug my nails into his shoulder. I was so close I could hardly breathe, and when it took me over, I came in a sighing gasp, clinging to him. Only then did he slide inside of me, rocking back and forth until I was full of him.

He laced his fingers with mine, and we moved slowly, savoring every moment. His movements were languid, erotic thrusts. Time had no meaning. He pulled out, turning us until we were on our sides, him behind me as he entered me once more. He plucked at my nipples, played with my clit, did anything to bring me closer to another climax.

And I orgasmed, one after another after another, until he couldn't take it any longer. He gripped my hip and drove deep as he came, too. At the last moment, he bit my shoulder.

In the shower, he went to his knees for me. We couldn't stop. It was like being a teenager again. Any little thing set us off, and before I knew it, he had me bent over in the shower with his fingers hard at work.

When the magic had worn down a couple of hours later, he handed me a thin silver chain. "This is for the ring, until I get it sized down for you. Unless you want to pick a new set—"

"No. I'd be honored to wear your family ring."

He smiled and threaded the ring onto the necklace before clasping it around my neck. He kissed me on the nape. "Thank you for knowing what that means to me."

I smiled, even though my heart hurt. "I'm just sorry your folks can't be there at our wedding. I know what it'd mean to me, if my mom could be."

"What about your dad?"

I sighed and shook my head. "He doesn't leave the nursing home. It's not that he can't, but because of his condition, he'd need a nurse to come with him, and that's so expensive. It's just not feasible." I shrugged, struggling not to dwell on it.

I had never planned my wedding as a little girl—it didn't seem like a big deal to me at the time. But I had always assumed my father would be there, and it hurt to know he wouldn't be. But I was happy to marry Casey and focused on what I could have instead of what I couldn't have. "All I need is you, Winnie, Nico, and Megan to be there."

He took my hand, kissing the back of it. "I know how important family is. They'll all be there. And Megan, too. And anything else you want."

"Right now, I want to see my baby and make sure Nico and Megan didn't burn the house down."

"Let's go now before I have to see what you look like naked on my couch."

I giggled and decided he should see that first.

Eventually, we pulled into the driveway of my house. I hadn't planned to spend the night at Casey's, but after everything that happened yesterday—his proposal, the game, Matthew's surprising approval—I couldn't bring myself to leave his side for a second..

I never wanted to leave him ever again.

I unlocked the front door, pushing it open to the unmistakable sound of clattering in the kitchen. Casey followed close behind, and we staggered to a stop from the sticky sight before us.

Winnie stood on a chair by the counter, pouring a box of cereal into my designated popcorn bowl with all the care of a four-year-old on a mission. There looked to be two other kinds of cereal already in the bowl. The counter was a mess—spilled cereal, milk dripping onto the floor, and a glistening trail of what I assumed was honey leading to the sink.

"Good morning, Winnie," I said, my voice equal parts amused and horrified. "What are you doing?"

She looked up, her face lighting up when she saw me.

She unintentionally stage-whispered, "Making breakfast for Uncle Nico and Megan!"

Our baby hadn't yet mastered the art of actual whispering, and I assumed she just woke them up.

Casey laughed softly beside me, his hand resting on the small of my back. "She's ambitious, I'll give her that."

My eyes darted to the living room, where Nico and Megan were sprawled out on the couch, still fast asleep. *What the...? Oh, screw it, at least they're clothed.*

Nico's arm was slung over Megan's shoulders, her head tucked against his chest. They looked so cozy that I almost didn't want to disturb them. Almost.

I walked over to the couch and kicked Nico's foot lightly. "Hey, Romeo."

He startled awake, his eyes blinking rapidly as he tried to figure out where he was. His cheeks flushed a deep red when he realized he was curled up with Megan. "Uh..." he started, shifting away from her as if that would make things less awkward.

The movement woke Megan, who sat up groggily, her hair a wild mess. She blinked at me, Nico, and then back at me, her cheeks turning hot pink.

"Morning," I said, smirking. "Did you two sleep well?"

"Gemma," Nico started, running a hand through his hair. "It's not what it looks like."

Casey walked into the living room, crossing his arms and grinning. "Oh, it's *exactly* what it looks like."

Nico faux-glared at him. "You don't get to talk. You snuck around with my sister behind my back for weeks, and now, you're coming in after a sleepover. I should get at least one Get Out of Jail Free card for that."

Casey raised an eyebrow, his grin widening. "Fair enough. But seriously, what's going on here?"

"It was nothing," Megan began.

I crossed my arms, my gaze darting between them. I wasn't mad, but I had to be clear about the rules when it came to my daughter. "You two better not have done anything on my couch. Winnie's in the next room and doesn't need that kind of education. Or mental scarring."

Megan's eyes widened, and she shook her head quickly. "No! No, we didn't do anything. We just...fell asleep watching a movie."

Nico nodded, his expression earnest. "Yeah. After we put Winnie to bed, we started a movie, and we, uh...I guess we crashed."

I studied them both for a moment, noting the way Nico avoided Megan's gaze and how she tucked her hair behind her ear, a nervous habit I'd seen a hundred times. Always around boys she liked.

There was tension between them, and it wasn't the awkward kind that came from being caught in an innocent situation. It was the kind of tension that came from wanting something you weren't sure you should want.

I decided to let it go—for now. "All right," I said, waving them off. "But you're on kitchen cleaning duty after you two dropped the ball on watching the kiddo this morning."

Chapter 39

Casey

I loved Gemma's house. It was cozy and cheerful without feeling too small. But my daughter's personality was big enough that they could have done with a bigger place.

Winnie's drawings hung from the fridge with care. With Gemma's relaxed way of looking at the world, I had the sense that I could make a mess, and it wouldn't be a tragedy. But a certain amount of pride was taken in her home. Pictures on the walls were dusted and leveled, gathered together by theme. Everything had a place and was at least mostly tucked there. Even the baseboards sparkled, and that was something I neglected.

It wouldn't be our long-term home, but I was glad to know my girls had a nice place for now. I planned to buy Gemma whatever house she wanted. All she had to do was point her little finger, and it was hers. But I'd let that be a wedding surprise. For now, I stood by, watching Gemma handle her household.

The smell of coffee mingled with the sugary sweetness

of spilled cereal and milk, and it all felt so wonderfully... normal. For someone like me, who had spent so much of my life on the road, in arenas, or alone in my own place, this kind of normal was everything I'd ever wanted. A family made of people who spent time together because they enjoyed each other, not because of obligation.

My family in Maryland was all right for the most part, but two of my cousins had married people who did nothing but passive-aggressively speak to one another or gossip about each other. One was from Connecticut, the other from Philly. My uncle had confided that they reminded him why he didn't like New Englanders, but I doubted that was how everybody in the tri-state areas acted. The sniping and backbiting made visiting a chore instead of something I looked forward to every year. Thankfully, there was none of that in Gemma's house. I doubted there ever could be.

Winnie was at the counter, enthusiastically pouring various cereals into a massive mixing bowl. Cornflakes, granola, chocolate puffs, golden pops, fruity loops—it was all going in, and Gemma watched with a mixture of horror and amusement as her daughter crafted what she proudly dubbed "Winnie Mix."

I tried not to fret about the health implications of her mix, but it was hard to turn off my coach's brain. "That is quite the recipe. Pretty sure she's getting her daily allowance of artificial color."

"She's really committing to the bit." Gemma folded her arms, shaking her head with an amused grin.

"She gets it from you," I teased, kissing her temple.

Gemma rolled her eyes but didn't argue.

We each took a bowl, and I prayed the artificial colors

wouldn't ruin Winnie's developing brain or Nico's gains in the gym. He and Megan were seated at the table, looking marginally less awkward than earlier, though they still avoided eye contact whenever they could. Megan stirred her cereal creation, while Nico leaned back in his chair, pretending to check his phone between bites of Winnie's Mix. Every once in a while, he stole a glance of Megan.

I kept waiting for him to turn on the charm like always, but he just kept silently pining. It was odd, to say the least. Nico Grimaldi had a reputation for a reason. He was a good-looking man, and women—especially puck bunnies—fawned over him. He could have any of them and had many times. But over a bowl of Frankenstein's imagination, he clammed up like he couldn't think of what to say to Megan.

She was a pretty girl, certainly, but I'd seen Nico with models draped on his arm. Rich women, thin women, full-figured women, old and young, they all wanted him. Megan, on the other hand, was picking at her breakfast like she'd eat it to make Winnie happy, but that was the only reason. Nico appeared to barely factor on her radar.

Until she spied him from her periphery and turned pink.

This mousy girl blushed like no one's business. Had they hooked up last night? Or was it just a movie night, like they'd claimed? I wondered if we'd ever learn the truth.

I sat beside Gemma on the couch, my arm slung casually over her shoulders. The TV was on, tuned to a morning news show that was currently featuring a segment about last night's game. Or at least, that was what I thought it was going to be about.

"And now, for the story everyone is talking about this

morning," the anchor said, a bright smile plastered on her face.

The screen cut to footage from the arena, showing the team skating into the heart formation at center ice. Winnie's tiny figure appeared in the spotlight, holding the bouquet of flowers. Then it shifted to me, down on one knee beside Gemma, as the crowd erupted in cheers.

My stomach sank. Was my hair really that gray all over?

"While the Atlanta Fire clinched a crucial playoff victory last night," the anchor continued, "it's what happened off the ice that's stealing headlines. Head Coach Casey McConnell proposed to journalist Gemma Grimaldi in a heartwarming moment that had the entire arena—and now the nation—cheering."

The screen shifted again, this time to Gemma's article about our relationship. The headline was overlaid with a banner reading *Love, Fire, and Ice.*

My jaw dropped. "It got picked up nationally?"

"Apparently," Gemma said, her voice tinged with disbelief.

"And it's not just the proposal," the anchor went on. "Grimaldi's article about her journey with McConnell and their daughter has been gaining traction across major outlets, with many calling it one of the most touching sports-related human interest stories of the year."

The screen filled with footage of the Kiss Cam moment again, and I groaned softly, running a hand over my face.

"This is surreal," Gemma muttered.

Nico leaned back in his chair, smirking. "I mean, it's kind of romantic. For an old guy like you."

"Watch it," I said, throwing my spoon at him.

To no one's surprise, he caught it.

Winnie appeared in the doorway, holding the massive bowl of cereal with both hands. Milk sloshed precariously close to the edge, but she somehow managed to make it to the table without spilling.

"What do you have there, kiddo?" Megan asked.

"It's my breakfast," she announced proudly.

Nico chuckled, scooting over to make room. "You sure about that? Might be enough breakfast for my whole team."

"I like cereal," Winnie stubbornly declared.

We joined them at the table, Gemma still shaking her head at the absurdity of that bowl. "Winnie, that's too much, even for you."

"Hockey guys need a lot of food to be big and strong," Winnie said, grinning.

Gemma's sharp gaze fell on Nico. He defensively said, "She wanted to know why I needed a whole bag of microwave popcorn last night, but she and Megan split one."

"You ate microwave popcorn last night?" I asked, half in a gasp. "You know the chemicals in that stuff will affect you on the ice. How many times do I—"

"Coach, we just won the Cup. I'm allowed to have a bag of popcorn. Do you really think what I did last night is worse than what any of the other players did to themselves at Smokey's to celebrate?"

I couldn't help myself. I smirked at Megan. "I don't know. Was it?"

She turned eight shades of red. "No. We told you. Popcorn, movie, dozed off. Nothing else happened."

"Sure."

Maybe she wanted to change the topic. Megan turned to Winnie. "You want to be a hockey guy?"

Her little head bobbed enthusiastically. "I wanna be just like Uncle Nico and Daddy."

Daddy. That word stole my breath. I teared up—I couldn't help it. I didn't know she'd call me that just yet. I'd thought...well, I didn't have a plan for any of that. I figured I'd roll with whatever she and Gemma decided. If that meant I was Casey to Winnie for the rest of her life, it was fine. I wanted them to be comfortable with me joining their family, whatever that took.

But Daddy, the morning after I proposed? It shook me in the best way possible.

Gemma gave my hand a squeeze. She must have known how it shocked me because the corners of her mouth upturned, but she didn't say anything. She knew to let me process what had just happened.

Winnie kept eating and bouncing in her seat like nothing had changed. But with that one word, my entire world had shifted. Was this what parenthood was like? Tiny, world-reshaping, welcome earthquakes every day? *Only time will tell.*

As we ate, the news coverage continued in the background. Every anchor had the same tone—gushing and celebratory. Nothing like what I'd expected, though I wondered if they'd be so generous if we hadn't won.

"What makes this story so compelling," one anchor said, "is the way both of them put themselves out there for each other. Casey McConnell risked his career for the woman he loves, and Gemma Grimaldi risked public backlash to set the record straight about their story. It's a modern fairy tale."

"Fairy tale," Gemma muttered, rolling her eyes. "I could have written better copy for them to read."

"Hey," I said, nudging her. "You're a journalist. You know how they spin things."

"It's still weird to hear it about yourself when you're a reporter. You're not supposed to become the story."

"It'll settle down as soon as they can sink their teeth into someone else."

She sighed. "I know. It's just..."

"Surreal?"

"Definitely."

I glanced at my phone, unable to resist checking the latest headlines. Sure enough, the proposal footage and Gemma's article were plastered everywhere. The win wasn't even the top story anymore—the proposal had completely overshadowed it. Which didn't make much sense.

I pulled up Whitney's number, my thumbs flying over the keyboard. *This media push about the proposal—your doing?*

She replied almost instantly. *Enjoy it, Coach. You deserve a break.*

I smirked, shaking my head as I showed Gemma the message.

"What does she mean by that?"

"She won't take credit outright, but I know it was her."

Another text came through.

PS—You should consider a wedding before the next

season starts. Gives you time to enjoy being a newlywed before reality hits again.

I read the message twice, considering her words. It wasn't a bad idea. In fact, it sounded perfect.

"What is it?" Gemma asked, raising an eyebrow.

I leaned over, kissing her temple. "I'll tell you later. Let's just enjoy today."

As the morning wore on, the odd nature of the situation started to fade, replaced by a warm sense of contentment. Sitting here with Gemma, Winnie, Nico, and Megan, it hit me again how special this was. Gemma had welcomed me into her little family with open arms, and each of them had done the same in their own way. I'd never experienced anything like it.

The world was buzzing about us, but in this little bubble, everything felt right.

Winnie giggled as Nico and Megan bickered over who had to clean up the remaining cereal mess. It had become clear the two of them were destined for each other. Gemma leaned against me, her hand resting on my leg as she watched them with a slight smile. I wondered when Nico and Megan might head down the aisle themselves and start a family.

Twenty-four hours ago, the world felt like it was ending. Gemma had thrown herself under the bus, and I had done what I could to pull her out, and none of it felt like enough. But life, such as it was, had fallen into place. This was my family now, too, in all their messy, imperfect glory.

I didn't know what I'd done in a past life to deserve them, but I was glad I did it. This was what I had needed all along, it just took a series of questionable choices to get me here. And I had one more to make.

Chapter 40

Gemma

My daughter—*our* daughter—was being adorable. Shifting my thoughts from mine to ours was a feat. I'd thought of Winnie as mine for the longest time. But I wanted to share her with Casey. I wanted to share everything with him.

Over breakfast, my brother and best friend had gone from awkward pauses to sly looks. I didn't believe for a second that all that happened was two people accidentally falling asleep, but I wasn't about to confront them in front of Winnie. Both because it was none of my business technically, and because all I could focus on was Casey.

His eyes held a spark of something mischievous, and the way he leaned casually against the counter made it clear he was about to say something big. With his arms crossed over his muscular chest, his shoulders looked even broader, and I got lost in salacious thoughts while I sipped my coffee. Without warning, he said, "Marry me."

I froze mid-reach for a refill, a laugh bubbling out of me

before I could stop it. "Well, I already said yes last night, so..."

He shook his head, stepping closer, his expression soft yet utterly serious. "No. Now."

His words caught me off guard, and I tilted my head, trying to understand what he was saying. "*Now* now?"

"Yes. Right now." He took another step toward me, and the intensity of his gaze made my heart flip. He smiled as he peered into my eyes, like he saw exactly how his nearness made me feel. "Whitney said something in her last text that I can't stop thinking about. She reminded me that we've only got the offseason before everything ramps up again. Once the new season starts, my schedule will be insane, and I won't have time to just enjoy being a newlywed. I want to spend more time with you and our daughter before that happens, and I want to do that as your husband."

I didn't know what to say. It was crazy and spontaneous. Could I just go get married? Who does that? Pregnant people, that's who. When I came down with a case of the pregnants, one of Nico's complaints regarding her father was that I should be getting married to him.

It was regressive as hell, and a part of why he spent less than an hour in LA when he came out to yell at me. I told him in no uncertain terms I was not marrying Winnie's father, and he started about how a child needs both parents. That was enough for me to tell him to leave. I was surprised when he did.

I was glad that we had worked that out. After that initial argument, he never brought it up again. I wasn't sure if it had bothered him in the intervening years, but he'd kept his thoughts to himself. He probably sensed that was the only way he would get to visit his niece.

But getting married to her father now? No invitations, no big party...no guests to cause a problem, no huge expense... "Isn't this kind of crazy?"

"Maybe. But do we care about that kind of thing?"

I huffed a laugh. "Not really."

"So, let's get married," he said, taking my hands in his. "Let's use the offseason to be newlyweds, to enjoy each other without the world pulling us in a million directions."

"But we need a marriage license."

"Not if we go to Vegas."

"Vegas?" I repeated, the word sounding almost absurd in the middle of my newly cleaned kitchen. I knew they'd cleaned up their act, but it was still Sin City. How could I bring Winnie there? Were there things for kids to do besides watch their parents get married?

He turned to Nico and Megan, who were perched at the table with bowls of Winnie's concoction in front of them. "You two," he said, pointing at them, "will you be our witnesses when we get married in Las Vegas?"

Nico's brows shot up in surprise while Megan nearly choked on a spoonful of cereal. "Vegas?" Nico asked, a quick grin spreading across his face. "Hell yeah, I'm in."

Megan smirked, shaking her head. "The moment you brought it up, you knew I was coming too, right? You get her, you get me, too."

"Wouldn't have it any other way." Casey grinned and turned back to me, his hands still holding mine. "So, what do you think? Let's get on a plane and get married in Vegas.

Right now. I don't want to spend another moment of my life not being married to you."

Tears welled up, and I took a breath to say the only thing that came to mind. "Yes."

He kissed me sweetly, making the world feel brighter. "You better get packing. I have some calls to make."

"Calls?"

"Someone has to make the reservations, and you'll be too busy overpacking to do them yourself."

I cocked a brow at him. "What makes you think I'm an overpacker?"

"Just a gut feeling."

I rolled my eyes at him and dashed for my room, my mind spinning with everything I'd need for an impromptu wedding. He might have been right about the over-packing thing. I fingered through hangers and drawers, pulling out dresses, shoes, and anything else I thought might work. My heart raced, but not with nerves. It was with pure, unfiltered excitement.

I was going to marry Casey. Not tomorrow, not next month—*today.* The thought sent a thrill through me, and I couldn't keep the grin off my face. "Okay," I muttered to myself, tossing a pair of nude heels into my bag. "A simple dress, something classic. Oh God, do I even have anything appropriate for a wedding?"

A knock on the door startled me, and I turned to see Megan stepping through the frame, her arms crossed and a knowing look on her face. "All right," she said, closing the door behind herself. "I need to ask—are you sure about this?"

"What do you mean?"

She gestured around the room, where clothes and shoes were strewn across every surface. "As much as I love the idea of shooting off to Vegas on a moment's notice, you're not exactly the spontaneous type, Gem. You're already deep in planning mode. I can tell. This is all happening *very* fast for someone like you."

I sat on the edge of the bed, my fingers curling around the edge of the duvet as I considered her words. She wasn't wrong—I liked making plans and knowing exactly what was coming. As a single mom, I'd gotten used to trying to keep order on my own. Sometimes it worked out, and sometimes it didn't, but having a plan was a comfort, even if it was just an illusion.

But as I sat there, my thoughts circling Casey and everything we'd been through, the answer came to me as clearly as if it had been waiting all along.

"It is fast," I admitted, my voice steady. "But it feels right. Casey and I...we just fit. It's like finding the missing puzzle piece—you just know when it's right. Hell, the first night we were together, we were in bed in under an hour. There's no timetable for love or marriage. I fell for him harder, faster, and deeper than anyone I've ever known, and it feels like it took us forever to get here, even though the real part of things happened in a blink. I think everything with us is fast because it's meant to be. We have five years to make up for."

Her expression softened, and I smiled, a thought hitting me.

"Kind of like how you and Nico—"

"Don't even start," she interrupted quickly, cheeks flushing a deep pink. My best friend had never been an easy blusher, but when it came to my brother, she radiated with color. She admitted, "I like Nico, okay? I've always liked Nico. And yes, he hasn't called me since you left town, and now...now there's something between us—"

"I knew it!"

She laughed. "But I'm not overthinking it. Whatever happens, happens. If it doesn't work out, then we can leave things at me being your best friend and him being your brother. This doesn't have to get weird or mean anything beyond what it is."

I smirked, recognizing the familiar pattern. Megan couldn't admit her feelings outright, but I knew. Whatever had happened to me and Casey was happening to them. The signs were obvious to anyone who knew them.

I couldn't have been happier about it. "Sure," I said lightly, zipping up my bag. "Whatever you say."

In the living room, Casey and Nico huddled over their phones, scrolling through flights with the intensity they usually reserved for hockey. Winnie was happily playing with her toys on the floor, completely oblivious to the whirlwind unfolding around her. I wasn't sure if she understood what any of this meant. When a wedding popped up in a cartoon, she watched it with little to no interest.

Would it be different if it was for her parents?

"Score!" Nico announced, holding up his phone triumphantly. "Flight leaves in three hours. Plenty of seats in first class, loads of time to get there, check in at the hotel and get you crazy kids hitched, along with all the other stuff you want to do. The hotel has the wedding package you wanted and, most importantly, availability."

"Perfect," Casey said, pocketing his phone. "Thank you, Nico."

I didn't know what I had expected, but it wasn't that. "Flights already?"

"And hotel rooms," Nico said with a wink. I was pretty sure that wink was for Megan, and I refused to think about it too much.

Casey crossed the room, took my bag from me, and set it down before pulling me into his arms. "Are you ready for this?"

"I've never been more ready for anything in my life."

His grin was infectious, and he kissed me deeply, making the world blur around us. My future husband had a magic mouth.

"All right, lovebirds," Megan said, breaking the moment with a laugh. "We've got a plane to catch."

"Did any of you geniuses think to pack a bag for Winnie?"

Casey smiled, walked around the corner to the foyer, and held up her Sesame Street suitcase. "All set."

"I knew there was a reason I was marrying you."

We called a rideshare for the airport drive. No sense in paying for parking if we didn't have to. This whole fiasco would be expensive enough as it was. The rideshare was one of those big SUVs with plenty of room for all of us to stretch out. Nico and Megan bickered over who got to sit where, while Winnie chattered happily in the backseat. I leaned against Casey, trying to find something to tether myself to in such a wild moment.

Casey held my hand tightly, his thumb brushing over my knuckles in a soothing rhythm. He had a tan line there from the ring, and I loved what that meant. That I was worthy of it. Of him. I glanced at my fiancé, my heart skipping at the way his eyes sparkled with excitement.

This was happening. We were doing this.

For someone who had spent her whole life planning, overthinking, and second-guessing, the spontaneity of it all felt exhilarating. As I looked around at the people I loved—Casey, Winnie, Nico, and Megan—I knew, without a doubt, that this was exactly where I was meant to be.

Epilogue - Gemma

I sat at the vanity, staring at my reflection, trying to take it all in. Not just the stellar makeup job that Megan had done for me, but everything that had led to this moment. How could I have known I had met the man who would become my future on that fateful night? I hadn't even wanted to go to the masquerade. I wanted to stay home and make sure everything was packed according to my list.

Instead, I met Casey.

Looking back on it now, there were clues. Every guy I met after him paled in comparison. Either they couldn't carry on a conversation to save their life, or they were mediocre at best in bed. I kept comparing everyone to the masked man I'd only known as Red. No one else could live up to that night.

Megan stood behind me, curling my hair with practiced precision. Her focus was intense, but every so often, she glanced at me in the mirror with a small smile, as if she couldn't quite believe this was happening either. "You're going to look amazing."

"You think so?"

She smirked, setting down the curling iron. "Gem, I've never been more sure of anything in my life. You're glowing, and you're not even married yet. Casey won't know what hit him."

I smiled at her in the mirror, though my hands still fidgeted in my lap. My dress was simple but elegant, ivory satin that hugged in all the right places, flowing down to my ankles. I couldn't wear anything I'd brought after I spotted this dress in the window at the hotel boutique. It was too perfect. The bouquet Casey had chosen—a mix of white roses and lavender—rested on the counter beside me, its scent soothing my nerves.

Casey had taken care of everything. He'd planned this wedding from start to finish, insisting I didn't lift a finger. Somehow, he and Nico managed to do the big parts while I packed a suitcase and the smaller details while we were in the air. They were miracle workers.

"You handle enough for everyone else, and come season, I'll need you to handle things for me," he'd told me with that teasing smile. "So, let me do this for you."

And he had. A spa day for me, Winnie, and Megan, a rooftop ceremony at sunset, and all the other details I didn't even know about yet—he'd handled it all, saying he had some surprises up his sleeve still to come. I wasn't a fan of surprises, but I'd gladly take whatever he gave me.

As she finished my hair, Megan carefully said, "We were never the girls who planned some big, elaborate wedding. But is this what you want for your wedding?"

I chuckled. "Well, it sets the tone for what I'll pick as my second wedding—"

She snorted a laugh. "I'm being serious. It's not too late to say this isn't what you want."

I turned around and held her hand. "Meg, I want this more than anything. You're right—we were never those girls who cut dresses out of bridal magazines or even thought about bouquets. All that stuff...it doesn't mean anything to me. But I'm getting a beautiful wedding, despite my lack of planning, after a lush spa day that I got to share with you and Winnie. My daughter and brother are here. You're here. I get to end the day with a husband who put all of this together for me, just so I could have a special day. I don't think there's much more I could want."

She smiled and gave my hair one last fluff, then stepped back, folding her arms as she admired her work. "Then I think you're ready to get married."

I stood slowly, smoothing the fabric of my dress as I turned toward her. She was right. I was ready for this. I didn't have butterflies or cold feet or any of that. I was happy and ready for more of this in my life. "Thank you. For being here, for doing my hair and makeup, all of it. This wouldn't happen if you weren't the best friend and babysitter in the world, and ready to take my baby whenever I needed you to."

She smiled and sighed. For a moment, she just looked at me, her tough exterior cracking. "You're going to be so happy, honey. And yes, I will babysit for her when you go on your honeymoon."

"I haven't even thought about a honeymoon." I laughed as I threw my arms around her, pulling her into a tight hug.

"Don't cry. You'll ruin the makeup."

I laughed, sniffling as I pulled back. "No promises."

"I was talking to me."

I laughed again, and she handed me the bouquet, then gestured toward the door. "All right, bride-to-be. Let's do this."

In the hallway, Winnie bounced on the balls of her feet, clutching her basket of rose petals like it was the most important job in the world. As soon as she saw me, she announced, "Mommy, I'm ready!"

I knelt down, adjusting the bow in her hair and smoothing the hem of her dress. Her dress was perfect because it was a similar one in her size but with sleeves. Megan had already done her hair into a pretty French braid and I let her wear pink lip gloss since it was a special occasion. "You look beautiful, sweetheart. You're going to do such a good job."

She nodded solemnly, her expression so earnest I had to bite back a laugh and a tear.

As we stepped onto the rooftop terrace, the cool evening breeze brushed against my skin. The sky was breathtaking, painted in shades of orange, pink, and gold as the sun began its descent. The terrace hosted several trellises and arbors, all woven with flowers and vines, and their scent carried on the breeze.

A green carpet path hooked right ahead of us, so we couldn't see where we'd meet my future husband, but violins played, and their music came from that direction. An attendant spotted us and signaled down the trellis-blocked path, and the music shifted from light and peaceful to The Wedding March.

Winnie took her job seriously, scattering rose petals with determined precision as she made her way down the aisle. I wondered if, in her mind, she was playing hockey. She glided side to side as she moved forward, looking like the cutest hockey player skating down the ice. With every flick of her little hand, she covered the green carpet with pink petals. Megan and I followed a few steps behind her, but as I looked ahead, I stopped in my tracks.

Full rows of people were seated on either side of the aisle, their heads turning as we stepped into view.

I grabbed Megan's arm, my voice a frantic whisper. "What's going on? Did we get the timing wrong? Or—are these people at the wrong wedding? Are we?"

Megan looked just as surprised as I felt. "I don't think so..."

And then I saw them.

Nico stepped out from behind a trellis near the rear row of seats, his grin so wide it nearly split his face. But it wasn't him that stopped me in my tracks. It was the man he pushed in the wheelchair.

My breath caught, my heart slamming against my ribs as I took in the sight of my father.

I couldn't move. For a moment, I wasn't sure if I was dreaming. My father—who hadn't been to an event like this in years, who never left the nursing home—was here. In Vegas. At my wedding.

What had they done to get him here on such short notice? What rules had they broken...hell, knowing Nico, what *laws* had they broken? The expense alone had to be astronomical. I couldn't believe they did this for me.

Megan gasped when she saw him. She had known him

as long as she'd known me and knew exactly how monumental this was. She murmured under her breath, "Oh my God."

Tears blurred my vision as I clutched the bouquet tighter, my legs trembling beneath me. Megan lent an arm for support, and slowly, I made my way to him, my eyes never leaving him, in case this was a mirage.

Everything else had been surreal. Maybe I was finally freaking out.

But when I reached him, I knelt beside his wheelchair. It was real enough. The man sitting in it was, too. I studied him, memorizing every detail.

Sparse gray hairs lay on top of his bare scalp, brushed and neat. Dad liked to keep a tidy appearance, even now. He wore a suit, much to my surprise. Navy and vintage. His hazel eyes were foggy, the lines of his face deeper than on my last visit. Maybe that was because he was finally outside, and I could see him better than in his dim room at the nursing home. They insisted he preferred it that way, but seeing him here and now, I wasn't so sure about that.

He squinted from behind his wire-rimmed glasses. There was a flicker of recognition as he looked at me, and that was all it took to bruise my heart. His good days were almost worse than his bad days. Getting glimpses of the man he truly was...well, it made the other days all the more painful. I knew I should appreciate the good days, but I missed him so much. Seeing him recognize me now, I struggled not to sob.

"I know you." His voice was still weak, but he smiled. "Gemmie."

A sob escaped me, and I covered my mouth, nodding as

I fought to compose myself. Hi, Dad," I said, my voice thick with emotion. "I'm getting married today."

"Well, I know that. Nickie told me." His lips curved into a wider smile, making one side droop just a little. He reached for my hand, his touch featherlight but warm. He was having one of his rare good days today by some miracle. I refused to waste one second of it.

"Will you walk me down the aisle?" I whispered.

He nodded, and Nico stepped forward, his expression soft as he placed a hand on the wheelchair's handles. "Let's do this."

Casey stood at the end of the aisle, waiting for me. I couldn't look at him yet. I knew I'd lose it. I wanted to run to him and cry in his arms, I was so damn grateful. Somehow, he had made this happen for me. He knew what it meant, and he made it happen for me. Before now, I had no doubts about becoming his wife.

But now, I would accept nothing less.

I stopped across from him and slowly looked up. His tux was classic black perfection, but he had a navy blue and gold pocket square. That had to be from Nico—a reminder of the team that had helped us find our way to each other. Twice.

Casey's expression was pure love, his blue eyes shining with unshed tears. I had never been happier in my life. As Nico pushed our father's wheelchair toward him, Casey stepped forward to meet him.

My father placed my hand in Casey's, his touch lingering for a moment longer than I expected. "Nickie says you're a good man."

"I try my best."

"You better take good care of my baby girl."

"It will be the honor of my life, sir."

I glanced back at the audience, and only then did I realize who they were. The team had come to support their coach. Even Whitney was there, and the owner, Matthew. A pair of twenty-something blondes flanked the elderly man, and I wasn't sure if they were his dates or his granddaughters, but everyone looked happy, and that was what today was all about.

Megan and Winnie sat in the front row with Nico and our father. The ceremony was simple, but every word was imprinted on my soul.

When Casey slipped the ring onto my finger, his hand was steady, but his voice cracked as he said, "With this ring, I promise to love, honor, and cherish you. Always."

I slid the ring onto his finger, tears streaming down my face. "With this ring, I promise to stand by your side through everything. Always."

As the officiant pronounced us husband and wife, Casey pulled me into a kiss filled with every bit of love we had for each other. The sound of applause brought me back to the moment, and I turned to see Winnie clapping the loudest, her little face glowing with joy. My father smiled faintly, his hand resting on Nico's shoulder.

For so long, I'd felt like pieces of my life were scattered and incomplete. But now, standing here with Casey, Winnie, Nico, Megan, my father, and the team, I knew everything was finally whole.

No more secrets. No more fear. Just love. And it was perfect.

THE END

Read more from the Pucking Daddies bestselling series, exclusive on Amazon:

The Spice Play: A Single Dad Hockey Romance
(Seb & Nelly)

The Fake Play: A Surprise Baby Hockey Romance
(Luke & Keke)

The Secret Play: A Silver Fox Hockey Romance
(Casey & Gemma)

Printed in Great Britain
by Amazon

58100772R00187